Justice Denied - A Harper Ross Legal Thriller

Rachel Sinclair

Tobann Publications

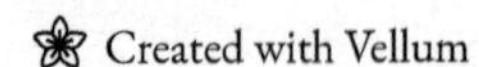
Created with Vellum

Also by Rachel Sinclair

For information about upcoming titles in the *Harper Ross Legal Thriller* series, sign up for my mailing list! You'll be the first to know about new releases and you'll be the first to know about any promotions!!!! http://eepurl.com/hBqhtr

Johnson County Legal Thrillers (Kansas City, Missouri)

Bad Faith

Justice Denied

Hidden Defendant

Injustice for All

LA Defense

The Associate

The Alibi

Reasonable Doubt

The Accused

Secrets and Lies

Until Proven Guilty

Emerson Justice Legal Thrillers (Los Angeles)

Dark Justice

Blind Justice

Southern California Legal Thrillers (San Diego)

Presumption of Guilt

Justice Delayed

By Reason of Insanity

Wrongful Conviction

The Trial

One

Taking Michael Reynolds on as a client made me want to vomit. I didn't want this creep anywhere near me.

Yet, the calculating part of me also saw how I could use him. I brought out my slinky and expanded and contracted it like an accordion while I stared at my ceiling. My mind started to race. Go to dark places. Corners of my brain that were better left unexplored. Deep down, I knew I needed to face what happened at the Sigma Chi house that night. What happened between Michael, his roommate Jim, and me. If I closed my eyes, I still saw him – tall and handsome, with huge dimples, big blue eyes and wavy black hair cut short on the sides and longer on top. He caught my eye from across the room, and I went over to him – a lamb being docilely led to slaughter.

Of course, my brain was swimming in alcohol by then. It usually was, just about every night, when I was in college. Bars ran drink specials every night of the week – quarter draws at this bar one night, dollar pitchers at this other bar the next. The best special of the week was the "all you can drink" for two hours on a Friday night at still another bar. I'd go there with my friends at 8 PM, drink all I wanted for one low price until 10 PM, and spend the rest of the night blasted and way, way, too friendly.

I went over to him, swaying to the music and barely able to stand. I said something to him. I don't know what. The details were hazy, and they were hazy even then. I said things to him I forgot two seconds later.

Before I knew it, we were grinding our bodies together on the dance floor. My hands were going through his thick dark hair, my teeth were caressing his earlobe, and my breasts were pressed against his pecs in the dark. His lips were soon on mine and his hands were grabbing my ass. *Let's go upstairs,* he said, and I nodded.

Tammy interrupted my reverie. "I heard about Heather," she said. "Congrats."

I nodded. Heather's case was already in the rear-view mirror. Funny how that worked – for three months, her case was all I thought about. I had a full roster of other cases, most of them minor criminal cases I pled out. But Heather's case was my only recent trial and I focused on it like a laser beam. It was central to my professional life. If it crashed and burned, I would've been devastated beyond measure. Not because I felt I had to win it, but also because Heather's life was hanging in a delicate balance.

"Thanks," I said. I swiveled in my chair, and looked out the window.

"Anything wrong?" she asked, looking concerned.

"Yeah. I mean, no. I mean..." I shook my head. What was I doing, taking Michael Reynolds on? Was my psyche so damaged I needed to sink him? How *would I* sink him, anyhow? There were any number of ways, but I wouldn't get away with any of them if he had a brain in his head. I could suppress evidence, invent damning testimony from witnesses and I could send him up the river with his prosecutor by getting him a terrible deal. But if he was smart, he'd know what I was up to and would turn me over to the Bar and appeal his case on the basis of ineffective assistance of counsel. I could certainly lose my license if I did everything to him I wanted to.

No, if I would sabotage him, it would have to be subtle. It

would have to be so subtle there wouldn't be any way he could know what I was doing. That would difficult, but not impossible.

"Harper?" Tammy said. "What's going on?"

I sighed. "You remember me telling you about a Michael Reynolds?" I shuddered just saying his name out loud.

Tammy sat down. "I think so. You mentioned something about him one time, although I forget the context."

"Yes. I'm sure I probably told you something about him. I don't think I gave you the entire story, though. I haven't told anybody the whole story."

Tammy looked worried. "What is the whole story? And why are you talking about him now? What's bringing him up for you?"

"He's coming in today. He's been accused of a crime. He called about a murder charge and wants me to represent him. Not sure what the facts are, though."

"I can tell you," Tammy said, picking up a newspaper. "I knew his name sounded familiar when you first said it to me. Here." She handed me the newspaper. "Front page."

I groaned. Another high-profile case. I was lucky with Heather, because the media lost interest in her case, after initially being all over it. As I read the article in the paper, however, I knew I wouldn't be so lucky this time. Michael Reynolds was the son-in-law of a Federal District Court judge. Said judge, whose name was Robert Sanders, was shot dead in his home. The article indicated that a random intruder was initially suspected to be the murderer, but Michael Reynolds, Sanders' own son-in-law, was arrested for the crime.

"This is a big deal," I said, reading the story. "A federal judge is murdered and this Michael guy is the lead suspect. The reporters will be crawling on this one." I questioned my motivation for taking this case. I spun around in my chair, realizing I'd have to be above-board with this one after all. Since the media would be all over this case, I couldn't maneuver the way I wanted to.

I wondered if I should just call him back and tell him not to bother. I couldn't quite understand why he called me, anyhow. Why me, out of all the attorneys he could hire?

"So, tell me about Michael. You were saying something about him."

I felt the anxiety, the cold tendrils I always felt when I thought about this guy, and shook my head. "Nothing, nothing. I knew him in college, that's all."

"That's not all," Tammy said. "There's something on your mind about this guy. I can sense it. I can see it on your face. You're as white as a sheet."

"I need to see my therapist." I took a deep breath. "I haven't seen her in awhile. I need to see her again tonight. Or sometime soon." I needed to get to the bottom on why I'd accept a case from Michael. I originally thought I needed revenge on him, so I'd try to throw it. Now I wasn't so sure. All I knew was that taking Michael on as a client was bringing up things I hadn't thought about in years. Things, buried deep within my psyche, were coming to the surface.

"Seeing your therapist is an excellent idea in general. You've been under a lot of pressure lately. I couldn't imagine always having people's lives in my hands all the time. But why are you bringing that up now? I just think that it's...a non-sequitur. I ask you about Michael Reynolds and you come back with needing to see a therapist. What's going on?"

I couldn't talk to her about it. I couldn't talk to anyone about it. I could barely talk to my therapist about it. I almost felt that if I spoke up about what had happened to me at that fraternity house that it would be true. That if I never said the word "rape" it didn't really happen.

I raised my eyebrow and looked down at the newspaper article. It was a long article, filled with details of Judge Sanders' life. He was appointed by President Clinton in 1994, rising through the ranks to become one of the most respected District Court judges in the country. He was 76 years old. His daughter, Christina Sanders, married Michael Reynolds some ten years ago. The newspaper article didn't go into the relationship between Michael and Judge Sanders - it simply indicated Michael was arrested for the murder. I had no idea why.

Tammy finally sighed. "You're hiding. You're always hiding. You'll just never let me in. Or anybody else for that matter."

I looked at her. "Don't you have a will to draw up? Or an estate plan?"

She crossed her arms in front of her. "What does that mean?"

"Nothing. It's just my way of telling you to back off. That's all."

"Oh."

"Why do you ask? Are you assuming I asked that question for some other reason?"

"Yeah. Sometimes I think you assume my job is easy. I assure you, it's not easy. It might not be as acutely stressful as what you do, but, trust me, it's not easy. I deal with millions of dollars and all the tax implications that go with everything I do. It's not as exciting or sexy as trying murder cases, but there are still high stakes."

I rolled my eyes. "Stop it. Stop trying to put words and thoughts in my head. I wasn't thinking you were beneath me. I've never thought you and I were anything but equals."

Tammy's face softened. "You're right. I'm sorry. I sometimes jump to conclusions." She paused. "The truth of the matter is, I'm kinda jealous of you. Drawing up estates all day gets pretty boring. I actually look forward to the few times I get to go to court for a will contest or something like that."

"Oh, God, don't be jealous of me. Trust me, you wouldn't want my job. I love it, I thrive on it, but it's certainly not for everyone. And look what happened with John Robinson. Look at how much turmoil that whole thing caused for me. Be happy you never have to deal with that."

"If you say so."

"I do." I looked at my watch. "I gotta move. I have a death case the State of Missouri has assigned to me." Death cases were occasionally assigned to private attorneys, even though the vast majority of them were assigned to the special division of the Public Defender's Office. The attorneys who did those death cases were the most dedicated I'd ever seen. I hated getting death cases myself. At least, I didn't like being assigned to them, because I rarely got paid enough for my time. A decent stripper at a high-dollar strip joint would make more hourly than I did for these cases. Hopefully this was one I could just plead out and wouldn't have to deal with too much.

Another reason why I hated being assigned cases like these was simple – I didn't have the chance to vet the person. I liked being able to choose who I represented. That was one of the perks of being a private attorney. When you're assigned to somebody, you never know who you'll get. The guy could be be crazy.

I had no idea just how crazy this one would be.

Two

I headed down to the jail, parking right in front. I went through the rigamarole of finding out where this guy was. His name was Elmer Harris, and I imagined what he looked like. I always pictured an Elmer as a guy who was a very slight build, maybe wearing glasses, probably sporting a bald head, probably with a stooped posture. I didn't know if my stereotype was accurate or not. More often than not, the person I met was opposite of the person I imagined.

The guard showed me where the guy was located, and I headed up there. I first had to go through a set of doors. The first door opened, and then you were in the middle, and you had to wait for somebody to open the second door. There were times when I got stuck in between the doors, and, for the first time in my life, I experienced claustrophobia. Five minutes would go by, and I was still stuck between the two doors.

This time, however, things went smoothly. One door opened, and the next door opened right away. I went down the corridor, found the elevator, and took it to the third floor. I walked past the metal doors that housed the inmates and got to another set of two doors. I pushed the button and one door opened, and then the next.

"Who are you here to see?" the guard asked from behind the bullet-proof glass.

"Elmer Harris," I said.

"Just a minute."

I took a seat at the small metal table and waited for Elmer to come out. I'd read the statement of information and some of the discovery on this case, and the guy seemed like a piece of work. He was a drug dealer and had a female partner. Apparently, the female partner was on the phone, allegedly talking to the authorities about Elmer, and he took the phone and beat her to death with it.

After looking through the police reports and interviews with witnesses, I had a feeling this guy was good for the crime. Pleading him out in exchange for life in prison, as opposed to the death penalty, would be most efficient.

Efficient didn't mean doable, however. I knew my clients well enough to know that getting them to take a decent deal wasn't always easy, no matter how good the deal might be.

I looked up and saw Elmer coming out and he wasn't anything like I'd imagined. He was a good 350 pounds with a head full of white hair and a full beard and mustache. He was dressed in an orange jumpsuit that seemed to strain because of his enormous girth, and grey hair on his chest peeked through the top of his jumpsuit.

Both his wrists were shackled and so were his ankles. He shuffled along slowly towards me and smiled when he saw me.

"Hello, Darlin'," he said. "How you doin'?"

I furrowed my brows at him. "Just fine. I wanted to meet with you before you're arraigned tomorrow."

He sat down. "Let me just tell you one thing about my case before all this bullshit happens," he said. "I'm good for this case. All day long. But I have an excuse for what I did. It's a good one, too."

I got out a pen and paper and looked at him. "Please, go on. What is your excuse?" I was humoring him, but that was my way. I usually wanted my clients to get out what they needed to and then would bring down the hammer. In this case, the hammer was a big one – he would get the death penalty unless he was willing to deal.

"Maria was my partner. My drug dealing partner. And the bitch-" He stopped himself abruptly. "I mean the young lady was turning me into the authorities. I beat her to death with the phone, but darlin', you have to know I had to do it."

I raised my eyebrow. "Okay. Elmer, you don't really think that's a legally acceptable excuse, do you?" I didn't know this man from Adam, but I knew he was a sociopath. Either that, or he was flying high on drugs at the time. Either way, he seemed to sincerely think that "I had to do it because she was going to turn me in" would be a legal justification for what he did.

He shook his head. "Darlin', it was self-defense. Pure and simple."

"Self-defense. How do you figure it was self-defense?"

"It was either my life or hers. If she turned me in, I'd be put away for fifteen to life. Isn't that what self-defense is all about? When it comes down to your life or the life of somebody else, you choose yourself."

This guy was, if nothing else, a bit of a creative thinker. But I had to disabuse him of his definition of self-defense. "It doesn't work like that. Self-defense is when your life is in danger right at that moment. Somebody has a knife, and they're lunging at you - you can kill that person. Somebody has a gun and they're pointing it at you - you can kill him. You can even kill somebody who broke into your home, even if they don't have a weapon and they're not really threatening you. But in this case." I shook my head. "Sorry, Elmer, no dice. Now, we need to talk about possibly getting a plea bargain out of this."

He shook his head. "No. No plea bargain. I want you to try this mother-fucker."

I groaned. I somehow knew he would say this. I calculated in my head how many hours this case would take, and how little compensation I would get from the state for trying it. I didn't like what I was calculating. I also didn't like that I was getting on a case with somebody who wasn't so good at listening or reasoning. That was the hardest part of my job – dealing with people who simply weren't rational. They all somehow thought they could beat the charge if only the jury could hear their story.

I swallowed hard and tried to find the angle that would dissuade this guy out of wanting a trial. With every client, it was different. Some could be reasoned with if they faced the death penalty and the plea was for anything less. Others could be bullied into accepting something. Sometimes it was best to flatter the client and let them know they were much more intelligent and worldly than the prosecutor and me.

Others just refused to listen to me and wanted to bulldoze ahead, no matter what I said or did. In those cases, it was best to withdraw from the case, but, since this case was assigned by the State, I didn't really have the choice to get off. I could only hope to find his angle, the words to make him realize the folly of taking the case to trial, and he'd agree to a plea.

I saw no other way. I could do everything I needed – discovery, depositions, investigations, the whole nine – but the fact was, he killed her. He admitted to it. There was no SODDI here, no justification. He needed to take any plea I could get, and take it with a smile.

He was still staring at me. Only now, he didn't have the same jovial expression he had when I first met him. His blue eyes were trained on me and they now looked dead. As if there wasn't a soul behind them. I shuddered, my blood running cold. I'd seen that look too many times. The last time I saw it was with a gang-banger who burned a guy alive in a car – Randall Thompson. Like Elmer, he told me he did it. Like Elmer, he wanted a trial. No plea bargain. When I informed him he needed to either plea his case or I'd withdraw, he lunged at me and almost strangled me. His hands were around my neck and he was squeezing hard. Thank God I was in the jail so the guard came out and got him off me in the nick of time. Otherwise, I probably would've been killed.

I took a deep breath. "Elmer, you admitted you killed her. And, no, you don't have a legal justification for doing it. I think I need to see the prosecutor and see what we can get for you. Bear in mind, that-"

He stood up and looked as large as a bear to me. I'm a slight woman – 5'9" and 130 pounds on a good day. I worked out as often as I could, lifting weights and running, but still...this man was easily 6'5" and 300 lbs, and wouldn't be intimidated by me or anyone else. "No plea," he said. "You get that persecutor, and you tell him we're going to trial. I'll just get up and tell the jury that I don't know what the hell the persecutor is talking about. I didn't kill that woman and I don't know who did." I noted his use of the word "persecutor" instead of "prosecutor," a term we defense attorneys jokingly used ourselves.

I sighed. I'd have to explain one more thing to him - I couldn't put him on the stand since I knew for a fact he killed the woman. "We can't win. I can't put you on the stand. Not when I know you did it. Now-"

All at once, he was enraged. I stood up and backed up, but he came at me. The gang-banger incident flashed through my mind as I put my hands up defensively. He charged me so I was up against the wall. I looked up at his face and his eyes were now wild. They were no longer dead and they certainly weren't friendly. I saw all his faces in one visit – he was friendly at first, then looked like a sociopath. Now he looked like a murderous demon.

I desperately looked over at the guard's station, and realized, to my horror, nobody was paying attention. They all looked pre-occupied with something else. Maybe there was a riot or perhaps just a lot of activity. I relied on them paying attention. When I was dealing with dangerous criminals, such as this Elmer, it was always imperative that somebody was diligent and looking out for me. Right now, nobody could see what was happening because nobody was looking in my direction.

He didn't attempt to strangle me, but, rather, he decided to rain body blows. White-hot pain shot through me as he smacked my body with his shackled wrist. The hard metal made contact with the bones of my chest and stomach, and I fought back tears. "You're going to try this goddamn case and I won't take a goddamn plea bargain. Do you hear me, you little bitch?"

Finally, there was a guard coming through the door. He had a stun gun in his holster and immediately tased the enormous man. Unfortunately, because of his size and girth, Elmer seemed not to feel the taser. He probably also had adrenaline coursing through his veins, which also meant that he wouldn't go down right away.

The guard tased him three more times before he finally slumped down on the ground.

"I'm very sorry, Harper," the guard, Scott, said to me. "We were dealing with a rising insurrection in one of the pods, and we should've been paying more attention to you."

I simply shook my head. "I have to go," I said, feeling shaken.

"Please stop by the nurse's station and get yourself checked out."

"I'm fine," I said. "Fine. I appreciate your concern, but I really have to get home."

"Harper," Scott said. "Do you need an escort to your car at least?"

"No. I'm a big girl. I'll be fine."

I staggered out to my car, hoping this whole thing didn't give me PTSD. After the incident with the gang-banger, I had nightmares for months. In my nightmares, I would always be cornered by an enormous man. I would be unable to breathe. I would be dead.

With shaking hands, I got into my car.

And promptly burst into tears.

Three

I returned to the office, feeling shaken but calmer after the incident with Elmer. This wasn't the first time my life had been threatened. I doubted it would be the last. The only bad thing was that I had to face Michael Reynolds and be mentally ready to do it.

My heart pounded as the clock approached 1 PM when Michael was scheduled. I looked at my right hand, and it was shaking. Why was I doing this? Why? Was I really nothing but a masochist? There was some reason I had to bring Michael back into my life.

My therapist had told me, over and over, that I needed to bring my demons out into the open and try to vanquish them. I never really vanquished this demon, and that was the reason for my depression, anxiety and bouts of alcoholism. Or so she said. I thought of my depression as something that had always been with me, off and on. A beast I couldn't get rid of, no matter how well my life was going. No doubt, my depression got worse after the incident in the fraternity house, but the darkness had always been with me in some form or another.

****

Michael arrived at my office right at 1 PM. I took a deep breath as Pearl announced him. "Harper, your new murder case is here," she said, calling me on the phone. "Michael Reynolds."

"Send him in." I took another deep breath. I would get through this. I would face this. I didn't face him in college or when he called me at my home five years after graduating to apologize for what happened. He was getting married and expecting a child and wanted to unburden himself. I simply listened to him babbling on the phone. I didn't say a single word. I hung up on him, and he never called me again.

I had never faced him before, but would face him now and take his case. If I found an opportunity, I'd make sure he fried. I wrestled with this, however, because if he was innocent, I'd ensure the real guilty party would go free.

I hoped he was really guilty. That way, I'd have the best of both worlds – I could ensure he got his just desserts, which would be a long prison sentence. If I knew he was guilty, I could ensure the prosecutor didn't go easy on him. That was the best way I knew how to get revenge on this guy. But if I thought he was innocent...I couldn't throw it. I just couldn't do it. It was against my ethics and against my conscience.

He walked through the door of my office. He looked different than I remembered him. When he raped me, he was an 18-year-old kid, slender, young, with a full head of dark hair. He was now 35, same as me, and it showed ever-so-slightly in the paunchiness of his gut. He still had a full head of wavy hair. He still had enormous dimples, and his blue eyes were as young as they were back in the day. He looked like a choirboy with his long dark eyelashes and easy smile. "Harper," he said, extending his hand. "I'm so glad you agreed to meet me. I was pleasantly surprised, actually."

"Sit down," I said, pointing to the chair before my desk. I got out a yellow pad of paper. "Did you fill out the new client intake sheet?"

He nodded and handed it to me. I looked at it, trying to calm my racing heart. My hand was shaking, and I turned away. "Tell me what happened," I said. "With Judge Sanders. Start from the beginning."

"Hey," he said. "Slow down. I called you specifically because I wanted to talk to you. I've never forgotten that night. I couldn't live with what I did. So, when I was arrested, your name was the first one I thought about. I remembered reading about your John Robinson case. You did an amazing job with that dude."

Oh, no, he didn't. He didn't just re-open *that* wound, too. "I don't want to talk about that," I said crisply. "I just want to know what happened with this case. I'm not promising I'll take your case. I'm not promising anything until I hear your story."

"Okay," he said. "But I hoped you would forgive me for what happened. I was wasted and stupid. It was something that I wish I could take back. I've wished that every day for 17 years."

"You won't get my forgiveness," I said. "Now tell me what happened. With your father-in-law. Why were you arrested?"

He finally sighed. "I don't know why I was arrested, to be honest with you. I don't know why. I was on the scene when the cops got there. Robert was in the house alone. Jane, my mother-in-law, was gone for the weekend, visiting her sister. My wife tried to call him for days. He was on medical leave from his job."

"Medical leave," I said, writing the words down. "What were his medical issues?"

"Nobody knew. He just started getting sick. Lost his hair. I mean, he was an older guy, 76 years old, but he had a full head of grey hair. He was exhausted all the time and bruised really easily. He also stopped eating, so he lost a lot of weight. He vomited a lot and had the runs. He also got severely depressed. When he got home from work, he started going to his room and just lay there in bed, watching television. He never was like that before. He used to play tennis three days a week and was part of a bicycle group that biked all over the city – the Prairie Village Yacht Club. Maybe you've heard of it?"

"Yes," I said, writing what he told me. I had heard of it – it was a cycling club that went on group rides several nights a week. I had even joined it myself once when I was cycling a lot. They were a neat group of people, and I got to know many professionals through that club. "So, he was active at one time."

"Yeah. But, about a month ago, he went downhill quickly. The doctors did test after test, but they couldn't find anything wrong with him. He was getting weaker and weaker, his bones were aching, he was vomiting, losing his hair, and he bruised when he barely bumped his leg." Michael shook his head. "So he was on medical leave."

"And your mother-in-law left for the weekend? Was there anybody around to care for him? Any nurse or anybody like that?"

Michael shook his head. "No. There wasn't anybody like that."

"Why not? He was that sick – why was he left alone?"

"I don't know. That's a good point." He didn't elaborate further, so I pressed on that point.

"Come on, Michael, it sounded like he was desperately sick. Why would your mother-in-law leave him that weekend without making sure somebody was there to care for him?"

Michael shifted uncomfortably in his chair and looked embarrassed. "I don't know."

I narrowed my eyes. "You're lying. This isn't my first rodeo, Mr. Reynolds, and I can always tell when my clients are lying." That wasn't entirely true – I had the wool pulled over my eyes on more than one occasion by some really adept liars I had defended in my career. But this guy was transparent. I actually was cheered by that because the worst thing in the world was to defend a client who was a superb liar, only to find out, halfway through the case, I'd been snowed all along. I would then be stuck with a dog of a case, even though the case looked good at the outset.

"I'm not lying," he protested.

"You are. Now tell me the truth. Why was your father-in-law left alone that weekend when he was having so many health problems? Serious health problems, it sounds like. Tell me the truth. I can't defend you unless you do."

He finally sighed. "I was supposed to look after him." He looked down at the floor. "I was supposed to."

"You were. And where were you?"

He looked out the window, his face bright red. "I was at the Marriott downtown. I was..."

"Staying with your mistress." I nodded my head. "Go on. I've already caught you in two different lies. One more strike, and you're out."

"What are the two lies?"

"You said you went to Judge Sanders' home because your wife had been trying to contact him. If she thought you were staying with him and looking after him, why didn't she just call you when she couldn't get ahold of your father-in-law? In fact, why was she so desperate to get in touch with him when she thought you were with him?" I raised my eyebrow, trying to get a read on this guy.

He shook his head and sighed. "She called me. She thought I was staying with her father. I obviously wasn't."

I nodded my head. "How many kids do you have?"

"Why is that relevant?"

"I just want to know. How many kids do you leave your wife to care for while you're away with your mistress when you're supposed to look after your father-in-law? And what ages are they?" I couldn't disguise my disgust. This guy was a tool in college. No, not a tool, a rapist. He raped me. I doubted I was the only one. Now he was cavorting with a mistress, telling his wife he would care for her sick father while leaving her home with a brood of kids to look after.

Michael Reynolds was making me nauseated.

"Five kids. The oldest is..."

"13. I know. I remember you calling and telling me you were expecting a child. That was the first time you asked for my forgiveness. I remember that well. How old is the youngest child?"

He sighed. "He just turned five."

"And the other three?"

"Ten, nine and seven."

I nodded my head. "So, your wife is home with five kids, four under the age of 10. And you're off with your mistress instead of caring for your father-in-law." I wrote this down.

"Listen, I never pretended to be a choirboy. I've made mistakes. That doesn't make me a murderer."

"I guess it doesn't. But go on with your story. One more lie, though, and you're out the door." I should have shoved him out the door, but I somehow couldn't do it. I was getting a perverse sense of pleasure watching him squirm as I pressed him on facts he didn't want to disclose.

He leaned back in his chair. "You're judging me."

"Damned right. You need me much more than I need you, and you're standing on my last nerve. You need to tell the truth because if you don't, I can't defend you." Of course, I was judging him. He was an amoral guy with a violent streak a mile long. That was the most important thing I learned in the years of counseling I had to go through after this asshat raped me – it was an act of violence. It had zero to do with sex. It was all about power, control, and violence.

He sighed. "Okay, okay. I was with my mistress at the time this happened."

"What's her name?"

"Why is that important?"

I rolled my eyes and threw down my pen. I crossed my arms as I stared at him. He stared right back for a few seconds, but after about half a minute of my staring him down, he looked away. I smiled as I realized I was intimidating him. That was a good sign. "Mr. Reynolds, I need the name of your mistress. That's your alibi, obviously." *Duh.*

"I, I, can't give you her name. She, she's married to the CEO of one of the largest companies in Kansas City. If he finds out what we've been doing, he'll divorce her and leave her penniless. That's in their prenuptial agreement – if there's any infidelity, she gets nothing."

"Guess she should've thought of that before she started sleeping with you."

Michael took a deep breath. "Maybe this wasn't a good idea to come to you with this. You've prejudged this whole thing."

"There's the door," I said, pointing to my office door. I wouldn't take his crap. He came in the door lying. That wasn't a good sign and didn't bode well for the case going forward.

He sat in his chair, not budging. He fidgeted for a few minutes and looked towards the door several times. However, he made no move towards it. He had no intention of leaving.

He finally leaned forward. "Harper, again, I'm sorry for what happened all those years ago. I need your help here, though. I'm being charged with something I clearly didn't do."

"Why me? There are attorneys everywhere in this city. Why do you want my help so desperately?"

"Because you're the best there is. I was stunned about what you could do with that John Robinson guy."

I shook my head. "I don't want to talk about John Robinson. That was not my most shining moment. In fact, it was my low point."

"Regardless, even though he killed somebody else, that you got him off stunned me. It stunned the city. The nation, really. I saw segments on that case on Fox News."

"It wasn't magical what I did. It was incompetence on the part of the prosecutor's office. Nothing more, nothing less. Any idiot could've gotten that guy off. I'm not that good, and I'm not that special. So, since we've already gotten off on a bad foot, I suggest you look elsewhere for legal counsel. I charge for this consultation, though, so you can pay that fee to my assistant, Pearl, on your way out the door."

Michael still didn't leave. "Okay, I'll give you all the information you need." He rolled his eyes. "This won't go over well with Kayla at all. Her husband will divorce her and leave her with nothing when this gets out."

"Not my problem. Now, your mistress' name is Kayla. What's her last name?"

"Stone. Kayla Stone. She's married to Gerald Stone. He's the

CEO of Stone Enterprises." Stone Enterprises was a chemical company based in Parkville, a suburb of Kansas City just north of the city.

I wrote down her name. "She'll be your alibi, so I must speak with her soon."

Michael smiled. "Does this mean you'll take the case?"

"I didn't say that. I should clarify – I'll need to speak with her *if* I decide to take your case. I haven't yet decided that."

"But you're willing to have an open mind."

I stood up. "Listen, Mr. Reynolds, I might take your case. I like a challenge. But I haven't forgiven you for what you did. I never will forgive you for that. You're why I've spent thousands and thousands of dollars on therapy. I still have nightmares about that night. I was a drunk for years because of what you did. I even went through a period when I had to be hospitalized for bulimia. All because of you and what you did. So, no, your apology isn't accepted. You're a disgusting piece of work, and you have changed little since you're sleeping with a mistress while your wife is dealing with a sick father and five kids at home. You're incredibly selfish, you're violent, and the sight of you makes me sick."

I sat back down and stared at him. I expected him to tell me off and leave the office, but he stared at me instead. "You might think I won't hire you because you said those things to me. Sorry, but I now know you're right for this case. I like that you don't take bullshit, including mine. I like that you tell it like it is. That's what I hoped for when I came to see you."

"Okay, then. My retainer is $50,000, payable in cash. I charge $500 per hour. This retainer will probably be exhausted by the time we get to trial, so you'll likely replenish it. That retainer will get about 100 hours of my time. It goes quickly."

He got out a checkbook. "Not a problem."

Of course, it's not a problem. He's married to a woman whose father was a District Court Judge. He's probably wealthy in his own right. Douchebags have no problem making money because they have no compunction in screwing people over to get to the top. "I didn't think it would be a problem. Please write me a check. I'll put the money into my trust account and give you an accounting of my time as I go along. Now that we got this straight, why don't you tell me the rest of the story?"

He sighed. "Well, okay. It's out in the open. My wife called me when I was at the Marriott with Kayla. She was worried about Robert because she couldn't get ahold of him. I don't know why she was so eager to speak with him, but she apparently was. I lied and told her I was out getting some fried chicken for Robert and me to eat for dinner, but, of course, I was at the hotel with Kayla. I rushed home and found him lying in the living room. He was shot twice, once in the chest and once in the head."

I kept writing as he spoke. "Okay, you lied to your wife about where you were. What time was it when you got to the house to find your father lying on the floor?"

"Midnight."

"Midnight. What chicken place is open at midnight?"

"Well, she called me at 11 PM," he said.

"What chicken place is open at 11?" Here was another hole in his story. Either his wife was the dumbest broad alive, or she didn't believe his chicken story. Maybe the wife wasn't so innocent, either.

"I don't know, KFC. Actually, grocery stores sell fried chicken, and they're open late. I didn't tell her where I was getting the chicken. I only told her I was out getting chicken."

"And your wife never questioned why you were getting dinner so late for you and your father-in-law? I mean, your father-in-law was 76 years old. I doubt he was used to eating at 11 PM."

"What does it matter if my wife believed my story?"

"It matters because I keep catching you in lies. I strongly suspect I'm catching you in another one. It may be insignificant, but you must give me every detail correctly. That's the only way I can piece all this together."

He sighed. "I told my wife I was getting chicken," he said weakly.

"I doubt she believed me, though. It was a stupid story, but it's the best I came up with on the fly."

I shook my head. "Your wife probably isn't stupid. Her father was a judge, and intelligence is generally inherited. I doubt she's a dummy. I'll go out on a limb and assume she knew exactly where you were when she called you about her father." That was a safe assumption, but why was that important?

"You're right. I mean, she's said nothing to me about Kayla. It's not like she spies on my emails and texts, but I imagine she at least suspects. But why does that matter?"

I tapped my pen on my cheek. "I don't know. I'll write it down, though. Maybe something will come to me. So you were with Kayla, your wife was at home and no doubt knew you were with Kayla and hasn't yet confronted you about your mistress. What happened when you got home and saw your father-in-law lying on the floor with gunshot wounds in his head and chest?"

He sighed and hung his head. "I called the police, of course."

I narrowed my eyes. "Okay, I'll assume you're innocent of killing your father-in-law. We'll get into why the police were so quick to accuse you later. Namely, we'll get into motive. But, for now, I'll assume you didn't have a thing to do with Judge Sanders dying." I took a deep breath. "Under that assumption, you were framed, big time."

"Of course I was." He seemed to get excited. "You believe me, then."

"I don't. It's my job to be skeptical. I told you I'll only assume you're telling me the truth. It seems somebody is framing you." I looked at the police report, which was in my file for this guy. "And I see the gun hasn't yet been recovered. But it will be. I can almost guarantee you this. It'll be recovered."

He leaned back, apparently not hearing my musing about the missing gun. "Who would frame me?"

"You got any enemies? Besides me, I mean?"

He rolled his eyes. "Where do I begin?"

"Where indeed? Let me ask you this. What you did to me in college – was I the only one?"

His face got red. "No."

"I thought not. How many other girls did you do that to?"

He looked at the ceiling. "Five."

My blood boiled. This guy needed to be in prison. He did. I had the chance to put him there, even if he didn't have a damned thing to do with his father-in-law's death. Society would thank me for ensuring this jackass went to prison for *something.*

I wrestled with this while I looked at him. "Five. Okay, I'll put these five women on your enemies list. I need their names."

"I can't give you those."

"You *will* give me those."

"No. I literally can't. They were randos from various parties. I didn't know their names then, so I certainly don't know them now."

I counted to ten and stared at the ceiling. Could I go through with this? All I needed was evidence this guy might've killed Judge Sanders. Then I could make sure he fried. If I passed him onto a different attorney, that attorney might ensure he went free even if he were guilty. I couldn't chance that. I *had* to stay the course. As hard as it was, I'd have to stay the course.

"Randos. The women you raped were randos. You can't even refer to them as human beings – you're dismissing them as randos. As if that makes it alright – you never got their names, so you don't have to feel guilty for what you did to them. Is that it?"

He paused. "You're right. I need to be more respectful of my language. Okay, they were women I met at various fraternity parties. I never knew who they were. I never had them in class or anything like that. I never saw them again. Is that a little better?"

"Better in what way?"

"Well, I'm not calling them a derogatory term like rando."

I took a deep breath. "Regardless, I'd imagine they know who you are. They're on your enemies list, whether you know it or not. Now, who else is on your enemies list?"

He swallowed hard. "This is hard for me to talk about."

"Boo hoo. You need to talk to me about this because I need to know who might go through the trouble of framing you. Maybe I can figure out if there's an intersection between these people hating you and them wanting your father-in-law dead."

"What do you mean by that?"

"It's like this. Let's say you know somebody who might want your father-in-law dead. He was a powerful senior judge who was quite liberal in a fairly conservative district. Let's just say somebody out there wanted him dead so a Republican could appoint his successor. That's a good theory. Now, if somebody wanted Judge Sanders dead because they didn't like the opinions he writes *and* that person also hates you – two birds, one stone. They get rid of the judge, and they get to frame you for the murder."

He leaned forward. "You're being awfully flippant about this whole thing."

"It's not my job to get emotionally involved with the facts. I need a list of people who hate you. From that list, I can glean who might also have a reason to kill Judge Sanders."

"I'll work on that list at home. It's a long list."

"I'm sure it is." You don't go through life being an amoral sociopathic douchebag without pissing off a lot of people. That was for sure.

"Is there anything else you need to know about?"

"Yes. Well, I'll just have to talk to the medical examiner, because it sounds like your father-in-law showed signs of poisoning."

He furrowed his brow. "Signs of poison? Really?"

"Really. Weight loss, hair loss, depression, aching bones, nausea – all this in a man who was previously healthy. The doctors couldn't find anything wrong with him. That all spells arsenic poisoning to me."

He cocked his head. "Huh. Nobody even thought about that."

"It can be undetectable. Unless the doctor is specifically looking for it, he might not find it. I'll have his body exhumed. I hate doing that."

"I see." He nodded his head as if the light bulb had just come on. "Poisoned. Somebody was after him long before he died."

"Well, it's possible it was more than one somebody. It's odd that whoever poisoned him didn't just let the poison take its course. Why go through the trouble of poisoning him if you're going to kill him with a gun?" That was another good question for me to ask. Another answer I needed to find out. Then again, maybe he wasn't poisoned – maybe it was all a coincidence.

"How would he have been poisoned, though? Janet would've gotten sick too if it was in the water at home. Same thing if they put it into one of the juices they drink at home. Why wasn't Janet sick too?"

I swiveled in my chair. "I'll go to his office and find out if something there might've supported the poison. Maybe he drank a bottle of scotch there and didn't share it with anybody."

"No. Robert didn't drink."

"Listen, I was an alcoholic. For many years, I was." I narrowed my eyes. "Mainly because of what you did to me, but that's neither here nor there. Anyhow, I was an alcoholic. I hid it well from most people, including my family. They never knew I drank at all. I'd go to dinner over there on Sunday and have not even a sip of wine. They all assumed I didn't drink wine with them because I didn't drink at all. The real reason was that I knew I wouldn't stop with a glass of wine or two. I'd be compelled to drink the entire bottle. I never wanted them to know about my compulsion, so I didn't drink around them. Your father-in-law was probably the same way."

"Okay," he said. "Find out if he was a closet drinker. Maybe that would explain where the poison would've come in. How the killer could've delivered the poison."

"I will."

He furrowed his brow. "Why will you do all this investigation? Why isn't the police force doing the same investigation?"

"Because they already arrested you. They'll hopefully do their own investigation, but they won't look very hard if they already have their man in custody. When working on a SODDI defense, it's my job to turn over every stone. That's the only way to convince the jury the police arrested the wrong person."

"SODDI defense?"

"Slang for 'some other dude did it.' That's what we're working with, here – a SODDI defense."

Michael picked up my paperweight and examined it. "Harper, I really meant what I said. I'm very sorry for what I did to you. I don't know why you're agreeing to represent me, but I'm grateful you are."

I pursed my lips. I knew why I'd represent him. If he was guilty, he'd fry. I'd make sure of it.

Even if he weren't guilty...I struggled with my desire to sink him anyhow. I remember reading a book by Albert Camus. It was called *The Stranger.* The narrator in that book was a nihilist. He had no empathy for anybody. No feelings. He laughed when a neighbor beat his girlfriend. He had no feelings for his mother, who had just died. He ended up in prison because he shot a man in self-defense. What I got out of that book was the guy deserved to be in prison, even if he was really innocent of murder – when you're that detached from the world and from emotions, when you have no empathy, it's only a matter of time until you commit murder for real. In a way, his ending up in prison was just a pre-emptive strike.

And so it was for Michael. He was a serial rapist. He currently was an unrepentant cheater. He had an enemies list. He was just a bad guy. Maybe he deserved to go to prison, whether innocent or not.

"Well, okay then." I looked at my watch. "I have a hearing, so..."

"I'll give your assistant a personal check. Would that be okay?"

"Sure."

At that, Michael left, and I stared at the ceiling. What was I doing? What was I getting into? Could I represent him? Could I sink him if he was innocent? Could my psyche handle this?

Whatever. I had a hearing to go to. Elmer's hearing. Fun, fun. I didn't mind Elmer, though, or guys like him. At least you knew what you were getting with a guy like him. But with a guy like

Michael...he was slick. Wily. Cunning. Smart. He might have killed his father-in-law. I would have to do my background check on him and his relationship with Judge Sanders. There was some reason the police were so quick to jump to conclusions. So quick to arrest him.

They must have known that he had a motive to kill his father-in-law – I would have to find out what it was.

Four

I got into court, and there was Elmer, sitting in the jury box with the other inmates. I wondered which Elmer I'd encounter. The charming one who called me darlin', or the unhinged beast who almost killed me.

I walked over to him and immediately found out which Elmer I was dealing with.

"Hey," he said, his gruff voice with the slight twang called out to me as I approached him. "You'll plead not guilty today, right? And ask for a trial?"

"I'll plead you not guilty because it's usually inappropriate to plead somebody guilty at the arraignment. But I'll still impress upon you the importance of pleading this out. The prosecutor's not messing around here. You could end up on the gurney before this is all said and done."

"So be it." He lowered his voice, aware that if he raised his voice to me, he would be immediately led out of the courtroom. This judge didn't take that kind of bullshit. "Listen, you bitch, I'm your boss. You're my fucking employee. I call the shots, and I'm telling you that you'll try this bitch."

I looked over at the bailiff, hoping he heard what Elmer was saying to me. I needed him to step in and help me if I needed witnesses as to why I needed off the case. Unfortunately, the bailiff wasn't paying attention to Elmer and me.

"I'll ask to withdraw," I said to him.

"If you do, you're a dead woman." His blue eyes had the dead look that creeped me out in the jail. "And you know what I'm capable of."

"You won't intimidate me." Over the course of my career, I'd been threatened by scarier dudes than this. There was the serial killer a few years back who I pled out. He regretted the decision to take the plea after he got the sentence and sent me threatening letters for six months afterward from his jail cell. He'd threatened to send his buddies after me if I didn't appeal, even though I'd explained, time and again, that you can never appeal a plea-bargained sentence. There had been the murderer who had cornered me in my office one night after hours. I pepper-sprayed his eyes, and he, too, threatened me for months afterward.

Now here was this Elmer guy, rougher than most and undoubtedly violent. But I couldn't let him and his words change my mind about him. I'd been around this job long enough to know a guy like him would threaten me no matter what I did. If I tried the case and it went down in flames, as a case like this undoubtedly would, and he got the death penalty, he would threaten me. If I pled him out, he would threaten me. If I withdrew from his case, he would threaten me.

No matter what I did, Elmer was a shit sandwich, so I might as well cut my losses early.

"I'll withdraw," I said.

"You can't. You've been assigned to me."

"I can. You attacked me, and I have a witness for that. And-"

At that, he stood up, leaped over the short wall between the jury box and the courtroom, and immediately tackled me. I could feel his blows raining down on me. I'd landed wrong, and this enormous man was on top of me, and because he was so enraged, he undoubtedly had the strength of ten men. I cried out in pain. I couldn't breathe, and I could feel something breaking. It might've been my leg. It might've been my ankle. All I knew was the pain was excruciating.

All at once, I could feel myself fading to black.

FIVE

I woke up in the hospital. I didn't quite realize what had happened. All I knew was that my sister Albany was next to me and talking to Tammy.

"What happened?"

"Hey, girl," Albany said. "You got attacked in the courtroom and now you're here. And I had to take time off work to ensure you made it home okay. You're such a malingerer."

"Malingerer? What you talking about?" Albany and I liked to rib each other as "malingerers" ever since we ended up in the hospital after a car accident, and each of us had a long recovery. I teased Albany about faking the injury so she could get out of household chores, and she did the same to me.

"I'm teasing. According to those in the know, meaning the other lawyers in that courtroom, here's what happened. You were in there with some fat ass, and he tackled you. You're here because he crushed you so bad you lost consciousness. You're the talk of the town now." She nodded approvingly. "You're my badass sister, so I knew that even a fat ass couldn't keep you down."

"Don't make me laugh," I said, feeling laughter coming and a tightness in my chest as I took gasps of air. "Seriously."

"Well, we need to get you out of here. Your kids are waiting for you to come home. Isn't that music to your ears? Your kids need you. Bet you never thought you could say that, huh?" She shook her head. "The things you do to get off a case."

"Am I off that case?"

"Of course you are," Tammy said. "Elmer got taken away and put into solitary. He had a guy assigned to him. I guess this guy will respect a man more than a woman, and he might not be as much of a douchebag. We'll have to see if that's the case, though. He might end up representing himself, so he can appeal any conviction on the grounds of ineffective assistance of counsel."

"How does anybody represent such a guy?"

"You tell me. Anyhow, I'll get the doctor in here so you can get the hell out of this hospital," Tammy said.

She left to find the doctor, and I looked at my ankle, which apparently was twisted. "This thing hurts like a mother," I said. "Too bad I can't take painkillers for it."

"Yeah. I'll get you hooked up with a decent acupuncturist," she said. "I have some good ones that do a great job with pain." That was Albany's focus – alternative medicine. She was into acupuncture and Reiki and saw a chiropractor once a week. I wished I had the time to pursue all of this, too.

The doctor came in, looked at my ankle, and said I was free to go.

Thank God. I had to get out of this place as soon as possible. Life was awaiting me, and I couldn't afford to take a break. Not with two young girls needing me, a murder case I was working, and everything else coming at me from all directions.

Albany drove me home. "Sis, I have to say, I'm worried about you."

"Me? Why?"

She shook her head. "You've got so much on your plate, it seems. I just don't want you to get overwhelmed."

"I'm not. Listen, this is my life. And this is actually what I like.

Being busy all the time. I don't want to think about things too hard. If I did, I might end up back at the bar."

"That's what we're all afraid of." Albany's hands gripped the wheel. "I know you have it all together, but it always seems you're on top of a house of cards. I just don't want it to collapse again."

I sighed. "So what would you have me do? Get a job at a grocery store? I have a mortgage from hell, and I need the income from these cases that are always coming in. I also have two girls at home and a nanny to pay. Now is not the time for me to be slowing down."

Albany put her hand on my neck and smiled as she drove on. "I'm only looking out for you. I wish you would've chosen a different profession. Any profession."

"I appreciate your concern. I do." I put my hand on her neck affectionately.

"You get too into your cases," Albany said. "I've always worried about that. I'm sorry to say it, but in your position, you can't afford to get emotionally involved. Most of your clients end up behind bars." She paused. "Except John Robinson. I've been worried about that one for a long time. I know it eats you alive."

"It does. I have Gina's kids with me, but that will never undo what I did in that case. Nothing ever will." I sighed. "And listen – I need to get passionately involved with my cases. At least the cases I believe in. I can't go into any of it half-assed because if I do, I'll lose every time. Being an attorney isn't a job for me. It's a passion. I need to keep it that way, or else I might as well get a job at McDonald's."

Albany chuckled. "Well, not McDonald's. You can do better than that. Hardee's, maybe, or Burger King. But not McDonald's."

"What you got against McDonald's?" I asked with a smile. "Ever since they started serving breakfast all day, they've been at the top of my list."

"I'll give you that. Apply for a job at McDonald's online today, and see what happens. I'll bet they'll take you. That could be your new life's calling."

"Nothing wrong with that. It's honest work."

We were at my house, and I gingerly stepped out of the car. "Well, I thank you for the ride."

"Do you need me to take you back to your car tomorrow?"

"Nah. You need to go to work. I'll just call Uber."

Albany nodded. "See you Sunday? For dinner?"

"Of course." Sunday dinner with the fam was something that I rarely missed. It kept me sane, even through all the turmoil in my life. "Love you."

"Love you too. See you Sunday."

At that, she drove off.

Six

I felt weird the next day after I got out of the hospital. My thoughts started to race, like I had never before experienced. I felt distracted and anxious. Like I wanted to jump out of my skin. I was also irritable. I knew that my job was, once again, getting me down. It always did, really. But having Michael as a client, combined with the fact that I was attacked not once, but twice, by that crazy bastard Elmer, was doing a number on me, mentally.

I went down the stairs and saw that Rina and Abby weren't there at the breakfast table. I counted to ten, not wanting to deal with their bullshit. I mean, Rina pulled this stuff all the time. She was slow to get out of bed, slow to get ready for school and really slow in eating her breakfast. But Abby was always there, right on time.

"Girls," I called. "Where are you? We gotta get a move on."

Abby peeked her head out of her bedroom door. "Aunt Harper, we don't have school today. Remember?"

"What do you mean, you don't have school today?"

"Don't you remember? It's a teacher's sabbatical day. They're all going to someplace in the Ozarks to learn stuff about teaching us better. We don't have school today."

I groaned. I totally forgot about that. "I see. Well, I guess I better call Sophia to come and watch you guys." For some odd reason, I felt angry about that. Why didn't the girls remind me last night? We had our usual dinner and the twins never said one word about not having school today.

"Thanks, Aunt Harper."

"You're welcome. And Abby...I guess this is something that I need to talk to you and Rina about tonight. But there's going to come a time, sometime soon, when hopefully you won't have to call me Aunt Harper anymore."

Her eyes got wide. "Why? Why don't you like to be called that anymore?"

"You'll see." I smiled. I was finally granted a hearing to adopt the two girls. I wanted them to call me "mom" as soon as the adoption went through. I was dying to hear them call me "mom," as a matter of fact.

Abby went back into her room, and I called Sophia. "Sophia, can you please watch the girls?" I asked her. "I'm so sorry, I totally forgot that the girls don't have school today."

"I'll be there," she said.

"Thanks." Sophia lived only a couple of blocks away, so I knew that she would be at the house shortly. "I appreciate that."

She arrived within 15 minutes. "Thanks Sophia," I said. "For coming on such short notice."

"Of course. I love watching the girls."

"I know you do."

When I got in the car, I realized that I was having a lot of problems focusing. My brain was too jumbled, my thoughts were coming way to quickly. One thought came into my brain, and then another and another and then another. None of my thoughts seemed to connect with any of my other thoughts, either.

I sighed. I would have to hunker down on Michael's case. He had emailed me his enemies list, and he was right about one thing – it was a long, long list. He apparently had screwed over quite a few people on his way to the top. Just like I had suspected.

Michael was currently a partner at VML, which was the largest advertising agency in Kansas City. He was responsible for millions of dollars of accounts from some of the largest accounts in the city. According to the form he filled out for me, he was making $550,000 per year. The list of people he gave to me who hated him were mainly people who he worked with. They were people whose ideas he stole – there were three different people who were angry with him because he took the ideas that they had and pawned them off as his own. There was one co-worker who was angry with Michael because Michael was running around with his wife. That guy was also one of the ones whose ideas Michael stole, so he had double reason to hate Michael.

None of these people, however, seemed to have cause to want to bump the judge off. I didn't want to dismiss them, but, at the same time, I needed something stronger to go on. These were creative types at the agency – copywriters and artists and people like that. They wouldn't have cause to kill a federal judge. If they wanted to get revenge on Michael, I imagined that they would find some other way of doing that.

The first thing that I wanted to do was to ask for an order to have Judge Sanders' body exhumed. I just couldn't believe that he was buried without an autopsy. That was ridiculous.

"Pearl," I said, calling my office. "I need a motion ASAP. I need to have a body exhumed."

"I'm on it," she said. "Who do you want to have exhumed and why?"

"Judge Sanders," I said. "He had signs that he was poisoned before he died. Yet there wasn't an autopsy performed on him. I need to find out if there was poisoning."

"I'll get right on that," she said. "Who would be the judge who would rule on this?"

"Judge Graham," I said. "She's the trial judge for this murder case. She would be the one who would rule on it."

"I'll draw that up."

"Thanks." I closed my eyes. "Listen, I would come into the office, but I don't feel like it right now. I don't know, I feel weird.

Antsy. Anxious. My thoughts are racing a mile a minute. I don't think that I'll be good right now. I think that I need to go to the federal courthouse and see Judge Sanders' chambers. I hope that they haven't cleaned it out yet."

"That's okay, Harper. I'll see you when you get here, whenever that will be. You don't have any new client intakes today, and you don't have court, so do what you need to do."

"Thanks, I will." I hung up and shook my head. *I have to see the judge's chambers. Damn that Elmer, hurting me like that. Damn Michael doing what he did to me. I wonder what Axel is doing today? Maybe he can meet me downtown for lunch. I don't get downtown all the time, except for court, so I hope that he can come and meet with me. God, I'm hungry. What's up with those girls not having to go to school anymore? I think that I need to work on a legal brief for that appeal I got going. I need to find somebody who can do the research for me.*

I blinked my eyes and shook my head. *Stop, Harper. Just stop. You have to focus. Focus. Focus.*

I saw the Federal Courthouse coming up ahead. It was a beautiful, stately building that was shaped like a giant horseshoe. It was fairly new, and it didn't look at all like a traditional courthouse. There weren't Roman columns or Roman architecture, but, rather, it was thoroughly modern. There were walls of glass in the back of the structure, and, in the front, it was all made of stone. I loved this courthouse and I missed coming to it. I sometimes got the chance to come down here when I had a federal criminal case, but, other than that, I never really got to see this place so much.

I walked into the enormous lobby of the courthouse and went up to the clerk who was behind the glass. "Hello," I said. "I need to go to the chambers of Judge Sanders."

The clerk looked at me and smiled. "Harper, I know that you're on this case, but you can't go back there. It's been cordoned off by the police. They've been investigating in there all morning."

I sighed. "Well, is there any of his colleagues around? I need to ask them some questions about Judge Sanders."

"You're going to have to make an appointment, of course.

Which judge would you most like to speak with?"

I didn't know who Judge Sanders was closest with. I really needed to find out if there was a liquor cabinet in his chambers somewhere - that would be the best place to put poison into. Considering that Michael told me that he thought that his father-in-law was a teetotaler, it would seem that, if Judge Sanders was a drinker, he wasn't an obvious one. Therefore, it seemed that I would have to figure out who was his closest friend on the bench. Only his close friend would know if he drank on the job or not.

"Do you know who Judge Sanders hung out with the most? I mean, if he were to meet a colleague after work, who would he call first to go out?" I hoped that the clerk might know that. They were always up on all the gossip.

"You probably want to speak with Judge Johnson," she said. "He and Judge Sanders were golfing and tennis buddies. He probably would have any answer you need to know."

"Thanks. Can you contact his clerk and get something set up? I really need to speak with him. Also, I would like a list of pending cases that he had in front of him." That was something that would important – if he had a case in front of him that was something that he would rule on and the ruling would adverse, I would imagine that somebody might want to bump him off for that reason alone.

"I can get that for you," she said. "Just let me print it out for you."

"Thanks."

I looked around as I waited for the clerk to print out the list of cases. There were people everywhere heading to the elevators and talking on phones. Talking to each other. And, somehow, everything just became a giant jumble. It seemed like there was only a morass of people. I couldn't hear individual conversations or even see individual people. They were only a conglomerate. I put my hands on my ears and squeezed my eyes shut tight.

"Here, Harper," she said. "Here's a printout of Judge Sanders pending cases."

"Thanks."

"I'll get in touch with Judge Johnson's clerk and let you know when would be a good time for you to meet with him," she said.

"Thanks."

She looked concerned. "Harper, are you okay?"

"I am. Why do you ask?"

"I don't know. You seem a little off. I hope you don't mind my saying that."

"I don't feel well. Thank you for that printout, though."

I walked out onto the street and the first thing I saw was a bar. A bar. I couldn't possibly go to that bar, though. Yet I wanted to. I needed to.

I got into my car and decided to do something else.

I drove down to the Country Club Plaza, which was the high-end shopping area of Kansas City. It was a crisp day in November, and I knew that, on Thanksgiving night, there would be untold thousands of people who would head down here for the Plaza Lighting Ceremony. That was the biggest annual event for the Kansas City area. Where some cities attracted zillions of people to see the lighting of the Mayor's Christmas Tree, in Kansas City, the masses of people came to the Plaza. It was an amazing thing to see the darkness of the beautiful buildings suddenly light up. Celebrities showed up to do the honors of pulling the lever that lit up the Plaza - real celebrities like Paul Rudd did the honors on occasion.

I parked the car. I always loved this shopping area. Kansas City was the sister city to Seville, Spain, and the buildings on the Plaza were designed in the Spanish style. Stucco facades, Spanish tile roofs and towers were the hallmarks of these buildings.

I walked into Talbot's, which was the department store that was the most prominent in the area. I was itching to spend some money, which was weird for me. I was always so thrifty with my money, watching every penny. I knew that I needed to be thrifty, even though I made really good money, because I had so many expenses. I had a mortgage, I had to save for retirement, I had all my usual expenses, I had a nanny, and I also had to save up money for the girls to go to college. I also had to pay for their private school – I had to send them to private schools because the Kansas City school district was so terrible. I had to save as much money as I could, so I tended not to spend very much money on things like clothing and jewelry and things like that.

Yet, when I went into Talbot's, I looked around and had the urge to spend a lot of money on things that I never thought about before.

I started at the Chanel makeup counter, and I got a makeover. I ended up buying all the products that the girl put on my face, including the skin care products, which was something that I never spent money on. I pretty much bought Noxema from Wal-Mart and put that on my face to take off my makeup. Yet, I bought everything that she put on me.

"You look beautiful," she said. "This eyeshadow really makes your green eyes pop. You have such peaches and cream skin, and these colors are beautiful on you."

I never thought of my complexion as being "peaches and cream." I was pale and I knew it. Out of everyone in my family, I was the one who most resembled our distant Scottish ancestors. The curly red hair, the green eyes, the pale skin – I looked like my great-grandmother who was right off the boat from Scotland. "Thanks," I said, looking in the mirror. The makeup artist certainly did a great job of subtly bringing out the color of my eyes while toning down any redness in my face.

"I'll take it," I said. "All of it."

After I moved through the makeup counter, I tried on clothes. Sweaters, pants, shoes, suits, hats, coats...Everything I tried on, I wanted, and I bought. I told myself that I earned this. I worked hard for this. I had to put up with people like Elmer and Michael and people like that. I had to have something for myself. I couldn't continue to deny myself the things that I really wanted.

The only problem was, I never wanted these things before. I never cared about clothes and makeup and jewelry and things like that. Yet, the second I walked through this door, I knew that I had to have everything I got my hands on.

Next thing, I went in to get my hair worked on. It had been way too long since my last haircut, and it was time to finally get that done. I ended up with a big, curly bob, which was quite a bit shorter than the long curly mop I had on my head before. I liked it, though.

Nails were after that. A spa pedicure and gel manicure, both in dark red, the color of blood.

I ended up looking in a full-length mirror and, for the first time in a long time, I actually liked what I saw. I turned around and admired my butt, which I worked hard on with squats and spinning. I liked the way that my legs looked in the flared trousers that I changed into after my shopping spree at Talbot's. I even liked the floppy brown hat on my head and my brand-new bright green peacoat, which was perfect for the chilly November evening that was falling.

"Axel," I said, calling my boyfriend. He was my boyfriend finally. We decided that we were going to be exclusive. I was falling in love with him, and he told me the same. "Let's meet for dinner. Here on the Plaza. Plaza III. My treat. I feel like splurging."

Axel laughed. "You certainly are a spontaneous one. I was hoping that I could come over to your house and fix dinner for you and the girls. But if you would like to go to the Plaza III, that's fine, too. But I can't let you buy."

"You have to let me buy. I just got a good murder case and I'm flush with cash." That wasn't actually true. I had a lot of murder cases and a lot of criminal cases, and I was never *that* flush with cash. I mean, I made a good living, but I was never one to blow any of it.

"I'll meet you, but I can't let you buy, Lass. Sorry about that."

"Lass." I smiled. That was one of the things that I loved the most about Axel – he was from Australia and I loved his accent and his use of Aussie colloquialisms. "I'll see you in about a half hour, huh?" Axel lived in the downtown area in a loft, so I knew that he could be down at the Plaza in a short period of time.

"I'll see you."

I went over to the restaurant and found a hostess. "I'm meeting somebody here," I said. "Can I go ahead and wait at the bar?"

"This way," she said, leading me into the bar area. She put a napkin in front of me. "The bartender will be right with you."

I took a deep breath, wondering if I could resist the urge to drink. I was constantly white-knuckling it. Every day, every second, was another day, another second, that I had to make a choice. Either keep on my sobriety or go off the wagon yet again.

But, somehow, the spending spree that I just did at Talbot's and the hair place and the nail salon took the edge off for me. I didn't have the need to have a drink. I smiled as I realized that I didn't want a shot of bourbon or whiskey or anything else on the alcohol menu. I put one of my packages on the bar and looked at the receipt. It was the bill from Talbot's, and I added everything up and was shocked that it all came to around $5,000.

$5,000. I've never spent $5,000 in one day ever in my life. Except when I bought my Beemer. I rationalized it, though. I earned this money, dammit. My life was stressful and I was constantly having to put up with nonsense from my clients. I needed something to make me happy, and, today, spending money was that thing.

In the back of my mind, however, I knew that something was wrong. Something was off. My brain was going haywire. It was as if I had drunk 100 Red Bulls and...that was it! In college, I took speed. Just once, because I needed to stay up all night studying for an exam. I wasn't used to stimulants, let alone a powerful stimulant like speed, and I ended up running up and down the six flights of stairs several times in a row. I couldn't concentrate on what I was supposed to be studying – I kept reading the same paragraph, over and over and over and over again, and I never absorbed any of it. I felt like I was flying high, yet, the next day, I completely crashed. Just totally crashed. I was eating lunch and, right there at the lunch table, I put my head down and fell right to sleep.

What is wrong with me? I haven't taken speed. I haven't even had a cup of coffee. I never drink coffee. I haven't even had a glass of tea. What's wrong with me?

Seven

Axel finally arrived and kissed me on the cheek. "Oh, lass, your hair is beautiful. I really like it. You look different, too." He stood back and looked at me. "You look like a model."

I laughed. "A model. A supermodel, huh?" I brought my sparkling water to my lips and noticed my right hand shaking wildly.

Axel noticed the same thing. He looked at my right hand and then looked at me. "Harper, what's going on?"

"I don't know." I shook my head. "I feel weird. I got this murder case, and I have this other murder case. One of my murderers put me in the hospital. He crushed me."

"What?" Axel stood up. "What do you mean he put you into the hospital?"

"Just what I said. He attacked me and put me in the hospital. Don't worry, I'm not representing him anymore."

"Harper, you have to be careful." He put his arm around me. "Seriously. I don't want to lose you."

"You won't lose me, silly. Listen, it comes with the territory. When you're a criminal defense attorney defending capital cases, you'll get these violent people who get really irate when you tell them things they're in no mood to hear. That's what happened with this guy. He told me he wanted me to try his case, even though he told me point blank he beat his drug partner to death with a phone as she tried calling authorities to turn him in. He told me it was self-defense." I laughed. "Self-defense. What kind of nonsense is that?"

Axel wasn't laughing along. He was sitting next to me at the bar, looking worried. "Harper, I have to ask you something. I don't want you to be offended. But I need to know." He looked down at his hands.

"Go ahead. Ask away. I'll tell you. I have nothing to hide."

He cleared his throat. "Are you drinking again?"

I shook my head. "No. Do you see this? It's sparkling water. Taste it since you probably don't believe me." I was irritated and had no idea why. Axel only asked me an innocent question – why did I feel he was giving me the third degree? Anybody would ask me the same question.

He put up his hands. "That's okay. I don't need to taste it. I believe you."

"Thanks." I took a deep breath. "Let's get a table. It's not crowded yet. The hostess can seat us."

He smiled, but I could tell something was off with him, too.

"What?" I asked him. "Why are you looking at me like that?"

"Like what, lass?"

"Like you think I'm on something. I'm not. I've never in my life taken drugs. I've never even smoked pot in my life."

"Let's change the subject. Tell me about your new murder case."

I took a deep breath. "I don't want to change the subject. I want to know what's going through your head. You're looking at me like you think I'm high. I'm not. I'm really not."

"I don't think you are. You're acting weird, though. You seem like you're on fast-forward."

That was how I felt, actually – as if I was on fast-forward. Like everything around me went faster and faster. I closed my eyes and heard a voice telling me that I was worthless, I brought all my hardships on myself, and everybody hated me. I put my hands over my ears. "Stop talking, just stop it." I shook my head. "Stop it. Stop saying those things." I suddenly felt like screaming.

I looked at Axel, who now looked really freaked out. "Harper, I think we need to cut this evening short. I still want to be with you tonight, but maybe not here. Let's go to your house. See your kids. For whatever reason, you seem a little...freaked out. I don't know why, exactly."

I nodded. "You're right. I don't feel well. Maybe things will stop spinning once I get home."

"Stop spinning?"

"Yeah. This restaurant seems like it's on a fast carousel right now."

We left the restaurant after I took care of the bill. I only drank soda water but left the bartender a $20 bill. "Keep it," I said to him. "You put up with me sitting here for an hour, so that's worth a big tip."

"Thank you," he said with a smile. "That's very generous."

Axel put his arm around me. "Where did you park, Harper?"

I furrowed my brow. I really couldn't remember. My car was somewhere on the Plaza, but where? "I don't know," I said. "I started out shopping at Lululemon. I remember that. And then I went to get my nails done and my hair cut. But I really can't remember where I parked my car." Was it on the street? Was it in a garage? Was it in a parking lot? How would I figure out where it was? This wasn't like me, either – I'd never completely forgotten where my car was.

Axel nodded. "That's fine, lass. I can drive you home and bring you back tomorrow morning to look for your car. Maybe you'll remember where you parked your car by tomorrow."

I felt spacey yet numb. "Yes. That'll be fine. Thank you, Axel."

We walked to his car, his arm around me. "You know, Harper, I like having you close to me. It's getting nippy already. It'll be cold soon. Let's get to your house, build a fire, and talk to your kids. You can tell me all about your new murder case, too. Maybe I can help you with that."

"Maybe," I mumbled. Axel opened my door. I got in and lay back on the seat. I closed my eyes, trying to concentrate on something. Anything. Yet I couldn't. My thoughts were coming in again, faster and faster, and I couldn't sort any of them out.

Axel said something but I couldn't process it.

"We're home," he said in a few minutes. My house was close to the Country Club Plaza so it took us only a few minutes to arrive at my doorstep. "I mean, we're at your home."

"Good. Thank you, Axel, for driving me home. Come on in."

I opened the door. Rina was waiting for me and had been crying. She immediately came up to me and threw her arms around me. "Aunt Harper, say it's not true. Say that you won't give us up. We're happy here. I'm sorry, Aunt Harper, I get bratty sometimes, but we'll be good from now on. We promise. Please, Aunt Harper, please don't give us up."

I had no idea what she was talking about, but, at the same time, I didn't feel like I could properly respond to her. I opened my mouth, shut it again, and looked at Axel. He was looking at Rina with an expression of concern on his face. "Harper, what is she talking about?"

"I don't know." I pushed Rina off me. "I really need to lie down. I-"

I sat down on the floor. I vaguely knew Rina was still bawling and Axel was comforting her. Abby, for her part, also was crying, but she stayed seated on the couch. Her head was hanging, and I could hear sobs.

"Axel, I'm so sorry," I said. "I know you were looking forward to hanging out with me and the girls and building a fire and everything, but I really need to be alone. You're welcome to stay and play a game with the girls. They'd really like that. But I don't think I'll be good company."

I went upstairs to my room and shut the door. I didn't even look at Axel before I went to my room. I didn't want to see his look of concern or, even worse, his look of being pissed off.

I went over to my desk and opened my laptop. I'd look at

Michael's enemies list again. For some reason, my mind suddenly cleared up. I was full of energy, perhaps more full of energy than I'd ever been before, but my thoughts were no longer jumbled. Instead, I had clarity. I could do anything. I'd win this case for Michael. I would do things right. Yes, I hated him more than I'd ever hated anybody. Yet, I was an attorney. I had an ethical duty to do all I could to ensure I won his case.

And I would win it. I had no doubt about that. I was Harper Goddamned Ross. If I had a case before the United States Supreme Court, I could win that, too. I could win anything at all.

That night, I stayed up all night. I carefully looked at all the pending cases in front of Judge Sanders when he was killed, and I felt this was a promising avenue to go down. Several companies were in court for various reasons – a pharmaceutical company was being sued for price-gauging; another company was in court challenging certain regulations as unconstitutional; there were several cases regarding environmental pollution.

I didn't see a smoking gun, however. Nothing in the list of cases jumped out at me. On the contrary – I found too many high-stakes cases where a certain company would lose millions of dollars in revenue if the judge ruled adversely. I also looked at the judge's record and saw he ruled on behalf of the "little guy" more than he ruled in favor of big corporations. Whether it was the Sierra Club suing on environmental concerns, a worker suing because a company violated safety laws, or an individual suing because he was denied worker's compensation, Judge Sanders seemed to have a bleeding heart.

That made me sad. I always favored the little guy sticking it to The Man, especially if The Man was a corporation screwing people over for a buck. I was a justice warrior at heart. Judge Sanders seemed to be a true populist, a judge for the people, and we needed more men like him.

Now he was dead. A Republican president would appoint his successor. There was a thread. But what was it?

After reviewing Michael's enemies list, I realized this list wouldn't bear much fruit. I could speak with everyone on the list and planned to, yet I couldn't see why anybody on this list would kill a federal judge just to frame Michael. It was drastic to kill a federal judge and would certainly result in the death penalty, which was what Michael was facing.

I'd think of something else. I had to get creative. The police weren't doing investigations – they had their man in custody. And that was where I'd look first – I had to figure out why the police immediately arrested Michael. There must be a history there. Something Michael wasn't telling me. That wasn't hard to believe – the slimy worm lied to me repeatedly when I first met him. I'd get his story, but it must come from other people. I'd have the complete picture once I put the puzzle together about who he was and the nature of his relationship with his father-in-law. Once I had the complete picture, I could anticipate the prosecutor's case.

First things first. I called Pearl. "Hey, Pearl, it's me. How are we coming along with the exhumation thing?"

"Not good. The daughter has filed a motion in opposition. The hearing is tomorrow at 1:30."

I sighed. While I anticipated this happening, it didn't make it any easier to deal with. "On what basis is she trying to deny it?"

"Her motion in opposition just says it would be unnecessarily painful for the family, and there must be extenuating circumstances before the court can order something so drastic. I mean, that's the argument in a nutshell."

I sighed. I didn't need this. The damn autopsy should've been done in the first place, and I had no clue why it wasn't. While I didn't blame Christina Sanders for not wanting her father's remains disturbed, this exhumation was necessary. If Judge Sanders was poisoned, that would be significant. It would mean the killer had access to the judge. He or she would be somebody with the ability to put poison in his drink, at a low level, for a long period.

That would narrow it down. Some greedy CEO with a big case might want to kill him to get somebody different to hear their case. But if the judge was poisoned...that would be a different ballgame altogether. What greedy CEO would have that kind of intimate access to Judge Sanders daily?

I walked downstairs and saw Axel sleeping on my couch. I approached him and put my hand on his cheek. He opened his eyes and smiled at me sleepily. "Hey," he said. "How are you?"

"I could ask the same." I sat down next to him on the couch. "I'm sorry about last night. I..." I shook my head. I couldn't explain why I was feeling so funky.

"No, no," he said. "Don't apologize. I was worried about you, so I spent the night. The girls are really upset, too. They have this idea you're going to give them back. I don't know why they have that idea, but they cried about it all last night."

I furrowed my brows. "I don't know why they think that, either. I-" Suddenly, the lightbulb came on. "Oh my God. I know why they think that. Where are they now?"

"Sophia took them to school. I called her because you were locked in your bedroom. I didn't want to disturb you."

"You could have. I didn't sleep last night. Not even for a minute."

Axel screwed up his mouth. "Have a seat, Harper," he said, patting the sofa next to him. "We need to talk."

I sighed. "Okay, but I have afternoon hearings, so I can't talk long. By the way, how come you're not at work right now?"

He shrugged his shoulders. "I'm doing investigations so I set my own hours. My department doesn't keep me on the clock. They're only concerned with whether or not I get my work done. But don't change the subject. I'm worried about you."

I nodded and sat down next to him. I put my head on his shoulder. "I'm worried about myself, too. Sometimes I feel I have a tenuous grasp on reality. Like I'm right on the edge of a precipice. I'm looking down, and if I fall off that cliff, I'll end up in the loony bin. I've always felt that way. You don't know how much I white-knuckle my sobriety. I don't think I've told you this, but I've suffered, on and off, from depression almost my entire life."

"I can see that about you," Axel said. "People who are perfectionists often suffer from depression. They have to do everything just right and set themselves up for failure. They can't handle failure, either. I've known people like that. My mother was like that." He sighed and looked in the distance. "She had a hard time handling the world. She was an amazing artist, very gifted. She didn't sell much, though, because it's a hard business if you want to make a living. But you should see some of her paintings. Her sculptings. She worked herself to the bone but never found an audience."

I put my arm around him. "Are you close with her?"

He nodded. "I was. She killed herself 11 years ago."

I closed my eyes, feeling his pain. Axel and I had something in common. He lost his mother. I lost everything the night Michael and Jim raped me. I could never get over that. I doubted Axel could get over losing his mother in such a way.

"I'm so sorry to hear that," I said to Axel. "Really. I couldn't imagine losing somebody in that way. My parents live here in town. I have three sisters and two brothers – two of my sisters are in town. I try to see them as often as I can. I couldn't imagine losing a loved one to suicide. You must be devastated."

He shrugged. "I am. It was tough because I always saw how much she tried to make something of herself. To make a name. She had my brother and me, but our father split when we were young. There wasn't a lot of money because Mum couldn't ever make it. That was tough for her. We grew up in Australia, so there wasn't really a dole for us. We had to make do with what there was, and there wasn't much. I always wished to do more for Mum, but I left home at 17 to come here. I came here on a student visa and then met Neila, my ex-wife, so I could stay. Mum killed herself 12 years after I moved to America."

I could hear the guilt in his voice. I knew what he was thinking without him saying a word. He abandoned his mother, in his view, leaving her lonely, destitute, and with nothing to live for. "Axel, it wasn't your fault. It sounded like your mother had a lot of problems."

"I know, mate. I know. But I'm worried about you. Last night, I saw you act in a way I'd never seen before. You looked different – your eyes were wide, and your face was flushed. And you acted strangely. Very out of it. I know you're not drinking. You told me that. I believe you. But I wonder if there was something else happening."

"What did you think was happening?"

He shrugged. "I don't know. But Mum used to act like that. Sometimes she'd lock herself in her room and paint for literally days. Not eat, barely drink water. She would just be in there, and when my brother Daniel and I would go into her room, we would see she had completed about twenty paintings. In about a week. We'd ask her what she was doing while locked in her room, and she'd tell us she was working around the clock. Other times, she would go to the pokies and lose any money she earned from selling her paintings."

I furrowed my brow. "Pokies?"

"Yeah, pokies. You put your money in, pull the lever, and hopefully, money spits back out. Pokies."

I smiled. "Oh, slot machines. I got it. So, she was a gambler?"

"Yeah. A gambler. She played the pokies, and she played cards. She didn't make much money, but what little she did went to the pokies and the cards. When she was like that, anyhow."

I shook my head. "I didn't do any of those things. I mean, I went shopping and spent a lot of money. More money than I usually spend. In fact, today, I'll take half of those things back. I don't need them and don't like spending frivolously. And, I admit, I stayed up the entire night looking over cases Judge Sanders was going to rule on and at some of his past rulings. I need to find the thread. It's a puzzle and one I'm determined to solve. But I feel okay right now. I feel fine."

He smiled. "You look fine." He kissed me, slightly biting my upper lip while his lower lip enveloped mine slowly. "You look very fine."

I nodded and put my arms on his shoulders. Axel and I were heading towards making love and I didn't know how I felt about that. The truth was, I hadn't been intimate with anybody since that night in the fraternity house all those years ago. That was 17 years ago - I hadn't let a man get close ever since. I didn't know how to talk to Axel about that. I wanted to make love with him. I was dying for that. He was sexy, sweet, handsome and smart. He treated me like a princess. I was falling in love with him.

Yet I was afraid of being intimate with him. I still associated sex with rape. My therapist had worked with me for years, but I still didn't feel whole.

By taking Michael's case, I could finally process what happened to me all those years ago. I wanted him to lose, yet, at the same time, I wanted to win. I was so conflicted about it...at any given moment, I had a different idea on why I was on his case. I swung wildly between wanting to sink him at all costs, to knowing I couldn't, to wanting to win, then back again. My therapist would have to help me sort all this out.

I had to find a way to get past what he did to me. To forgive and let go. If I didn't, I'd screw up this relationship with Axel. Thus far, it was the healthiest relationship I'd ever been in. I couldn't mess things up.

"Well," I said, looking into his beautiful eyes. "I need to get to work. I have hearings this afternoon and need to start investigating my new capital murder case."

He smiled. "Let's go and find your car."

I furrowed my brow. What was he talking about, find my car? My car was right out front, wasn't it?

Then it hit me – no, my car wasn't out front. It was somewhere on the Plaza. I couldn't find it yesterday.

I was really crazy yesterday. I hoped not to feel like that again. I had too much on my plate – I couldn't feel like that and do my job.

Eight

The next day, after a full day of hearings, depositions and client intake, I knew I'd have to deal with Rina and Abby. I felt awful they somehow thought I'd abandon them. I had no idea why they would think that, but I had to reassure them.

I picked up a pizza on the way home. It was a mushroom pizza, because I knew that was their favorite, and I picked it up at D'Bronx, our favorite pizza joint. I loved that little deli so much – it had become a Kansas City staple over the years. They were famous for their enormous sandwiches and their absolutely amazing authentic New York pizzas.

I got in the door and the girls attacked me. They both came up to me and wrapped their arms tightly around me. "Aunt Harper," Abby said. "We've been dying to talk to you. We wanted to talk to you yesterday, and you didn't want to talk to us and we've been paranoid all day long. Talk to us, Aunt Harper. Please."

"Okay. Look, I have pizza. Let's eat and we'll talk. I'll tell you whatever you want to know."

I put the pizza on the center of the table and the two girls got out three plates. Sophia left, because she always had to get home to her own children, and I sat down with the girls.

Rina put three pieces of pizza on her plate and Abby glared at her.

"What?" she demanded from Abby.

"Nothing. You're always complaining about being fat, yet you're taking three pieces of pizza."

"Hey," I said to the two girls. "First of all, Rina, you're not fat. Not in the least. You're beautiful and I don't want to hear about being overweight. If you become overweight, we'll talk, but only because I'd be concerned about your health if you gain a lot of weight. But you're a rail." Rina was 11 years old, 5'2", and probably weighed less than 100 pounds. There was always a ton of pressure for girls to look like the cheerleaders and the popular girls, which usually meant they couldn't have any extra pounds. I wouldn't have that, though. I'd nip that stuff in the bud.

Rina stuck her tongue out at Abby, who gave her a dirty look. "But Aunt Harper, if she keeps eating like this, she'll get fat. That's what I'm saying."

I rolled my eyes. "You do you, Abby. Let Rina be. As I told her, if she gains weight to where she becomes overweight, we'll figure it out from there. For now, she's beautiful, she's growing and she doesn't need your nagging."

Rina smiled. "Thank you, Aunt Harper."

"Not a problem. Now, we're all sitting at the table. I know why you two girls think I'm ready to let you go. I feel awful I was misunderstood. But I told Abby yesterday the two of you might not have to call me Aunt Harper for long. What I meant was that I finally have a hearing for your adoption. The court will just use the home study they did before, and Alexis is on board with it. There shouldn't be any obstacles to my adopting you two. I guess what I meant to say was that I hope you'll soon call me Mom."

The two girls were quiet, just staring at me. Then I saw Rina had tiny tears in her eyes and Abby put her arm around her. "We're going to have you as our mom? Really?" Rina's voice was tiny, which was not like her at all. "I just can't believe it. I..."

Abby came over to my side of the table and hugged me from

behind. I put my hand on her arm and closed my eyes. These girls were a part of me. I could never let them go. Not now and not ever.

I stood up and spread my arms. Rina came over and I wrapped my arms around her and Abby. Rina was now sobbing. Her arms were around my waist. She was crying and so was Abby. "We're going to have a mom. You don't want to give us back. I was so scared."

"Shhhh," I said. "Why would you ever think I'd give you back? I would never do that. I love you two. I..."

Rina just shook her head. "I know kids in foster care, and they go from one home to the next. I was so afraid that would happen to us. We love it here, Aunt Harper. We love it here, and we want to learn everything you do. At least I want to learn. I want to be an attorney just like you. But that's not why I want to stay here so bad. I just love you, Aunt Harper. So does Abby."

Abby nodded her head silently in affirmation of what Rina was saying. "We love you. And we will be good."

I put my arms on both girls and slightly pushed them off me so I could look them both in the eye. "Hey," I said to both of them. "I don't want you to think you're on pins and needles here. You guys will mess up from time to time, but that doesn't mean I love you any less or I'll send you back. I don't want either of you to ever imagine you have to be perfect or good or any of that, because if you mess up, I might send you back to foster care. That won't happen. I just want the two of you to be yourselves. Okay?"

The two girls nodded their heads silently.

"Now, let's dig into this amazing pizza."

The three of us sat down, and Rina rapidly ate the first piece of pizza while Abby slowly and deliberately ate her pizza with a knife and fork. "This is my favorite pizza of all time," Abby said.

"Mine too," Rina said.

"So, how was your day?" I asked them both. I always tried to ask them how their day was, and they generally told me what happened that day – both good and bad. Rina was more likely to dramatically tell me all the gossip at school, and Abby more or less stuck with what was going on in her classes and what homework she had.

"Oh my God, Aunt Harper, today was like the best day ever in school. The best day ever," Rina said dramatically.

I smiled. For her, any day where there was some kind of juicy gossip happening was *the best day ever.* "Tell me about it, Rina. How was today the best day ever?"

"Well, we had a substitute teacher in biology class and that teacher was such a moron. I mean, totally clueless." She rolled her eyes. "But it was so much fun, 'cause we didn't do much but watch a stupid movie. It was this old movie where these people get really little and small and go into this dude's body to do stuff. They get attacked by red blood cells and all these cool things."

I nodded my head. "*Fantastic Voyage*. I remember it well. I'm surprised they still trot that old movie out for your generation. I loved that movie, though."

"Yeah, it was alright. I just loved that class today, because it's so boring every other day. And I don't have any biology homework, so it's all rad."

I smiled. "Any other reason why today was the best day ever?"

"Yeah. Amelia Stone broke up with Alex Carter. They were like the popular kids and they've been going together for three years now. That was like whoa!" She made the motion for *mind blown.* "I mean, really."

"Three years? How old are they?"

Rina shrugged. "I don't know, they're in the 8th grade."

I tried to suppress a laugh. "So, they've been hot and heavy since the 5th grade then. They were a regular Elizabeth Taylor and Richard Burton couple."

"Who are they?" Abby asked.

"Oh, Lord. Looks like the two of you have a lot to learn. Now, I know that this'll be boring for you, but the two of you need to learn about actors from the golden age. Tell you what, this weekend, we'll watch some movies. *Bringing Up Baby* with Cary Grant and *National Velvet* with a young Elizabeth Taylor. I think you'll love both of those movies. Later on, I'll expose you to movies with Audrey Hepburn, James Dean and Marilyn Monroe. At the very least, you girls need to know those actors. Otherwise..." I shook my head. "You just have to know these actors."

Rina shrugged her shoulders. "If you say so, Aunt Harper. We'll watch whatever you want to watch as long as it's not boring."

"Oh, you won't be bored. Now, Abby, how was your day?"

"It was fine." Her face brightened. "I wanted to ask you if I can start playing an instrument in the band. It's early enough in the semester that I can get in if I want. I want to play the flute."

"The flute it is. We'll go shopping for it."

"Thanks, Aunt Harper."

"Band geek," Rina said.

"Hey," I said to Rina. "There's nothing wrong with playing an instrument. I played the flute myself when I was her age. I wasn't very good at it, but I played it. It was a lot of fun."

Abby made a face at Rina, and she punched her in the arm.

I rolled my eyes. "None of that. Now, I know you girls have homework to do, so after dinner, you need to get on that. I'm here to help you with whatever you need."

Rina groaned. "I hate homework."

"Of course you hate homework. Trust me, in your life, you'll do a lot of drudgery you'll hate doing. I hate doing depositions, taxes and paperwork. Life isn't supposed to be all fun and games." I raised an eyebrow. "Now, let's get these dishes done and you two girls need to get to studying. Once you're done studying, you can do whatever you want. But homework comes first."

We all did the dishes and the girls went to their rooms. I retired to my office and looked over some case law on Michael's case before I fell asleep right there in the chair, fully clothed.

Guess I was tired.

Nine

"You're doing what?" Axel asked me. He was over at my house, hanging out and watching movies with the girls, who each had a friend over, and me. We were in the kitchen, doing dishes, while the girls were plopped down in front of the TV, watching some PG-13 movies, the only movies I allowed them to watch, aside from G and regular PG movies. "Do you mind repeating that for me?"

I drew a breath. "I'm representing the guy who raped me in college."

He shook his head. "You never told me you were raped." His face looked pained. "I'm very sorry to hear that. But I don't understand. He's been accused of murdering his father-in-law, and you took his case? What are you thinking, Harper?" He bit his lower lip. "Why didn't you go to the police when it happened? And why don't you go to the police right now? There's no statute of limitations on rape. That's what you should do, Harper, not try to get him off on this current crime."

I scrubbed the dish I was working on and put it into the dishwasher. "Axel, you know better than that. Hell, *I* know better than that. You know what happens in those rape cases. The victim gets dragged through the mud. I was traumatized enough by that happening. I wouldn't be re-victimized by the prosecutor bringing in witness after witness who would testify I was dirty-dancing with Michael that night and that I was blasted beyond recognition. That I was wearing a short skirt and a low-cut blouse. I would not have my character assassinated. It would be 'he said, she said' the entire way, and I didn't want to deal with it."

Axel raised an eyebrow. "That was completely selfish, Harper. You let the bloke get away with it. Now he's accused of murder. Are you so sure he didn't kill Judge Sanders?"

I shrugged my shoulders. "No. Of course not. But trust me, if I find out he did it, I'll ensure he gets his just desserts. That was one reason I took the case – I can ensure he doesn't walk if he's guilty as sin. And, yes, I've thought a lot about sinking him even if he didn't do it. But I can't do that – if I do, the real people will go free."

I sighed and put my hands on the edge of the sink. "Axel, I'm having issues with this. I won't lie. But a part of me feels that representing him will help me put what happened behind me. I've been carrying it around with me all this time. My therapist has told me the rape is behind a lot of my issues." I peeked out of the kitchen into the living room and ensured the girls were preoccupied and couldn't hear me. "And we need to talk about that."

Axel nodded. "Let's go out back," he said. "I think I know what you'll say to me."

I got on my coat, and Axel did the same. The weather was getting colder and colder by the day. Soon there would be snow on the ground, and the big oak tree in the backyard would have white branches. I was looking forward to it, yet dreading it at the same time. I loved the snow because it reminded me that Christmas was around the corner. Christmas was always my favorite time of year. It meant family gatherings, holiday specials and Christmas-themed movies on the Hallmark Channel, which I loved.

Yet I hated the snow because I hated driving in it and the city was terrible about clean-up. The snow plows would pile the snow on the sides of the streets, and I'd have to scrape my car because I didn't have a garage. And I did a lot of walking because I usually had to park far away from the courthouses downtown, and I hated walking through the snow.

But tonight, the air was crisp but not cold. Even so, I felt a chill. I didn't want to have this talk with Axel, but I knew I had to.

We sat down on the backyard chairs, and I wrapped my coat around me tight. Axel was looking at me, and I could almost read his thoughts.

He took my hand, and I smiled. "Uh, Axel, I wanted to talk to you before things went further. I know you are probably going to want to, uh, make love at some point. But I..." I shook my head and felt tears coming to my eyes. "I haven't been intimate with anybody since the rape. I've pushed every guy away from me because I just can't bring myself to make love with anyone. My therapist has tried working with me about it, but I've been having problems. I associate being intimate with fear, degradation, intimidation, and pain. I'm so sorry." By that time, I was crying, hot tears running down my cheeks.

Axel nodded. "I understand, Harper. I do. Of course, I'd like the two of us to make love at some point, but it doesn't have to be right away. I can wait as long as you need me to."

I took a deep breath. "What if you have to literally wait forever? What if I can never get there? It's been 17 years, and I haven't so much as dated a man since then. I can't even think about doing that with a man. I just don't know..."

He put his arm around me and kissed me on the forehead. "It's okay, Harper, really."

"No, it's not. You deserve a real relationship. I can't hold you back like that. I might never get to where I can make love without wanting to freak out. That's not fair to you." My heart was breaking because I was falling in love with Axel. Yet, I just couldn't hold him back. I would see my therapist this week and try to work it out again, but I didn't think I could. And if I couldn't, how could things go forward with Axel or any other man? They couldn't. I hated that fact, but I had to face it. Axel and I were going to only be friends.

I hated Michael that much more. He screwed me up, maybe for life. Because of him, I couldn't be normal. He made me sick.

"Harper, I won't give up on this." He looked down at the ground. "I'm falling in love with you. And your girls. You're worth waiting for. You'll figure it out. You're strong. I believe in you, Harper. And there's no need to rush anything."

He put his hand in my hair and kissed me softly. I closed my eyes, feeling the tingling yet also feeling the fear. My heart was pounding, and I felt my entire body shaking.

I pulled away. I didn't want to lose control. I didn't want to go further.

"I'm falling for you, too," I told him. "But-"

"No buts. Seriously, I'm a very patient man." He kissed me again and then kissed my forehead. "But I don't see why you're putting yourself through this. Representing him. How can you be unbiased?"

I took a deep breath. "I'll admit it. I want him to fry. I'm hoping he's guilty so I can make sure he fries. That would give me the most emotional satisfaction."

"But if he's not guilty? What happens if you find, beyond any doubt, he had no hand in killing that man? What then? You'll represent him and I know you'll give it your all. Or, worse yet, what happens if he did it and the jury finds him not guilty? Like with that John Robinson bloke. How will you handle that? I'm worried about you, Harper. I won't lie. I'm worried about you, anyhow. I don't know why you were acting odd the other night. I think you should see a doctor."

I shook my head. "I'm okay. I've suffered from clinical depression for most of my life, and I take meds for that. I felt weird the other night, but I feel fine today. But I'll see my therapist. I have to get my head straight about this Michael thing. It's bothering me, and I must understand how I feel about it."

Axel kissed my forehead again, and I sighed. "Thank you for being so patient with me. I hope to get past this and get on a better footing. I know you won't wait forever, though."

He smiled. "I'll wait as long as you like. You're special, Harper. I mean that."

At that, Rina poked her head out the door. "Brianna's mom is here," she said. "To pick her up."

I nodded and stood up. "I better greet her. You can hang out back here or come on in."

Axel followed me into the living room so I could see Brianna off.

I was relieved to have this talk but worried at the same time. He said he'd wait for me.

But what if I could never get there?

Ten

The next day, I decided that I would do the investigation of Michael with an eye towards proving to myself that he was guilty. I *wanted* him to be guilty. I *needed* him to be guilty. It would give me great satisfaction to make sure he went down. Yet, if I thought for a second he was innocent, I couldn't sink him. I was too ethical for that.

I was restrained, however, by my Sixth Amendment duty to Michael. I was bound by ethical rules to give Michael a zealous defense, even if he was guilty as sin. That was always the hardest part of my job, even though, usually, if a person was guilty, I could just plead him out. I could possibly plead out Michael, too, if I thought he was guilty.

Yet I wanted to try the case. I wanted to try it and see the jury stand up and find him guilty. If that happened, I would derive immense satisfaction. If I pled him out, it wouldn't have the same effect. I wanted him to be humiliated in front of the jury and the people in the courtroom and the media, which was ramping up interest in this case.

If I pled him out, it would just be me, the prosecutor and the judge in the courtroom. That wouldn't be as fun for me.

I shook my head as I made my way to my car. Fun for me. I

would have fun if the jury found him guilty. What kind of person was I? My psyche was so tangled up, so haywire, and I didn't know which way was up.

One thing I knew, however – my investigation would be geared towards eliminating possibilities, not trying to find if Michael didn't do it. I wanted to make sure I crossed every T and dotted every I, so I could prove to myself Michael was guilty.

I started with going downtown to the police department to talk to the cops on the scene. I would also talk to Christina Sanders to find out what the relationship was between Michael and Judge Sanders. That was important to me, because I knew there was some reason the cops were so quick to arrest Michael for the crime. Yes, he was on the scene. But he called the police. Since he called the police, why was he so quickly suspected of killing the judge?

I also wanted to talk to Christina, because I had a suspicion about her, as well. She was one of the people I wanted to eliminate.

I went to the police department. I had previously made an appointment to see Officer Murphy, who was one of the officers on the scene. I wanted to talk to him and get a feel for why he was so quick to make an arrest.

"Hello, Harper," Office Chris Murphy said when I went to the police headquarters to see him. "It's great to see you."

"You too, Chris," I said. He offered me a donut and I politely took one and started to eat it. "I guess you know why I'm here."

"Of course. You wanted to talk to me about that Michael Reynolds case." He took a bite of his donut. "That was a bad deal, I tell you what."

I brought out my trusty yellow pad and pen and prepared to make notes. "It was. But tell me about it. You arrested him on the scene. Why? He told you an intruder must've killed Judge Sanders, and he wasn't home when the judge was killed. He basically got there and found the judge dead. Yet you and your partner didn't even hesitate to arrest him. There must be some reason for doing that."

Chris nodded. "There was, Harper. He was on the scene. Plus, his story add up. And he strikes me as being slick, that one. Rich assholes are usually up to no good."

I sighed. This wasn't what I wanted to hear. I wanted to hear Officer Murphy had a good reason for arresting Michael, but he didn't. Unfortunately, every reason he gave me for arresting Michael didn't pass muster. It could all be explained away perfectly.

"Officer Murphy," I said, addressing him formally, even though the two of us were friends. "If he killed the judge, he probably wouldn't have called the police when he found his father-in-law. He's smart enough to not be so obvious, don't you think?" I shook my head and took another bite of the donut. This wasn't going well.

"Well, that's right, unless he goes the other way with it." He pointed at me. "There's a kind of reverse psychology these people use with us all the time. They try to be really obvious, for the same reason you just said – they think they'll never be suspected because they called us to the scene. It's just as likely he did it and tried to make us think he didn't."

That made sense to me. I represented people in the past who admitted to me they did it, even though their actions were similar to Michael's. They would call the police, yet they were guilty.

It didn't usually work, however, with the cops. It did work with jury arguments, though – show how illogical it would be for my client to kill somebody and then immediately call the cops. I got more than one person off with that very argument.

More than one guilty person, to my ever-lasting shame.

"You mentioned earlier his story didn't add up. Why do you say that?"

He shrugged. "It was just a hunch I had. I think the little bastard was lying. He told me he was out at the supermarket buying fried chicken. That's just about the dumbest thing I've ever heard. The deli case closes at 9 at the local Hen House, if it stays open that late."

"Did he have fried chicken when he came in the door?"

"Yeah. He had a little box of chicken, but I looked at it, and it was cold as ice. He bought some chicken, alright, but hours earlier. But he was eating it when we got there."

I made a note about that. I wondered why Michael went through the trouble of buying the chicken earlier and then tell the cops he was out buying the chicken when the judge was killed. What a ridiculous story to tell.

"What else struck you as odd?"

"Nothing, really. I interviewed the mother and the daughter, and they both told me Michael wouldn't do something like that, but I have my doubts."

I sighed. "Tell me the truth. Did you just arrest him because you had nobody else to arrest for this crime? If it was a random intruder, as he told you it was, then it'll make your job much, much more difficult. And the media has been all over this case – you're under a lot of pressure to make an arrest. It's a federal judge who was bumped off. If you didn't make an arrest, you'd be hounded night and day until you had somebody in custody. So, there Michael Reynolds is, you think he looks good, and you arrest him for the crime. Boom, you're done. Is that it? He never confessed. So, what else do you have?"

I was disappointed. I thought the police had so much more than this. But, it seemed like I hit the nail on the head – a federal judge was knocked off, and, if Michael's story was believed, the culprit was a random intruder. It was much less work for the police to arrest Michael, so that was who they arrested.

Nothing more than that, apparently.

Officer Murphy's silence spoke volumes. "Listen, Harper, I'd like it if you didn't judge me about this. We get a lot of pressure from the powers that be when things like this go down. Yes, Michael was convenient to arrest."

"And you guys aren't looking at anybody else?"

"No. We have our man."

I stood up. "Well, I guess we're done here. Thanks for the donut."

I left his office feeling out of sorts and angry. I couldn't believe

Officer Murphy was so lazy as to just arrest the first person he could, without doing the necessary work to find out who really did it. There were people with motives – anybody who had a case in front of Judge Sanders really had a motive to kill the judge. Yet the cops never even looked at any of them.

Why?

I went to the office. "Pearl, I need to get Christina Sanders in here for a deposition."

"On it," she said. "What else do you need done?"

"I need for you to take a closer look at all the cases Judge Sanders had pending in front of him. And get Anna on the phone. I need her to do some hacking work."

Pearl got busy doing all these things and I went into my office. I had an appointment to see Judge Johnson, who was Judge Sanders' buddy. I had to find out more about the judge's habits and see if he had any suspicion on anybody who might've targeted the judge.

Pearl came into my office. "I did all those things you asked me. Let me take a closer look at the companies in Judge Sanders' court. I'll give you a run down and let you know if I see anything suspicious."

"Thanks."

I stared out the window, looking at the Country Club Plaza below me. My mind was on Michael and Axel and Elmer and, somehow, these three men melded in my mind. Michael raped me, Elmer attacked me and Axel...sweet, lovely Axel. He was completely innocent of any crimes against me, yet I couldn't bring myself to really love him because of men like Michael and Elmer and all the other men who had attacked me physically and mentally throughout the years.

I had my first appointment with my therapist that evening. The first one in a long time. I looked forward to it, dreaded it all the same. I didn't quite know what to tell her. I hoped she could straighten me out. I was confused about so many things in my life.

I looked at my watch and realized that my appointment with Judge Johnson was coming up. "Pearl," I said, "I need to go and talk to Judge Johnson. Keep looking over those cases and let me know if anything stands out for you. I'll be back in a couple of hours."

"I will, girl. I'll see you soon."

I got to the Federal Courthouse, went in and immediately got on the elevators. I went to the eighth floor, where Judge Johnson had his chambers. "Hello," I said to the receptionist who sitting behind the desk in the judge's suite. "I have an appointment with Judge Johnson at four."

She nodded. "Harper Ross," she said, looking at her appointment calendar. "He's expecting you."

"Thanks."

I went back to the chambers and found Judge Johnson. He was an African-American man, about 6'5" and very slender. His head was shaved and he dressed impeccably. Even though he was always in his judge's robe, and nobody really got a chance to see his actual clothing, he always made sure his suits were pressed and clean, his shoes were buffed and he even had a little handkerchief in his pocket.

"Hello Ms. Ross," he said, standing up. "It's good to see you."

"And you," I said. "You're looking well."

He nodded. "It's difficult circumstances, but I've been holding my own. Holding my own. Please have a seat."

"Thank you." I sat down. The chambers were opulent, much more opulent than the judge's chambers on the state circuit court level. The ceilings were high, the walls were paneled in walnut and the windows were floor to ceiling. The room was enormous and, on two of the walls were bookshelves that had every legal book and treatise imaginable.

"Now, what would you like to ask me about Robert?" he asked.

I didn't quite know how to approach this subject. I didn't want to tell him my suspicions about the poison. "I haven't been able to see Judge Sanders' chambers," I said. "So I couldn't ascertain if he had anything in there, as far as drinks might go."

"Drinks," he said carefully, as if he had no idea what I was getting at. "Like a water receptacle, that sort of thing? He had one of those."

I shook my head. I didn't want to know about his "water receptacle," because the culprit couldn't have poisoned that without poisoning everybody who drank from it. "No," I said. "Did he have a liquor cabinet?"

He furrowed his brow. "No. No, he didn't. Some of the other judges do around here, but not Robert. He didn't drink, as far as I know. At least, he didn't drink while he was here." He paused and looked at me for a beat. "Why do you ask?"

"It's just a question I needed to ask. I also wanted to ask if Judge Sanders expressed any concern about anybody. Has he any criminals in front of him who've threatened him? Any civil cases he was concerned about?"

Judge Johnson shook his head. "We all get criminals who threaten us. Comes with the territory. But he hadn't gotten death threats. That much I can tell you. If he did, he could've asked for security detail. As for civil cases, what are you asking? Are you wondering if maybe a civil defendant or plaintiff might've been involved in his murder?"

"It's something I'm investigating," I said.

Judge Johnson chuckled. "You've been watching too much television, I'm afraid. I wouldn't be too concerned about civil defendants putting a hit on any one of us."

"You don't think they would have motive? There are multimillion dollar lawsuits being filed in this court every day. Companies stand to lose that amount of money. Judge Sanders was known to be very pro-plaintiff and he routinely ruled against large corporations. I can see a motive right there. A motive as old as time – greed."

Judge Johnson made a little temple with his fingers and then his face broke out into a smile. His smile was blinding, charming and disarming. He laughed again a little bit. "I suppose you're right, Ms. Ross, but how will you figure that out? He's had hundreds of cases and hundreds more have been filed and have drawn him as a judge. It would be a needle in a haystack, really, to try to figure out which one of those companies might have had motive to kill Robert." He shook his head. "Good luck with that. The police aren't investigating this any more, because they've got their man."

"Yes. About that. What do you know about the relationship between Judge Sanders and Michael Reynolds? Did he talk much about that?"

Judge Johnson furrowed his brow, like he was lost in thought. "He didn't get along with him, I don't think. He complained Michael wasn't treating his daughter very well. It seemed Michael had a taste for the ladies."

"Did Christina know about this? That Michael was stepping out on her?"

"I get the feeling maybe she didn't know so much about that. But Robert did. He hired a private investigator to follow Michael around. That was how he found out about Michael's affairs. He wanted to present Christina with this information, but I don't think he got the chance."

I wrote down what he was saying. This actually sounded bad for Michael, especially if Robert and Michael had words about it. "Did Judge Sanders confront Michael with what he knew?"

"Yes he did. Three days before he died, he told Michael he had a dossier of information about him and the affairs he was having and would go to Christina and tell her everything."

"What was in his dossier?"

"Pictures of him and his mistress out on the town. He wasn't very discreet about it, either."

I cleared my throat. "Do you know who his mistress was?"

He leaned forward. "Yes. Her name is Ariel Winthrop. She's an heiress to the Winthrop diamond fortune."

Ariel Winthrop? I'd seen her picture in the society section from time to time. She was married to a trust fund baby. A playboy type who didn't have to work. Michael Reynolds was somebody who got around quite a lot. So far, there were two mistresses I knew about – Ariel Winthrop and Kayla Stone. I wondered if that was significant.

I didn't know. What was significant, as far as I was concerned, was that the judge and Michael had a strained relationship and the judge was about to reveal all to his daughter about Michael's messing around.

Might that be a reason for Michael to kill him?

I knew the answer to that – people have killed for reasons such as that, and for much, much less. I made a note of that on my pad.

"What else can you tell me about the relationship Michael had with Judge Sanders?"

"Well, I think Robert never approved of Michael, even before he realized Michael was stepping out on Christina. He thought Christina could've done much better than Michael. He personally thought Michael wasn't smart or kind enough to be with Christina. Michael would berate Christina in front of people, such as in family gatherings. He would say rude things to her right in front of everyone, and, if he was angry, he would yell at her in front of everybody. Robert would never stand for that, of course, so he would berate Michael for yelling at Christina, and there was serious tension in that family because of that dynamic."

I furiously made notes. "Were you present for any of this?"

"No," he said. "I was Robert's best friend, however, so I heard all about these quarrels."

I nodded. Somehow, none of this surprised me. Michael obviously had poor impulse control. A serial rapist could never boast about having excellent control over his emotions or impulses. I was slightly surprised, however, that Michael would show his crazy around his father-in-law.

"What about Christina? Why would she put up with Michael's bad behavior?"

He shrugged. "The heart wants what it wants, I guess. I hardly think Christina Sanders is the only woman who loves a man beneath her in station and behavior. I doubt she'll be the last, either."

I leaned back in my chair. "Would you characterize Michael as being a bad boy?"

He chuckled. "You mean like a guy who rides motorcycles, has tons of tattoos and drinks 45s while he rides through the streets?"

I laughed, too. We seemed to have the same stereotype in our heads. "Yes, something like that. Except no motorcycle and, instead of wearing a leather jacket, he wears an Armani suit. He might have tattoos, though."

"I know. You're talking about attitude. Did Michael have the attitude of a bad boy. That's what you want to know, isn't it?"

"It is."

"Then the answer is yes. And, from what Robert told to me, Christina has a way of picking these types of men. Poor Robert was at his wit's end about that. His beautiful daughter, educated at Yale, popular in her private school growing up – why she always went for the loser, he never knew. That was how he termed these boys and men – losers. Now, Michael isn't exactly a loser, but his attitude made him one. I guess some women just like men who will punish them somehow."

"How well do you know Christina?"

"Not very. I met her at some parties Robert had in his house. I haven't really spoken with her one on one, though." He paused. "Why did you ask me earlier about the drinking thing?"

I felt like I could confide my suspicions in him. He'd find out sooner or later anyhow, as the toxicology report would be in and I had a hunch arsenic poison would show up in the judge's system. "I think he was being poisoned," I said. "And I'm trying to figure out the source. If the judge had a certain bottle of liquor he didn't share with people, that would be the perfect vehicle for the poison. Other than that, I don't know. It would have to be put into his food and drink at his house. Which actually would lead me right back to Michael."

Not that this was a bad thing. I actually was hoping the

poisoning took place at the judge's house. That way I could build my case against Michael.

But maybe not. There was always Christina. She possibly would poison her father. Why that would be, I didn't quite know just yet. There was something there, and I'd have to figure that out.

The judge seemed to start thinking about my words. He was nodding and the expression on his face was that of somebody trying to access a distant memory. "You know, he has a mini fridge in his chambers. Or he had one. It was in a closet. He was a health nut, and he had this plastic jug in that refrigerator that he drank out of. It was some kind of green drink he brought into him fresh each week. He ordered it from the mail order and it was delivered to him. Nobody else drank that but him, mainly because nobody else liked that sort of thing. It had kale in it, broccoli and all sorts of green veggies." He chuckled. "I hope you don't mind my saying, but that stuff tasted rank."

I laughed out loud and nodded my head. I knew the kind of drink he was talking about, and it *was* rank. No doubt about it.

"Was that the only thing he more or less drank exclusively?"

Judge Johnson paused, considering the question. "Yes," he finally said. "That would be the only thing. But he also kept yogurts and cut-up vegetables and things like that in that refrigerator. He was very much a health nut." He looked sad. "I guess that's the irony of it all. You do all you can to make sure you live to be a ripe old age, only to have somebody cut you down. It's not fair."

No, it wasn't fair. Life wasn't fair, but being murdered in your prime *really* wasn't fair.

I stood up. "Thank you, Judge Johnson. I know you have a lot of cases you need to tend to, so I won't take up any more of your time."

"Thank you for coming to see me," he said. "I appreciate knowing you're diligent in finding out who might have done this. If the police won't do this kind of investigation, I'm very happy somebody else is. You have to bring whoever did this to justice. There's nothing worse than having justice denied."

I nodded my head, thinking that, if Michael somehow walked free from this case, it would be the ultimate case of justice denied. He deserved to be in prison, if not for the murder of Robert Sanders, then for the lives he destroyed through his serial rapes and serial philandering.

He was a bad guy, and I secretly hoped I could be instrumental in hanging him for it.

Eleven

After work, I met my sister Albany, because she wanted to go to my therapist with me. I hadn't seen my therapist in quite a long time, and I knew that seeing her would probably shake me up, so Albany wanted to come with me and wait in the waiting room while I poured my guts out.

"Hey," she said, picking me up at my house. "I wanted to give you this. For luck and strength." She handed me a crystal and I held it in my hand. I wanted to believe the crystal had some kind of magical powers, but I couldn't. My brain was always too logical to believe things like that. Nevertheless, I clutched it tightly and smiled at her.

"Thank you."

"You're welcome. This crystal has been blessed by a very powerful psychic. I've also been lighting candles for you every night. I'm telling you, I'm worried about you, sis. Everybody is."

I sighed and felt tears coming to my eyes. I didn't tell Albany about representing Michael. She probably would've brained me. She didn't know I'd been raped. I didn't tell her or anybody else, because I didn't want to deal with my family nagging me to go to the cops. I would never do that, so I just kept quiet.

"What does this crystal represent?"

"Strength and luck, just like I told you. When you hold it in your hand, your holding the power of Mischka Wilson, my personal psychic. You might laugh, but she's told me things that came true, right on the money. She's the real deal."

"I'm not laughing."

"You're holding it in, I can tell."

She was right about that. I wanted to laugh out loud, but I didn't want to hurt her feelings, so I had to stifle it. "No, I'm not."

"Yes you are, but that's okay." She reached her hand towards mine. "I'm glad you're getting back to therapy. It did you good before. I'm a firm believer that everybody should have regular therapy if they can afford it."

"Me too. Especially people in my profession. I admit, it takes a lot out of me."

She nodded. "How is your new murder case going?"

I swallowed hard, wanting to tell her the truth, but holding back. "It's going fine, I guess. I'm doing some of the preliminary investigatory work, as the cops aren't investigating anymore. They were under a lot of pressure to make a quick arrest, so they arrested my client. I don't believe he did it, though."

"Well, even if he did it, you'll still go balls to walls to represent him, as you always do. No judgments, but how do you do that, sis, and look at yourself in the mirror every night?"

Good question. "No judgment? That sounds like a judgmental question to me."

She shrugged. "It's not meant to be, but I can never understand representing guilty people. Plead them out, get them off the streets, but don't try to walk them."

I looked out the window, thinking of John Robinson, Gina and the two girls. I shuddered a little. "Maybe I'll plead this one out if I find out he did it."

She headed to the parking lot of my therapist's building and parked the car. "Let's go," she said. "I'll be waiting for you when you get out of there. I have a feeling you'll have a lot to say to your therapist. I don't know why I have that feeling, but I do."

We went up the elevator and we found the door to my therapist. Her name was Dr. Teresa Rosen. She was a 30ish woman who dressed modestly in sweaters and slacks, and usually wore her blonde hair up in a tight bun. She was attractive, fit and extremely easy to talk to.

"Harper," she said, coming out of her office and giving me a hug. "I haven't seen you in so long. I'm very happy that you're back, though. I actually was thinking about you before you called for an appointment. I see your name in the papers from time to time, and I've always wondered how you've been holding up."

I hugged her back. "Are you ready for me?" I asked her.

"I am. Hello, Albany," she said, giving Albany a hug as well. "It's very nice to see you, too. It's always good for my clients to have a support system."

I followed Dr. Rosen back to her office. She went over to her fish tank, which sported all manner of saltwater fish, and put a pinch of food into it.

I was always fascinated with her fish tank, because she kept some of the most beautiful fish I'd ever seen. There were enormous fish that were blue with bright yellow fins, and coral reefs swaying in the water. There were vibrant clown fish, with their distinctive orange and white patterns, and delicate sea horses which bobbled alongside brilliantly striped fish.

I watched the fish, mesmerized, while Dr. Rosen sat down behind her desk. "You always liked watching the fish," she said with a smile. "I bought some new ones since you were here last."

I nodded. "I worked in a pet store when I was 16, and the saltwater fish always fascinated me. But I know how hard it is to maintain this tank, so hats off to you."

She smiled. "It is a challenge, but once you get the hang of it, it's not so bad." She hesitated. "But I know you didn't come here to talk about the fish."

I sighed and hung my head. I was embarrassed to admit to her what was on my mind, even though I needed to tell her all about it. I needed to have *somebody* help me try to puzzle out what I was doing with Michael's case. It certainly wasn't coming to me.

"No," I said, "I didn't come here to talk about the fish. But the fish certainly are a nice bonus."

"Of course." She nodded her head. "Now, Harper, why don't you tell me why you made this appointment. It's been years since we last met. There must be something on your mind."

I nodded and swallowed hard. The words just weren't coming to me, for whatever reason. I leaned back on the sofa and crossed my arms. My breathing was labored and I was on the verge of tears. I guessed that telling Dr. Rosen what was on my mind was more difficult than I'd ever imagined.

"Um," I began. I picked up the paperweight on the coffee table in front of me and I examined it. "I'm having problems processing a case. I'm..." I trailed off. Would she judge me for taking Michael on as a client? Would she judge me if I told her I really wanted to sink him and make sure he ended up behind bars? She couldn't go to the Missouri Bar and tell them the truth about my motivations on this case, because of professional confidentiality, so I didn't have to worry about getting into professional trouble for telling her the truth. Yet, I was having difficulties admitting it. I really had difficulties admitting failings to anyone, so how could I tell her I was trying to deliberately fail on this case?

"Go on," she said. "You have a case you're working on, and you're having problems processing it because..."

I swallowed hard again and tried to control my shaking. "I'm having problems processing it because the defendant is Michael Reynolds."

She nodded her head. "I see. The man who raped you in the fraternity house." Her poker face was impassive, which drove me crazy, because I couldn't tell what she was thinking. I didn't like that.

"Yes. The man who raped me in the fraternity house."

She leaned back and made notes. "Tell me about the case. What's he charged with?"

"He's charged with murdering his father-in-law, who also happens to be a judge."

"Yes," she said. "Now I remember reading about this case in the paper. He came to you to ask you to defend him. Why do you suppose he would choose you for that?"

I shrugged. "I've pondered that question myself. I don't really know. He said it was because of my reputation and the fact that I've been able to win some impossible cases. I guess that's true, because I have won some cases that seemed unwinnable at the outset."

"Well, I'm certain that's true, but let's try to unwind what you're really thinking about why he would have chosen you, out of all the attorneys in the city, to represent him."

That was a question I hadn't really considered. I just took it on face value that he chose me because he felt I was the best person for the job. "I don't really know. Maybe he chose me because he unconsciously wanted to make amends. He says he does. Want to make amends, that is."

"Do you believe that?"

"No. I don't believe that."

"Then why do you believe he chose you because he wants to make amends?"

I shrugged. "I guess that was just the first answer that popped into my head. It's probably wrong, though."

She made some more notes. "What are some other possibilities?"

I pursed my lips and shook my head. "I don't really know."

She nodded her head. "Well, let's move on. I suspect you're here because you're questioning why you would take the case. I am correct about that?"

"Yes," I said. "That's exactly why."

"Tell me your thoughts on it, and then I'll give you my theory."

I took a deep breath. "I want him to fry. I desperately want him to go down in flames. I'm afraid that if a different attorney took his case, he'll get away with killing the judge. If he's guilty of the crime, I want to make sure he doesn't get out of it."

She nodded her head. "But only if he's guilty of the crime? What if he's not guilty of the crime? How will you feel when you secure his freedom? And how will you know for sure he's guilty or not guilty? That question can never be known beyond a shadow of a doubt, unless the person actually confesses. How are you untangling those questions in your head?"

I looked out the window. "I want him to be guilty," I said softly. "So I can make sure he gets the justice coming to him. I want him to die in prison." I hung my head. "I'm his attorney and I want him to die in prison. I'm having a hard time squaring that desire with the ethics that I practice under and with the oath I took when I was sworn into the Missouri Bar. I'm bound to represent him zealously, no matter if he's guilty or not, but, in truth, I'm trying to find a way to make sure he goes to prison for life."

Dr. Rosen was correct about one thing – I never would know if Michael was guilty or not guilty. I could only find evidence that would point one way or another, but, unless he came right out and told me he did it, it would be impossible to prove with 100% certainty. Juries convicted with evidence beyond a reasonable doubt. The term *reasonable doubt,* however, didn't mean 100% certainty. It simply meant that the evidence showed that the defendant most likely committed the crime.

She cleared her throat. "Here's my suspicion on why you took this case. I believe you took it because seeing justice given to Michael will help you finally move on. What he did to you has led to some deep-seated issues that you and I have tried to work through, but, as of yet, we haven't been successful in working through them together. When you stopped our therapy before, you told me it was because you felt you weren't making progress. I wonder if you took this case to get closure on your feelings about the rape."

"Yes," I said. "I think you're right about that."

"I am worried, however, about what will happen if he's found not guilty. I worry that such an outcome will cause you to regress even further."

I sighed. "I've considered that possibility."

She nodded her head. "You might consider withdrawing from his case," she said. "For the sake of your mental health. You're gambling that the outcome won't be what you want. You need to think about the possibility that you will never see Michael get the justice you want for him."

I bowed my head and felt hot tears coming down my cheeks. "I know," I said softly. "And I might never have a decent relationship. I still can't bring myself to even think about being intimate with a man. I have a man now, a man who says he loves me and will wait for me, but he won't wait forever. I'm afraid that if Michael is found not guilty and he walks away, I might never be free. Might never feel safe. Might never feel the unjust will be punished."

She nodded her head. "And how do you feel knowing that, in your past, you've defended guilty people who have gone free? How does that fit into that dynamic?"

I blinked, seeing she was getting at the crux of the matter. She was stabbing at the heart of why I was feeling so loathsome about myself. I was raped and my rapist was still walking around free. Nothing happened to him – in fact, he apparently went on to rape multiple other women. Yet I defended criminals. I celebrated when I got a not guilty verdict for them, even if the person was actually guilty. I liked to think that most of my clients who went free through my efforts were actually innocent, but I knew that wasn't always the case. John Robinson was one example, but I was sure there were others.

I was willfully blind and I had to be to do my job. I had to always imagine, no matter how much my gut was telling me otherwise, that my client was innocent. Factually innocent. If I didn't tell myself that, I couldn't do what I did. I couldn't put all my effort into somebody I knew to be guilty, even though I was ethically bound to do just that.

Was I a whore? I went to the highest bidder and took cases in a mercenary fashion – if they could pay my bill, I gave them representation, come hell or high water.

John Robinson was the one exception to my willful blindness

notion. I knew him to be guilty, and I gave him my all. And look what happened there. He murdered Gina Caldwell, and now her girls were in my custody. I was going to adopt Gina's girls, and I loved them, but they really needed to be with their mother. They couldn't be because I did my job too damned well.

"I don't defend rapists," I said, knowing that was a weak excuse. No, I didn't defend rapists, but I defended murderers, arsonists and people charged with assault. I defended people who got behind the wheel, blind drunk, and killed multiple people with their car. I defended drug dealers who dealt drugs to children. I defended all manner of loathsome scumbags, and I did it all without really examining why. Why I would be so willing to be a part of these people being returned to the streets?

She nodded. "Michael is a proxy. Have you ever thought about that possibility?"

"What do you mean?"

"You were victimized by Michael. You're in a profession where you defend people who have hurt others, as Michael hurt you. I wonder if you want to make sure Michael gets a long prison sentence not just because you want to see justice done in his case, but also because you secretly feel guilty for all the other clients you've managed to set free. Clients who you suspect, if not know for sure, were guilty of the crimes for which they were charged. In that way, Michael is a proxy for all the other clients you've managed to set free."

I pondered her words. They made sense. Maybe she had a point. Maybe I secretly felt shame for working so hard to set criminals free, so I put all my shame onto Michael. Let Michael pay for what he did, and maybe I could assuage my guilt for all those other clients who went on to walk the streets after I took their case and secured not guilty verdicts for them.

"Maybe," I said.

She nodded. "Again, I want you to imagine how you will feel if Michael goes free and you're part of the reason why. If he goes free and then goes on to hurt somebody else, as he hurt you. How will you feel if that happens?"

I felt a knot in my chest as I thought about that possibility. It was a cold knot, bound up in fear and loathing and anger. My heart started to pound and I felt nauseated.

I finally took a deep breath and looked Dr. Rosen directly in the eye. "I will feel like hell, but I'll really feel like hell if I withdraw from the case and find out another lawyer makes sure he walks free. I think this case is better in my hands."

She nodded. "It sounds like you have your mind made up."

"I do. But you're right. I'll be devastated if he walks free."

We talked for the rest of the hour about what had been going on in my life. I told her about John Robinson and the girls and how I felt about all that. I never got over what had happened there, although I was somewhat mollified by the fact I had the girls at my house. I would rather that Gina be alive, however. I was quite sure the girls felt the same.

After our session was over, I walked out of the office feeling slightly better, but only slightly. I would still walk into the lion's den and represent the scumbag Michael. I was playing with fire. I knew that.

But if it all worked out, it might be the first step to freeing me.

Twelve

The next day was the day of the autopsy. I was down at the Medical Examiner's Office, as was the prosecutor in the case. April Todd was an experienced prosecutor with 20 years under her belt, but I had felt, and so did many others, that she was rapidly burning out. That worried me. I needed her on the top of her game so that Michael got his just desserts.

"Okay, Harper," she said, joining me by sitting next to me on the chairs just outside the ME office. "Why don't we exchange some dates on when we can get our discovery into one another. I just got a notice from the trial court, and this trial is set for February 10 of next year. I'd like to close discovery by January 15. Would you be able to do that as well?"

"I would. Do you have an offer on this case?"

She shook her head. "I haven't been authorized to give an offer just yet. As of now, my boss isn't backing off the death penalty. She might never back off that, either. Unfortunately, Judge Sanders was a close friend of hers, so I think she's taking it personally. Looks like we'll try this thing no matter what."

I sighed. I was hoping for a plea bargain. One that was decent, which meant I could talk Michael into taking it. I certainly didn't anticipate there not being a plea bargain possibility at all. "That's rather unprofessional, isn't it? Your boss won't authorize you giving a plea offer on this case just because she was friends with the victim?"

She shrugged. "Yes, I agree with that, but here we are. I don't want to try this, either. The media has been all over it. We've been contacted by every news organization there is, even some of the national ones. There's even talk of allowing cameras in the courtroom. I hate when the media gets involved, and they're very much involved in this one. It's not every day a federal judge is murdered, after all."

"I haven't been too inundated with media requests," I said. "Actually, I haven't been at all."

"Just wait," she said. "You just entered your appearance on this case. The media hasn't had the chance to harass you. You better run for cover on this one, especially if it goes south for us. You'll get blamed for it."

I knew that to be true. It was true in the John Robinson case, and it was bound to be true in this case as well.

"What discovery do you anticipate you'll be giving me?" she asked. "And, by the way, the gun has been recovered. They recovered it from a landfill."

"I knew it would be. As for discovery, I pretty much just plan on doing depositions. I don't anticipate doing much more." Usually, I would get experts to go through the crime scene in cases like this, to show my client wasn't present in the room when the person was killed. They had ways of showing this by estimating when the footsteps of the client hit the hardwood floor. I'd usually have some kind of forensic analysis done on the gun and bullet, to show glove prints on the gun. A well-paid expert can trace the glove prints to a certain pair of gloves, for glove prints were similar to fingerprints.

Not that I wouldn't introduce an expert to testify to the glove prints. I would only do that if the glove prints at the scene of the crime could not be matched with any pair of gloves Michael owned. If they matched a pair Michael owned, then I might go ahead and bring in the expert to testify. That was one way that I could make sure Michael went down. I could feign innocence pretty easily if the expert testified the glove print matched Michael's glove. I could simply tell Michael I thought the expert would testify the other way.

"Only depositions? You won't do forensic analysis or anything like that?"

"I don't anticipate doing that."

"Okay then. We plan on bringing in the cops on the scene. We'll also bring in the testimony of Christina Sanders."

"Christina Sanders. What will she testify to?"

"The relationship between your client and Judge Sanders. She doesn't want to testify, so I'll probably treat her as hostile, but I think she has a lot to say about how Michael Reynolds and Robert Sanders got along. Which wasn't well, to say the very least."

I nodded my head. "Anybody else? Who else you going to call?"

"We're still doing our investigation, and, to tell you the truth, who we call will depend on how this autopsy goes. Obviously, if it turns out the judge had been poisoned for a matter of months, there'll be more investigation into how that fits into the overall scheme of things. I'll definitely let you know, however, who we'll call and what evidence we plan to present."

The Medical Examiner came out and the two of us stood up. "Our preliminary examination indicate signs of poisoning in the system of the judge at the time of death. That is only the preliminary finding. We will have to send tissue samples for further analysis, but I'm reasonably confident the judge was, in all likelihood, poisoned."

I nodded. I knew this was coming.

I left the office and called Michael. He had to know what was going on, and I wondered if he'd supply me with some kind of explanation on who he thought poisoned the judge and why.

Speaking with him made me sick, but I had to do it. I still needed to make sure I did my job.

I only hoped "my job" would end up in a conviction for the scumbag.

Thirteen

"Robert was poisoned?" Michael asked me when he arrived in my office. "Seriously?"

"Seriously," I said. "He was poisoned." I narrowed my eyes. I would have to figure out, from Michael, if there was an alternative explanation for the poisoning. I hoped he did it, but I needed to rule out other people. "Do you have an explanation for this, Michael? From where I sit, you and Christina had the best access to the judge. The two of you would've been able to administer the poison to him. Nobody outside your circle would've been able to do that for such a long period of time. The only other person who might have been able to do that would've been your mother-in-law, Ava."

Michael's eyes got wide and he shook his head. "It wasn't me, of course. As for Christina, I don't know if was her or not. I can't imagine my mother-in-law would do it, either. I don't see why she would do something like that."

I raised an eyebrow. "I see you answered that question very different for your wife and for your mother-in-law. You said you didn't see why Ava would poison your father-in-law, but you just said you don't know if Christina would do it or not. There's a very subtle difference in those two answers."

He leaned back and appeared to think about my words. "I don't know who else would've done it. I mean, Robert had a domestic servant. Her name is Anita Gonzalez. She lived with Robert. Maybe she did it."

I sighed. "Why would Anita Gonzalez kill your father? Did she have any motive at all?"

He shrugged. "Who knows? Maybe Robert was diddling her. That could be. You never know what goes on behind closed doors."

That made me sick. It sounded like Michael was trying to toss poor Anita under the bus. It made me twice as suspicious that Michael was responsible for poisoning the judge. "I guess I'll have to look into that. I need Anita's phone number, because I'll have to interview her. I'll also interview Christina."

I had the feeling Michael was putting up Anita as a smoke-screen.

"Here," he said, writing down a phone number on a piece of paper. "Call her. Talk to her. I doubt you'll get straight answers, though. Not when Ava is still alive and employing her. Anita has reason to lie. And you might try to bring a translator, too. She knows very little English." He chuckled.

That was okay that she didn't know much English, because I spoke fluent Spanish. I lived in Mexico for several years in my youth, so I knew I could communicate with her.

"I'd like to speak with your wife at the same time," I said. "I'd like to arrange a time when Anita will be there at the same time Christina is. What day and time would be good for that to happen?"

He shrugged. "My wife visits Ava twice a week. Wednesday and Sunday evening. She goes over there, has dinner and watches movies with her. That's especially important now, because Ava has had a hard time accepting Robert's death. She's very lonely these days. If you go over there either of those evenings, you should catch my wife there and you can also talk to Ava. Ava had nothing to do with the poisoning, that much I can tell you."

His answers still made me suspicious. He kept reassuring me his mother-in-law couldn't possibly have anything to do with the poisoning, but he didn't seem to want to give me that same reassurance about his wife. Why?

"I'll make an appointment with Anita," I said. "For Wednesday evening. Hopefully I can talk to everyone I need to talk to when I visit that evening."

"I hope so too. You need to get to the bottom of this." He shook his head. "Poisoned. Wow. I never would've thought that would be the case."

"You never did? Seriously? The thought never crossed your mind? A healthy man who biked and golfed and ate fruits and vegetables gets deathly ill, and you never even considered why?"

"Not my job," he said. "It was the job of the doctors who gave him his physicals. Why didn't they find out Robert was being poisoned? Seriously. They were the ones who dropped the ball."

Why indeed? I would have to find out more about that. Either the doctors who examined him were incompetent, or there was something much more nefarious going on.

"Well, I hope to get to the bottom of all of it."

Later on that day, I summoned Anna to come over and do some hacking for me. I had a hunch, and I'd go with it.

She appeared at my office in all her tattooed gloriousness. Her hair was growing out, little by little, and she had taken to dyeing parts of it a shade of bright purple that looked like it took hours to get right. Nevertheless, the purple in her hair made her look even more kick-ass sexy. I often thought that, if I ever decided to swing that way, Anna would be the woman I'd "swing" with.

"What do you need for me to do?" she asked.

"I need you to see if you can find any kind of medical records on Christina Sanders," I said. "She's the daughter of Judge Sanders, so hopefully you can find the trail on her. I don't have much more information on her, though."

She nodded. "It's helpful her father was a federal judge," she said. "I should be able to find her records. What are you looking for in particular?"

"Psychiatric records," I said. "I need to know if she has had any kind of mental disorders."

"On it."

I loved that Anna never questioned why I made my requests. I had a hunch that Christina Sanders had a reason to have her father killed. Maybe Christina herself did it.

While Anna worked in the other room, I examined some of the cases Pearl had culled for me. These were the cases Pearl thought could bear fruit. These were all cases where corporations had a lot to lose by being in front of Judge Sanders, as well as some criminal cases. My hunch, however, was that the corporations would be the most likely culprits in doing this.

One company was a prominent pharmaceutical company. They were involved in a patent dispute and were being sued for $50 million. I shook my head. That one sounded promising, but I was looking for a case where there was a chance for punitive damages. One of Judge Sanders' case I looked at involved punitive damages, and he awarded them to the tune of $1 billion. In the case of a patent dispute, the only possibility was for regular damages, not punitive ones, so that company wasn't all that likely, in my eyes, to do something drastic like bumping off the judge.

Another company was involved in a class-action wage dispute. That one was more promising, because the suit called for $500 million in compensatory damages and over $1 billion in punitive damages. I put that one to the side. I'd have to examine that one much more closely.

For the rest of the afternoon, I pored over pending lawsuits, looking for clues on who might have the motive to murder the judge. Besides the wage dispute lawsuit, there was a lawsuit against a power company whose warehouse exploded, killing 18 people. That company was being sued because it had 150 safety violations they hadn't corrected, so the punitive damages would potentially be exorbitant in that one. Any judge would award punitive damages in that case, but Judge Sanders probably would have awarded more punitives than usual.

Around 3, Anna came into my office. "Knock knock," she said with a smile. "I have the information you're looking for."

"Come on in," I said. "Hit me with what you got."

She cleared her throat. "Christina Sanders appears to be somebody who has a lot of mental problems. To say the least." She handed me some medical records. "Here's where she was hospitalized for anorexia. Five times she was hospitalized for that. She also has a long record of psychiatric care. She's been in and out of psychiatric facilities since she was 15 years old." She shook her head. "Poor girl."

I looked at the records. They were only records of hospitalization and the basic reasons why Christina was admitted to the hospital each time. Which meant I didn't access to the reasons why she was admitted to psychiatric facilities, just that she was. I was intensely curious about this, and I made a mental note to scrutinize Christina much more when I went to see her. I needed to rule her out, as I needed to rule out those companies. I still wanted Michael Reynolds to be guilty, but I knew that, for my own psyche, I needed to do the necessary investigation to feel satisfied that he probably did it.

I also thought there was the possibility that Christina and Michael might have been in cahoots in killing the judge. Christina might have wanted him dead for personal reasons, while Michael might have wanted him dead for reasons of his own.

"I'll speak with Christina tomorrow," I said. "And I'll also speak with Anita Gonzalez, the domestic servant for the Sanders' household. I'm slightly suspicious that Michael is trying to throw Anita under the bus for this."

"Only slightly suspicious?" Anna asked. "Didn't you say the judge had been poisoned? Who could've done that?"

"Michael, Christina and Anita. Of the three, I admit, Anita seems to have the best access to the judge and could've monitored the poison consumption the best. That's because she lived with

Robert and Ava." I sighed. "It makes sense she might've done it, because she was in the best position to know what Judge Sanders ate or drank exclusively. That's important – there had to have been something in Judge Sanders' house that nobody else ate or drank but him, and Anita could've figured that out."

I also knew here were things in his office only he consumed. I couldn't discount that. I'd have to figure out who in his office had constant access to the judge and had the motive to kill him.

Fourteen

The next day, I went to see Christina and Anita at Judge Sanders' home. Anita was a pretty Mexican woman, dark-skinned and raven-haired, with a quick smile and slightly curvy figure. She wore a typical maid's uniform – a grey dress with a white apron, with comfortable white shoes. She spoke perfect English in a thick accent. If I had to guess, I'd imagine she was in her late 20s.

"Hello," she said, "Ms. Ross. Come on in." She waved her arms into the living room, and I walked in. The house was elegant and beautiful, located in the Mission Hills area, a ritzy suburb of Kansas City. The houses on the block were mansions and this house was no different. It was an enormous Tudor-style home, with pitched roofs and white walls, located on acres of land. The house was easily worth $1.5 million. I these homes and what they went for, and that was what I estimated this house's worth to be.

"Thank you," I said, walking into the enormous living room area with the vaulted ceilings that rose some fifty feet. The judge and Mrs. Sanders apparently had traditional taste with regard to furnishings, as the living room was marked by Queen Ann antique furniture and oil paintings that appeared to be extremely good Degas and Renoir knockoffs. Degas was actually one of my favorite painters – I loved his portraits of ballerinas. I also loved Renoirs, especially his portraits of garden parties.

"You wanted to speak with me?" She asked, a smile on her beautiful face. "About Mr. Sanders?"

"I did." I looked around. "Is Christina around? Or Mrs. Sanders?"

Anita shook her head. "No. They're out to dinner. I wanted to speak with you with them not around. They'll be back around 9 tonight, though, so you can speak with them then."

"Are they expecting me?"

She shook her head. "I'm terribly sorry, Ms. Ross, but I didn't tell them you were coming."

I raised my eyebrows, wondering what was going on. She wanted to speak with me in private and she didn't tell Christina and Mrs. Sanders I was coming. Somehow none of that sat right with me.

"Would you like some tea?" she asked.

"Please."

She left and came back in ten minutes, a tray in her hand. On the tray was a tiny tea kettle with matching tea cups. The cups and kettle both had flowers embossed on them, with gold trim around the edges. It was as traditional as the rest of the surroundings.

I took a sip and Anita sat down next to me.

"Thanks," I said, and then I brought out my pad of paper and pen. "I wanted to speak with you, because, well, the preliminary results are back from the autopsy of the judge and it showed the judge tested positive for arsenic poisoning. The final results won't be in for several weeks, but those were the preliminary findings. I'd imagine the final findings will be similar."

She nodded. "That doesn't surprise me." She ducked her head and a single tear ran down her cheek. She shook her head. "Mr. Sanders was very sick, very sick. No doctor could find what was wrong with him." She took a sip of her tea. "Nobody spoke with me about it, of course. They never really think about me being around. They don't hardly notice me. I guess they believe I don't listen to what they say, but I do. I never show it, of course, but I hear everything they say."

I furrowed my brows and leaned back in the chair. I suddenly remembered that Michael had warned me that Anita didn't speak very good English. However, here she was, speaking perfect English to me. I wondered if the Sanders family didn't know how much English she really could speak and understand. If they truly thought she didn't know what they were saying, Anita could be an excellent asset to tell me what I needed to know.

And what I really needed to know, more than anything else, was something, anything, that could hang my client.

"I see." I put my hand on my chin as I studied her. She was a wily one, that was for sure. She came off as a subservient woman, all smiles and submissive posture. But she had a great deal of intelligence, I could tell. I wondered if the Sanders family knew just how intelligent she was. "Anita," I said. "Let me ask you a question."

"Okay," she said. "You can ask me anything. I can tell you most things you want to know."

"The first thing I'd like to know is whether or not the Sanders family knows you speak very good English."

She shook her head, but she had an amused look on her face. "No. I got this job through a referral, whose name is Alejandra Hernandez. She worked for the Sanders for fifteen years, but had to quit because she got married and started a family of her own at home. Before I applied, she told me to act like I could only speak broken English. Mrs. Sanders, Alejandra said, prefers authentic Mexican women to work in the home, and that would mean Mexican women who do not speak good English." She smiled and shrugged. "Who knows why? I suspect it has something to do with her showing off for her friends that she's open to diversity. That's very important for her – to be seen as somebody who has all different types of people around her."

That was odd, but not that odd. Mrs. Sanders could very well have been just a little bit eccentric. I would have to speak with her to get a read on that.

"So, as far as the Sanders knew, you only speak limited amounts of English?"

"Right." She smiled and laughed. "Silly. They're very silly people."

"Sounds like it. It also sounds like you probably heard a lot of dirt over the years coming from this house."

She nodded her head. "Yes. That was what I was saying. I was always around – cleaning, cooking, serving. They spoke freely around me, because they didn't know I could understand what they were saying. And ay caramba. This is one rich family that has many skeletons in their closet." She touched my forearm for emphasis. "They always say the wealthy people are crazy, and this family is probably crazier than most."

Crazier than most. That sounded interesting, to say the very least.

"What do you mean?"

"Well, let me see. Judge Sanders apparently has a different family. Had a different family. They live across town, in Parkville. Mrs. Sanders found this out several years ago. Mr. Sanders would leave the house for days at a time. He told Mrs. Sanders that he had to go to Washington DC three days a week, and Mrs. Sanders believed him for years. Christina knew better, but she never told Mrs. Sanders that Mr. Sanders didn't actually have to go to Washington DC all that often."

I wrote down what she was telling me, wondering how it was relevant. If it was relevant at all.

"A different family. By that you mean a parallel family, or it was a family he had before he was married to Ava Sanders?"

"Parallel. It wouldn't have been much of a scandal if it was simply a family he had before he married Mrs. Sanders. But this was particularly scandalous when this came out. And Mrs. Sanders was furious, to say the very least."

"Scandalous," I said. "Tell me about this other family."

"He has three kids with this other woman. Her name is Carmela Adams. She's Latina, although she was married to a white man, which is why her first name is Latina and her second name is not. That made it that much worse, of course – Mr. Sanders was having a long-term affair with a Latina woman, and he was having children with her as well."

"Three children." I sighed. "Michael never said a word about this to me. He never told me there was another family the Judge had across town." I wondered about this. Maybe he never thought I'd find out about it, but why was he hiding this other family? That peculiar, to say the very least.

Anita shook her head. "I don't know, but that whole thing blew up several years back. They could never get a divorce, though, because Mr. Sanders likes to live here in this palace, and he never could if he divorced Mrs. Sanders."

That struck me as odd. "You mean Mrs. Sanders was the person who has the money in this family? Not Mr. Sanders?"

She nodded her head. "Right. Mr. Sanders makes around $200,00 per year. That's a good salary, of course, but it's not enough of a salary to live here in this house in this neighborhood. He grew up poor, too, so he doesn't have family money. Mrs. Sanders' family is old money from the East Coast. She's an heiress to a shipping company."

I narrowed my eyes and wrote things down on my paper. "Mr. and Mrs. Sanders have been married for how long?" I had access to that information, but not at my fingertips, and I was too preoccupied to look it up.

"Fifty years. They got married when they were both 17."

I closed my eyes, suddenly realizing there was yet another suspect to look at – Mrs. Sanders. "When did she come into the money? Do you have any knowledge about that?"

She shook her head and I would have to look into that.

I could feel the case slipping away. With every revelation, it became more and more clear Michael probably wasn't guilty after all. That knowledge made me sick. I wanted so badly to sink Michael, but I couldn't do it if I knew somebody else was guilty.

A part of me wanted to quit. Not dig any further. To try to

come up with some concrete evidence Michael did it, any evidence at all, and ignore all the exculpating facts I found out. Yet I ethically and morally couldn't do that.

I would have to find closure some other way.

I made notes to find out more about the Sanders' finances. I specifically needed to find out when Mrs. Sanders came into her inheritance, and if she somehow converted her inheritance money into joint assets. If she took the inheritance money and put it all into a separate account, with only her name on it, she was entitled to keep all that money, except for the interest earnings during the course of their marriage. It would be considered to be separate assets and Judge Sanders wouldn't be entitled to any of the money in the event of a divorce. But if she got her inheritance and put it into a joint account, or joint stocks and bonds, or real estate the two held jointly, or even if she took that money and put it into any kind of assets at all, the inheritance would've been converted into joint property. And that would mean Judge Sanders would be entitled to half of that if they divorced.

I knew enough about property division in dissolution of marriage cases to know Mrs. Sanders had reason to kill Judge Sanders. She was probably angry enough to do it. I had to put myself into her shoes – she finds out her husband, the man that she'd loved since she was 17 years old, was having a long-term affair with another woman. He had three kids with this other woman, and he lied to Ava by telling her he was going to DC three days a week. She finds out the truth, and feels not only betrayed but stupid and played. She believed his lies and apparently never bothered to check to see if he really had to go to DC each week.

And what if he asked for a divorce? What if Ava told Robert it was her or the other family, and he chose the other family? What then? If there wasn't a prenuptial agreement, then Ava was faced with the prospect of giving Judge Sanders half her fortune. That would be insult added to injury, to say the very least. That was the bad part of no-fault divorce, which was the law in Missouri – even though Judge Sanders apparently was acting atrociously, running around on his wife, he still would be entitled to half of what she had in the event of a divorce.

If I were in Ava Sanders' shoes, I probably would've killed Judge Sanders. Nobody could blame her for doing that.

"Okay," I said. "Do you know that happened after Mrs. Sanders found out about Mr. Sanders' affair?"

She shrugged. "Nothing, really. They had a huge argument, but Mr. Sanders told Mrs. Sanders he couldn't stop seeing Carmela. He told Mrs. Sanders he had a family with Carmela, and he couldn't just abandon the three children they had together." Anita shook her head. "And, oh Lord, that didn't go over well. There was a lot of screaming going on for many weeks. Weeks of constant fighting and screaming and throwing things at each other. Well, Mrs. Sanders threw things at Mr. Sanders, although Mr. Sanders never threw anything at her. Every time Mr. Sanders left the house and did not come back for days on end caused another huge fight. He would come back in the house and Mrs. Sanders would violently scream at him to get out."

"Did he get out?"

"No. He told her this was his home, too, and she couldn't force him out." Anita shook her head. "Oh, boy, that was a problem, too. I heard Christina talking to Mrs. Sanders, and she told Mrs. Sanders needed to divorce Mr. Sanders. Mrs. Sanders said she couldn't divorce him, although I never quite understood why. She said things like she wanted to stay with him because her friends looked up to her because she was married to a federal judge. But I think there were other reasons, too."

Yes, there were other reasons why Ava could never divorce Judge Sanders. I had a feeling I was probably right – her inheritance was converted into marital property and she wasn't about to give him a thin dime.

"So, there was that," I said. "The other family he had. What else can you tell me about this family?"

Anita shook her head and started to speak in Spanish. She didn't know I could understand every word, but, from what I could tell, she was cursing and not really communicating anything important.

She lowered her voice. "His daughter. Christina." She shook her head. "Oh, my. Mr. Sanders had been doing inappropriate things to her since she was 12 years old."

I bowed my head. I had a hunch about that. I thought that might have been the reason why she was anorexic and had been in and out of psychiatric facilities. Maybe there were other reasons why she had so many mental issues. I'd have to ask Anita about that.

"And Mrs. Sanders didn't suspect this, either?" What was this lady's problem? Her husband had another family and he was sexually abusing his daughter, and she never suspected a thing. Really?

"Oh, no. Mrs. Sanders knew all about what was happening with Christina and her father. But she pretended not to. I overheard conversations between Mrs. Sanders and Christina, and Christina told her what her father was doing to her. Mrs. Sanders shut her down every time Christina tried to say a word about it. Now, I truly think Mrs. Sanders had no idea that Mr. Sanders had another family or that he was having an affair with Carmela. I don't know how she could've been so naïve, but she was."

Maybe not naïve. Maybe she was willfully blind.

I cleared my throat. "And what about you? Did he try to make any indecent approaches to you?"

"No," she said, shaking her head. "He never made any indecent approaches to me. I would've quit if he did. I don't play that, mamacita." She smiled and shook her head again. "No way."

I mentally cleared Anita as a suspect in my head. But both Christina and Ava were looking more and more likely.

And if Ava did it, that cleared up another aspect nagging at me. I wondered how somebody could've poisoned Judge Sanders without also poisoning Ava. They both probably drank from the same milk jug. Probably drank from the same pitcher of tea. If they drank wine, they probably shared the bottle of wine. It would be highly unusual for a married couple to not share the same drinks.

Then again, maybe not. Perhaps they lived separate lives, ever since the Judge was found to be messing around with Carmela Adams.

But that was probable – they shared the same milk jug and tea pitcher etc. If somebody else was surreptitiously poisoning Judge Sanders, there would a good chance Ava would be poisoned as well. But if Ava was the one who was administering the poison...

"Tell me about how they lived. Did they live separate lives after Judge Sanders was found out?" I looked around, seeing this house was a good 6,000 square feet. It had different wings. It would be extremely easy for a married couple to live completely separate lives in this home. If that was the case, anybody could've poisoned the judge, because he might have his own separate refrigerator full of his own separate food.

"Of course," she said. "Mr. Sanders was banished to the east wing. He moved out of their bedroom and that wing is an entire other house, really. It has its own kitchen, its own living room, three entire bedrooms. It's a house within a house. That was where Mr. Sanders had to live."

Back to square one. That meant anybody who frequented this house could've poisoned Judge Sanders. That included Anita, Ava Sanders, Christina Sanders and Michael. All of them visited the house on a regular basis. Any one of them could've done it. Anita and Ava had the most access, because they were there every day, but there was also the chance Christina or Michael could've done it.

"How often did Christina Sanders and Michael Reynolds visit this house?"

"Every week. They came over for dinner once a week."

"Did Mr. Sanders have anything in his own special refrigerator only he drank or ate? Did he buy milk by the gallon, or make pitchers of tea, or did he have bottles of unopened wine? Something he drank every single day?"

She nodded. "Yes. He made a pitcher of tea every week. A new pitcher of tea. He drank two glasses a day, sometimes more. He also drank milk in his coffee every morning."

Bingo. That seemed to be the best vehicle for poison. He had his own milk and his own pitcher of tea.

What was good was that, in my mind, Michael was still a suspect. I didn't quite know what motive he had to kill Judge Sanders, but he still might've killed him. He still might have. I didn't have all the pieces of the puzzle just yet, but I would .

"What kind of relationship did Michael Reynolds have with the judge?"

Anita shook her head. "Not good at all. I served all their meals, and, just about with every dinner, there was some kind of fight between Mr. Sanders and Michael. Michael would yell at Christina, would curse her out and insult her, right there at the table, and Mr. Sanders would yell at Michael. They always brought their children here, too, and they had to witness Michael saying horrible things to Christina. He took pleasure, it seemed, insulting her right in front of everyone."

"What kind of insults?"

"He called her fat, Miss Piggy, said she shouldn't take extra servings of food. He called her stupid, bitch, stupid bitch, told her she was a bad mother, accused her of having sex with his best friends. You name it, he said it to her, right in front of everyone."

I thought about Christina, who appeared to weigh about 120 lbs. She had problems with anorexia in the past, too. And he was digging at her right where it hurt her the most – she apparently had a dysmorphic body image to begin with, so he knew that if he called her fat in front of everyone, he would be harpooning her right through the heart. Maybe she also was insecure about raising her children. If he said things about her being a poor mother, then that, too, would be putting a dagger right into her core.

Michael apparently hadn't changed since college. He was still just as sleazy. Still a bad, bad guy. I wouldn't be surprised if he was still raping women, too.

"What did Judge Sanders say to him when he was saying these cruel things to Christina?"

"They almost came to blows just about every week. But Michael and Christina would always be back the next week, because Mrs. Sanders wanted them to visit and bring the grand-kids." She sighed. "There was always a lot of tension whenever Michael and Christina came to visit. I dreaded their visits for that reason."

"What else can you tell me about the relationship between Michael and Judge Sanders?"

"Well, Mr. Sanders knew Michael was cheating on Christina. I heard many conversations between Mr. Sanders and Michael, where Mr. Sanders was telling Michael he knew about Michael's affairs. He told Michael that if he didn't come clean, he'd tell Christina all about what Michael was doing."

That was more promising. It was duplicative of what Judge Johnson told me in Judge Sanders' chambers. That gave me more of a motive for Michael to have killed the judge.

That gave me another idea – I would have to figure out exactly what Michael had to lose if he was forced to divorce Christina. As with Ava and Robert Sanders, perhaps Christina was the one with the money. I'd have to figure out if there was a trust fund set up for Christina, one that maybe Michael didn't have access to. That would mean Michael would have much to lose if Christina divorced him. He was an executive at an ad agency. He was highly paid, but he certainly wasn't paid enough to live the kind of lifestyle he was living. His house was also in one of the ritziest parts of town – he lived in the Hallbrook area, which was where business owners, CEOs, sports stars and major drug kingpins lived.

So, there was yet another theory of the case I formulated – one that was as plausible as any other. Michael killed Judge Sanders because Judge Sanders was threatening Michael with telling Christina about his affairs. If Christina divorced him, he'd be forced to come down in his lifestyle, and he had no desire to do this. So, he killed the judge.

While this was a good idea, it wasn't a sure thing. It wasn't even that good of a theory. I had to have something more solid, more of a smoking gun. Only then would I feel comfortable undermining Michael in his case. Only then would I feel right about sinking him.

It certainly wasn't a sure thing in comparison to everything else. Christina had reason to kill the judge. Ava certainly had reason to kill him. All three of these people – Christina, Ava and Michael – had means to poison him.

But, even if I figured out who poisoned the judge, I couldn't figure out one thing – why was the judge shot? Why wasn't the poison just allowed to run its course? And why was Michael so open about telling me about the symptoms the judge exhibited? That made zero sense to me, if Michael was the culprit. The ME might've missed the arsenic poisoning if I didn't alert her to it, and I only suspected poisoning because Michael told me about Robert's sickness. Arsenic poisoning is usually undiscovered in autopsies unless the ME was looking for it specifically. So, with Michael telling me about Robert being sick, it led to the ME making a definitive finding about the poisoning when perhaps that wouldn't have been the case before.

Maybe it was all just a sick kind of reverse psychology again. Just like I suspected Michael *didn't* kill the judge because he called the police, maybe the same principle worked when Michael told me his father-in-law was sick. Maybe he figured I wouldn't suspect him of poisoning his father-in-law because he was open about his Robert's sickness. It would've looked as if he had something to hide if he didn't tell me about Judge Sanders being sick, but I found it out later on independently.

This could all just be a game.

FIFTEEN

The next day, I wanted to dig into everything I learned from Anita, but, unfortunately, Rina stopped me from doing any of that. I got a call from her school – I was commanded to pick her up. She had been suspended for fighting in the schoolyard.

As much as I wanted Sophia to tend to this little crisis, I knew it wasn't her duty to do so. It was mine. I was the guardian, soon to be the adoptive mother. I'd have to deal with it all on my own.

It's not a big deal. God knew I was suspended more than once when I was in school. Once for fighting, and once for smuggling in a flask of alcohol. I was *that* kid. The kid who started trouble. I even had purple hair, just like Anna had now. I gave my parents so much grief...Now, I guess it was my turn. I gave my parents hell, now Rina was doing it to me.

Turnabout is fair play, after all.

I went up to her school, Pembroke Hill, parking right in front, and went into the main building. Her private school was situated on acres of land in Leawood, Kansas. This was a school where millionaires sent their children, and it cost me an arm and a leg to foot the bill. I was determined to foot that bill, though, because I wanted Rina and Abby to have the best education. I wasn't a millionaire, of course – far from it. But the girls didn't have their mother, so, in a way, my sending them to this fancy school was my way of making that up to them. I never could get over the guilt that they didn't have their mother because of me.

I probably never would.

She was sitting in the office of the headmaster, her arms crossed in front of her. Her little legs were swinging back and forth, back and forth, underneath the chair. She saw me, glared and then looked away.

I shook my head. She was giving me attitude, and I wouldn't having that. "I'll go and talk to the headmaster," I told her. "I'll be right out."

She shrugged and said nothing at all.

I went into the headmaster's office after she summoned me in there. She motioned me to sit down, which I did.

She grimaced as she looked at me. "I'm so sorry you had to come down here," she said. "This obviously isn't the best of circumstances."

"No, it never is, is it? Parents aren't summoned to the principal's office unless something no good is going on. What did she do?"

"She got into a fight," she said. "I've spoken with the other girl involved, and the family of that girl. I've also spoken with Rina. Now I'm talking to you." She looked out the window, as if afraid to tell me what she needed to.

"Okay," I said. "She got into a fight. What was the fight about?"

"How much did you tell the girls about how you came into their lives?" she asked me.

My heart started to pound and a knot formed in my stomach. "I got into contact with their social worker and she agreed I could be their guardian, so I petitioned the court and they came to live with me. That was what happened originally. Then they were taken from my house, because the guardian ad litem on that case didn't approve of my adopting them, and-"

She shook her head. "I understand the guardianship process," she said. "That wasn't what I asked, however." Her eyes were on me. They seemed accusing, although I probably was imagining that. "I was wondering if you ever sat down with the girls and explained why you were interested in them."

I knew what she was getting at and I was ashamed. I never told the girls the truth. I never told them I was the attorney for the man who killed their mother. I never explained that John Robinson, their mother's killer, never would've been free if not for me. I meant to tell them. I did. But the time just never seemed right. Never seemed right.

I hoped never to face it. Maybe somehow, someway, we could live our lives together without them ever finding out why I was interested in them. I knew that wasn't realistic, but it was my fantasy.

I felt like I was facing an angry boss who was trying to get answers about what I did wrong. I didn't like that feeling, to say the least. "What do you know about why I became interested in them?" I was stalling. I didn't want to answer her questions.

"Well," she said and then paused. "I don't really know. I only know Rina got into a fight with a student by the name of Brianna Leigh, and Rina has been crying ever since. I've talked to Rina, asked her about why she and Brianna got into a fight, and she said Brianna said something that made her extremely angry."

I dreaded to hear just what Brianna said to Rina, but I knew I had to hear it. "Go on. What was this horrible thing?"

"Brianna told Rina that you defended her mother's killer. However, I don't think that's correct. I remember reading about the murder of Rina and Abby's mother, and I distinctly recall he's being defended by a man. That case is still pending, from what I understand."

"It is. It'll be tried in the spring."

"Right. But you aren't on the case, are you?"

I looked out the window. "No. I'm not. I would never defend that...man. Never."

She nodded her head. "Well, then, maybe Brianna was incorrect."

"No. She's not."I sighed, feeling that familiar white-hot knot forming in my stomach. "I defended their mother's killer. He was an earlier client. He was accused of murdering his business partner. I got him off on a technicality. So, in a way, I'm responsible for their mother being killed. That was probably what Brianna was talking about." I looked down at my lap, not wanting to meet her eyes. I felt shamed. Shamed by what she was surely thinking about me, and shamed by what I was thinking about myself.

"Oh, I see." She nodded. "That was what Brianna was talking about. I think you'll have to have that conversation with your girls. Rina already knows, and I'm quite sure she's probably texted Abby about it. I don't want to lay judgment on you, so please don't misunderstand. But I'm curious on why you never told them the truth earlier. They were bound to find out sooner or later."

I sighed. "I didn't want to lose them. I guess I've been living in a bubble of my own making. I've been wanting to believe that somehow the topic would just never come up and they'd never have to know the truth."

She nodded and sat back in her chair. "You're not alone in dealing with unpleasant things. People, in general, want to put bad things off and pretend the bad thing won't come back around on them. Don't feel bad about that. But trust me, it's always better to get on top of things. When you don't, they come out in other ways, and everything is that much worse."

I knew that. She didn't have to tell me that. It didn't change the fact, however, that, as she said, it was human nature to avoid bad things. She was also correct, unfortunately, that when you avoid bad things, they just get much worse.

I stood up. "Thank you Ms. Hayden," I said. "I'll have a talk with my girls."

I went into the waiting room, where Rina was sitting. She looked up at me, glared and then looked away.

I held out my hand. "Let's go," I said. "I know we need to talk. We'll talk when we get home."

She shook her head. "No. I won't go anywhere with you. I've already called Abby, and she agrees. I'm calling our social worker next. Danny O'Hare. I'll tell him that me and Abby can't stay with you one day longer. We'll go back into foster care, but we're okay with that. We won't stay with a murderer."

"Rina, please, let's just go home and talk about this. We'll get some pizza, your favorite kind, and we'll talk about it."

"*Now* you want to talk to us about it. *Now?* What about the first time you met us? Before we ever came to stay with you?" She shook her head. "All this time, I thought you brought me and Abby to your house because you loved us. Turns out that's not true at all. You brought us in because our mom would be alive if not for you."

Her words stabbed me in the heart and I felt like I couldn't breathe. She was absolutely right and there was nothing I could say in my defense. Any words I had would sound hollow in my ears, so they would also ring hollow in Rina's ears.

"Rina," I said. "I know you're angry, but I'm your guardian. You're my charge. Abby is too. You have to come with me."

"No I don't. I'm calling Danny to ask him to take me and Abby away and put us into a new foster home until they can find somebody else. I can't stay with somebody who would do something like you did. I mean, how can you defend a man like that, Harper?"

I sighed and squatted down so I was eye to eye with her on her chair. "Rina, I didn't know he would do something like that. And it's my job."

"Your job? Your job is getting scumbags off so they can get right back out there and do it again. That's your job, Aunt Harper, and I was wrong when I told you I want to know what you do. I don't anymore. I would never do something like that." Her arms were crossed and her little legs were still swinging back and forth.

I stood up. "Rina, you won't get in touch with Danny tonight. For now, at least, you're in my custody. I have to take you home."

"No. I won't go home with you and you can't make me." She

balled up her fists and her face got red. "You can't make us come home with you. Abby's with me." She motioned to the door, and there was Abby coming through it.

Abby didn't say anything, but came up to me and wrapped her arms around my waist. "Aunt Harper, say it's not true. Say you didn't represent that awful man who killed our mom. Please, Aunt Harper. Tell me it's not true."

"It is true, Abby," Rina said, "and I know it's true because I just asked her about it and she's not denying it. So we know it's true."

"Is that why you wanted us?" Abby asked. "Because you felt guilty? You felt bad? You knew our mother wouldn't have been murdered if not for you? Is that why?"

"No, of course not. I became your guardian because..." I would lie to the girls, in a way. Abby and Rina were right – if it weren't for that John Robinson thing, I wouldn't have the girls in my home. I never had the desire to become a foster parent, much less an adoptive parent, and I originally took the girls out of obligation. However, although it started out that I wanted the girls because I felt obligated, I needed to keep them for a much different reason.

I needed to keep them because I loved them. I bonded with them. They had become a part of me. If I lost them, it would be like I lost a limb. So, I would just have to lie to them.

"Why?" Rina demanded. "Go on, Harper, why did you become our guardian? Why?"

"I was interested in fostering children. I met the two of you and I knew you were the ones meant for me."

"Bullshit!" Rina shouted. "Stop lying, Aunt Harper, please. Just stop lying to us. We're not dumb. That doesn't make any sense at all – you randomly wanted to foster a child and you somehow, someway, picked out two girls orphaned because what you did. Gee, what a coincidence." She crossed her arms, tapped her feet and glared at me. "We may be only 11, going to be 12 soon, but we're not stupid, Aunt Harper. We know the truth. You only came for us because you felt responsible that we no longer have a mother. Admit it. Just admit it."

"That's not true," I said weakly, but I knew I was defeated. "Okay, that was true at first. That was the original motivation for taking the two of you. But, I swear, I'm only keeping you in my home because I love you both very much. I'm only adopting you because I love you both. I hope you believe me about that."

"We don't," Rina said, standing up and stomping her feet. "We don't believe you about that. How can we believe anything you say anymore, Aunt Harper, when you lied to us all along?"

"I didn't lie. I just didn't tell you the whole truth." I felt shamed, embarrassed and frightened the girls would really leave. Not that they had that choice. Obviously, they couldn't just up and leave. There would have to be hearings and the social worker wouldn't take them away because of this. There was no way the girls would be allowed to leave. Rina obviously thought she could leave , but I knew better.

"You didn't tell us the whole truth? That's the same as lying. Our teachers always tell us that's the same thing. You must think we're stupid, Aunt Harper."

"No, I never think you're stupid."

The headmaster, Ms. Hayden, came out of her office. "I'll have to leave soon," she said. "Is there anything I can help you with, Ms. Ross?"

"No," I said. "We're just leaving."

Rina reluctantly got to her feet and I inwardly sighed with relief. I tried to grab her hand, but she refused to give it to me. I put my arm around her shoulders, but she literally shrugged my arm off.

Abby grabbed my hand and squeezed it tightly. "Aunt Harper, I forgive you. I know you were only doing your job. Rina will get over it, too."

How could Abby forgive me so quickly? If I were in the same position as the girls, I would've acted just like Rina. What I did was unforgivable, full stop. I was grateful Abby was so fine with it, but I didn't deserve her forgiveness.

"Stop it, Abby," Rina says. "You can't just forgive her like that. She's the reason why we lost our mother. She is."

"Rina, if Aunt Harper didn't take on John Robinson, somebody else would have. She was just doing her job."

Rina walked rapidly on ahead, dramatically flinging open the door of the office suite and then running down the hallway and, just as dramatically, flinging open the door of the school. I quickened my pace, afraid to lose track of her. Abby was still holding onto my hand, so the two of us practically ran out the door of the school.

I felt a sense of relief when I saw my car and saw Rina standing beside it, her backpack on the ground.

I got to my car and opened the door, and the two girls got in – Abby got in readily. I sat in the driver's seat and Abby was next to me in the passenger seat – ordinarily, both girls sat in the back, but Abby chose to sit next to me. Rina continued to stand outside the car, looking around, and I kept checking on her, making sure she didn't bolt.

She finally, finally, opened up the back door and slid into the car. She buckled her seat. I put the car into drive and drove out of the parking lot.

"So, Aunt Harper," Abby said. "You were talking about maybe getting me a flute this weekend. Are we still going shopping? There's a music store some of the kids are telling me about. It's nearby The Plaza. I'm really excited to start learning to play."

I chuckled, happy at least one of my girls didn't hate me. "Of course. I said I'd take you to get a flute this weekend, and I'm as good as my word. I hope you'll be better at playing the flute than I was. I'm sure you will be. You seem musically inclined."

"She's not," Rina said. "She's a terrible singer and she has awful taste in music, too."

"Rina," I said. "That's not nice to say. She hasn't even gotten a new instrument and you're already downing her."

"It's okay, Aunt Harper," Abby said. "I'm just going to show her I'm serious about this. I don't know how to play an instrument yet, but I've always wanted to learn."

"Ha. Don't believe her, Aunt Harper, about that. She only wants to join the band because she likes a boy in there. His name is

James Arness, and he plays the trumpet. Trumpet players are gross. They take that tube out and their spit gets all over the floor. James is gross."

I suppressed a smile. "Rina, if Abby wants to join band because she wants to get to know a boy, that's her prerogative. As long as she enjoys being in band, it's not my business why she wants to learn how to play the flute."

"Thank you, Aunt Harper," Abby said. "And I don't want to join the band for James." She looked out the window. "I mean, I like him. He doesn't know I'm alive, but I like him."

"That's right, Aunt Harper," Rina said. "She likes that boy and she'll join the band just because she wants to see him every day. That's a bad reason for joining, Aunt Harper. She'll quit and you'll buy her a flute for nothing."

"Now, Abby, how do you know he doesn't know you're alive?"

She faced me and I saw tears in her eyes. "I just do. He never looks at me and never talks to me. He's like dating this older girl who's in the ninth grade, but I hear they don't like each other any more." She shrugged. "So I guess there's hope."

"There's no hope," Rina said. "No hope at all."

"Rina," I said in a stern voice. "That's enough."

I looked in my rear-view mirror and saw Rina sitting in the back, crossing her arms and looking out the window with a pissed-off look.

We arrived at our house and Rina ran out of the car, up the stairs to the front door, and went in the door and slammed it behind her. Abby and I walked into the house, Abby holding my hand and leaning her head on my shoulder. I let go of her hand and put my arm around her shoulders. "I'm so sorry, Abby, for not telling you earlier about John Robinson."

"That's okay, Aunt Harper," she said. "But tell me that's not the only reason why we're with you. Tell me that's not the only reason you wanted us." She hung her head and I saw tears threatening to flow.

"Of course not, Buttercup," I said. "You girls are here because I love you both. Rina will realize that too, again."

"I know," she said. "Rina will get over it."

I sighed.

I certainly hoped she did. I couldn't take much more stress.

Sixteen

Christina Sanders was scheduled for a deposition this afternoon, and I had to prepare for it. I was lucky to live in a jurisdiction where criminal depositions were allowed - I knew that wasn't the case with every jurisdiction. But, in the 16th Circuit of Jackson County, Missouri, the defendant was allowed to depose anybody, whether or not their testimony would be material to the case and whether or not they would be available for trial. So, even though I might be on a fishing expedition with Christina, I could still depose her, which I would do.

There was something I'd have to uncover from her and I had to get her under oath. I knew she didn't want to come and answer questions from me, but there wasn't a thing she could do about it. She couldn't quash the subpoena I issued for her deposition, because she didn't have cause to do so.

She arrived in my office right at 3. Her blonde hair was newly cut into a sharp bob and she was wearing a fur-lined trench coat over a green dress with a pair of Gucci gold pumps on her feet. She looked effortlessly chic and incredibly thin. I couldn't believe Michael actually called her fat and "Miss Piggy" and got away with it. It told me everything I needed to know about her self-esteem that she would allow her husband to say such awful things to her, right in front of everyone.

Not to mention, she was as far from fat and being "Miss Piggy" as anybody could possibly be. The woman probably weighed 120 lbs, even though she was a good 5'7".

"Okay," she said, coming in the door. "Let's just get this over with." She looked around. "Where is my husband? Isn't he supposed to be here?"

"No," I said. "It's only me, your attorney and the court reporter. Would you like a cup of coffee or a bottle of water?"

"I'll take a whiskey if you got it. Straight up." She didn't smile, so I didn't know if she was serious or not.

"I don't have whiskey here," I said.

"Why? Don't you drink? Michael said you were quite the drinker in college. I figured you'd have a fully-stocked bar around here somewhere."

I cleared my throat. "No," I said. "I don't drink. Not anymore."

She snorted and took off her coat. "Oh, God, how do you get through the day if you don't drink?"

I had the feeling Christina wasn't the duped wife I thought she was.

I also suddenly felt compassion for Christina. She was talking just like I used to. Like her, I used to never imagine a day when I *didn't* take a drink. And, even now, I craved liquor like I craved sunlight. I could never touch it again for just that reason. "It's difficult, believe me."

"Yeah," she said. "I believe you." She looked at her watch. "Where is that goddamn Ryan? He's always late." John Ryan was Christina Sanders' attorney. "Yeah, go ahead and give me some boring water or iced tea or whatever you got."

I went to my mini-fridge, got her a water bottle and I handed it to her.

She took it without a word of thanks and looked at her watch again. "How long is will this take?"

"About two hours."

She rolled her eyes. "Ms. Ross, I have five kids. Five. Couldn't you have scheduled this damned thing a bit earlier?" She got out her phone. "Yeah, Hayley. You'll have to pick up all the kids today. Sorry about that." She nodded. "I'll see you when I get home." She looked at me. "My nanny. I'm sure you know about that. You have two of your own, don't you?" She narrowed her eyes. "I hear you're watching two girls orphaned by your scumbag client. That true?"

"That's really none of your business."

She snorted again. "Oh, but it is. It is. You see, I don't want the same thing to happen here. I don't want my husband to walk out of that courtroom a free man. I hope I've made myself perfectly clear."

I sat down, wondering what her game was. "I don't understand?"

"Oh, I think you do. Perfectly." She raised an eyebrow. "Do you ever question why Michael would come to you, of all people in the world? Out of all the attorneys in the world, he chose you of all people?"

Did she know my history with Michael? I just stared at her, wondering how much she knew. Suddenly, Christina Sanders was *much* more interesting to me than I ever thought she would be. "No, why? Why did he choose me?"

She crossed her arms. "Take a wild guess. I'll put it this way. My husband is broke. Broke. I've been very careful to keep our finances separate. I know the drill, unlike my mother, who was stupid enough to take her inheritance and put it into joint assets. I haven't done that. I came into this marriage with a lot of money and I'm leaving it with just as much. So I hold the purse strings. I paid your fee, Ms. Ross. He doesn't have two nickels to rub together. I told him he had to hire you or go with a Public Defender."

I narrowed my eyes. "Why hire me? Why did you want me?"

She smiled. "I know what happened with you and Michael and Jim in college. My husband has been very open about what a scumbag he was. He told me all about it after my father was found dead. He was very concerned his past would get out with the media, so he wanted me to know. The second he told me about what he did to you, I knew you were the one I wanted to represent him."

My wheels were turning. I wasn't quite sure how to take Christina. She obviously wasn't the fool I thought that she was. She wasn't the wet blanket, the doormat, that Anita portrayed her. She was cunning. That wasn't necessarily a good thing.

I had to get the truth.

"Why? You know about his raping me, and you wanted to hire me. Why?"

"You know why." She raised an eyebrow. "My husband is guilty and I wanted to give you the satisfaction of making sure he got his just desserts in this case."

My heart started to palpitate as I watched this woman. The inescapable conclusion was that *she* killed her father, framed her husband, and then enlisted me to make sure he went to prison and not her. Either that, or she was covering for her mother.

"Ms. Sanders," I said.

"Please, call me Christina."

"Christina. I think you know better than that. You know I can't just throw this case if he didn't actually kill your father. I'm ethically bound to give him the best defense possible."

"Ethical shmethical," she said. "I'm telling you he did it. Now you just have to figure out how to make him fry for it."

"Well, nevertheless, I need to go forward with this deposition."

"Go ahead, ask away. As soon as my attorney gets here, we can get the show on the road. Where is the court reporter, anyhow?"

"She's running late, too."

"How convenient." She smiled. "May I smoke?"

I didn't want her to, but I nodded.

She lit up, her fingers elegantly holding the end of the cigarette. She raised her face to the ceiling, smoke billowing out of her red-lipsticked mouth.

She watched me. "You know I'm right," she said. "You smell blood in the water. What's so hilarious is that my husband has no idea why I wanted you to be his attorney. He didn't want to hire you. No way. I told him it was you or nobody."

"How is he broke? I don't quite understand?"

She rolled her eyes. "Guess mistresses cost a lot of money to keep. Well, that and the fact that he likes the cards a bit too much. God knows he has no interest in our kids. Or me, for that matter." She looked sad, just briefly, but only briefly, because she was soon back to smiling.

Just then, her attorney came in the door. The court reporter was right behind him.

"Party's over," Christina whispered to me. "Hello, John," she said. "Let's get the show on the road."

We went into our conference room and set up. The court reporter got out her machine and prepared to type. "I'm terribly sorry I was late," she said. "I wanted to call, but I forgot my phone at home. You probably think I'm so unprofessional."

"No, it's fine."

Christina raised her eyebrows. "You were late and so was my attorney, and you guys ended up walking in at the exact same time. Admit it, you're sleeping together."

She smiled wickedly.

I was starting to really like this woman.

John Ryan rolled his eyes. "That's enough of that. Ms. Ross, are you ready?"

"I am," I said. I fidgeted in my seat, wondering if I really wanted to still drag Christina through the mud. I strongly suspected she killed her father, but I didn't want to see her punished. I wanted to see Michael punished for it, whether he did it or not.

"Please state your name for the record."

"Christina Sanders."

"Ms. Sanders, do you understand you will be put under oath, and, just like in a courtroom, you must tell the truth under penalty of perjury?"

"Yes. I've done these before."

"Then do you promise to tell the truth, the whole truth, and nothing but the truth, so help you God?"

"I do."

We went through preliminary questions about her age, her relation to the victim, her relation to the defendant, and other such sundry items.

I then decided to get into the meat of the matter.

"Ms. Sanders, are you aware your father, Robert Sanders, was being poisoned?"

"I do now."

"What do you mean, you do now?"

"I guess the medical examiner did his thing and he found poison in my dad's system." She looked down at her hands, and, again, I saw a look of sadness cross her face, then vanish. When she looked up again, she, once again, looked impassive.

"Were you aware your father was having health problems in the last month of his life?"

She rolled her eyes. "Of course I was. I went to the doctor's office with him every time. They could never find anything wrong with him, so they sent him home. He got weaker and weaker and sicker and sicker and, somehow, nobody even thought to look for poison in his system." She looked annoyed. "That doctor is next on my list. I've already filed a malpractice lawsuit against him."

"Who had access to your father's food and drink?"

"Me, Anita Gonzalez, my mother and Michael Reynolds. And my kids, I guess. We all went to visit Mom and Dad every Sunday."

"Who, in your view, would be the person most likely to have poisoned your father?"

"Michael Reynolds."

"And why is this?"

"Because Michael was the one who administered dad's pills."

My ears perked up. This was one thing that hadn't yet come up. "Your dad's pills? What pills were those?"

"My dad took medication for his heart and diabetes. That was why he was always drinking health shakes and things like that. Why he only had fruits and vegetables in his work fridge. He was trying to get his health issues under control without pills. But my husband took care of that."

"Walk me through this. Your father was staying in the East Wing, correct?"

"Yes. My mother banished him after she found out about his other family." She rolled her eyes and shook her head. "Turns out my father couldn't keep it in his pants, either. He had a lot in common with my husband in that way."

"So he's staying in the East Wing. He has his own kitchen in the East Wing, is that right?"

"Yes."

"Who else had regular access to this kitchen?"

"Nobody. He was the only person who regularly used that kitchen."

"Nobody. Nobody ever drank drinks out of his kitchen or ate food out of his kitchen. Is that what you're telling me?"

"That's what I'm telling you."

"Now, tell me about how Michael administered the pills to your father."

She shrugged. "My dad didn't like to bother with such things. I put Michael in charge of making sure dad's pills were in their little pill box things you buy in drugstores. It has little compartments for each day. In my dad's case, it had compartments for morning and evening for every day."

"And how did that give Michael access to your father's food and drink?"

She rolled her eyes. "It's pretty simple. My mother never went to that other kitchen. Neither did I. Michael did, because that was where we kept the pill boxes he filled up every week. He had a reason to be in that kitchen. Mom and I didn't have a reason. So, Michael was the one who was in the best position to put poison in my dad's food and drink."

That was making sense to me. But I wasn't sold. I still thought Christina was hiding something. It was all too perfect. If she killed her dad, she framed him perfectly, got the right attorney to represent him and had the right story as to why Michael was the only one who had decent access to Judge Sanders' food and drink.

"Do you have a prenuptial agreement with Mr. Reynolds?"

"What do you think? I kept my maiden name, as you noticed. It's pretty obvious I want to keep things separate from him. So, yes. We have a prenup. If Michael and I divorce, he'll get diddly squat. He won't even get the house, because my father bought that for me before we were married and made sure only my name was on the title. All my inheritance money was put into a separate account before we were married, too. I've been careful to never put any money into a joint account of any kind."

I nodded, thinking that was significant, although I wasn't quite sure why.

I cleared my throat. "Ms. Sanders, I need to ask you some delicate questions."

"Yes," she said. "Yes, my father sexually abused me. That was your question, wasn't it?"

"It was. When did this abuse occur?"

She shifted in her seat uncomfortably. "When I was 15 years old. It happened only once, though. My mother stopped it after that."

That story didn't quite comport with the story Anita told me. She indicated this was an ongoing thing.

"Only once." I shook my head. "Would you be surprised if I told you that Anita Gonzalez told me it happened much more often than one time?"

"Well, she's a liar," Christina said. "She hates me and she obviously wants you to think I had a reason to kill my father because he was abusing me. She obviously wants to take the attention off my husband. That won't work, though." She glared at me and whispered to her attorney.

"What about your mother? She found out your father had an entire other family living in Parkville. Another woman and three kids with her. How did that make you feel?"

"Like crap. How would you feel? My mother didn't deserve that treatment. She didn't deserve that at all. My mother is a good person, and I'd really appreciate it if you don't bring her into this mess. She's gone through enough." She raised her eyebrows at me and I got her drift. She wanted to limit the exposure to her mother, because she was determined her husband would pay for this murder. Nobody else but him.

"Did your mother want to divorce your father?"

"No, she wanted the other family to move in with us, so she could be a sister wife to my father's whore." She rolled her eyes. "Of course she wanted to divorce him. But she couldn't divorce him, because she'd have to give him half her fortune. So, she didn't divorce him, but banished him to the East Wing."

"Okay," I said. "Here's how I see it. You have a reason to kill your father. Your mother has a reason to kill your father. The one person in your family who didn't have a reason to kill your father was Michael Reynolds." That conclusion was inescapable. I wished it wasn't, but it was. Michael had no clear motive for killing the judge. Christina and Ava Sanders both did.

"Oh, but he had a motive. He did."

She swiveled in her chair as she watched me.

"What was his motive?"

She looked down at the table. "You're just going to have to ask him."

"I'm asking you. You indicated he had a motive. I'm asking you what it is."

"This deposition is over," she said.

"Ms. Sanders, what, in your view, was your husband's motive for killing your father?"

She shrugged. "He's a bad guy. A bad, violent guy. That's motive enough."

I sighed. "Ms. Sanders, that's not motive enough. Not under the law."

She looked out the window. "You'll find a motive. You just have to dig a little deeper."

"Help me out here. If there's a motive, I need to know what it is."

She looked me directly in the eye. "I don't know what it is. All I know is that he did it. You're going to have to find out why."

I wouldn't get anywhere with her. I knew it and she knew it.

"Okay. This deposition is done here."

The court reporter folded up her equipment and John Ryan packed up his briefcase. Christina, for her part, remained at the table. It looked like she wanted to speak with me, but I didn't want to talk to her anymore about the case. If she wasn't under oath, whatever she told me she could deny on the stand. If she wanted to speak with me, she'd have to do it under oath.

She finally stood up. "It's been real," she said. Then she winked. "You'll find your motive. I have faith in you. And once you do, you make sure the prosecutor knows what it is, too. They're floundering over there and they don't know their ass from a hole in the ground. They're under a lot of pressure, too, because of who my father was. Find the motive. Everybody wins in that case."

As she left, I sat at the conference table, feeling stunned. What just happened? Did Christina really come in here and tell me she was behind my hiring because she wanted her husband to go down? She did it. I was sure of it. She did it and she was framing Michael.

Or maybe not. Maybe Michael *did* have motive. So far, however, it seemed that the only people who had motive were Christina and Ava Sanders.

Ordinarily, in a case like this, where it was so obvious that other people were most likely the murderers, I would call the police and tell them to look in a different direction, away from my client. They might do it if I called, and they might not. But I usually tried to at least get them looking in that direction.

In this case, however, I didn't do that. I'd follow the evidence where it led, and I had no desire to cut things off prematurely.

Christina wanted me to sink Michael.

So did I.

Seventeen

I got home and found something most unpleasant on my lawn. Well, not on my lawn, but on the street in front of my lawn. A group of reporters were standing there, apparently waiting for me.

I sighed. “Hello guys,” I said. “I don’t know why you’re here, because you know I can’t speak to any of you.”

They started to shout questions at me. “Is it true the judge was poisoned? Did your client kill that judge? Is it true the judge had a different family while he was married to Ava Sanders?” These were all questions that were shouted at me as I made my way up to my door. I wouldn’t talk to them. I *couldn’t* talk to them. If they were court reporters, which they probably were, then they had to know I couldn’t speak with them.

But one question, shouted above all the others, made me pause. Made me pause and actually made me want to turn around and answer the question. “Is it true your client is a serial rapist?”

My heart pounded and I wondered where that information leaked from. I immediately thought about Christina and how she somehow knew about what happened to me in that fraternity house. I wondered if she also knew about the other women Michael raped. He told me there were five other women. I wondered if there were more. Maybe they came forward after Michael was charged with murder? I had no knowledge they had made anything public.

I shook my head and rushed into the house before I could say anything that would sink me. I wanted to stay on this case now. I *needed* to. Christina indicated the prosecutor's office was dropping the ball, and they would possibly need my assistance in making sure Michael got what was coming to him. I couldn't afford being forced off the case by the judge because I went to the press and told them anything about this pending case. I wanted to confirm that reporter's question about Michael being a serial rapist, but that would have disastrous consequences for the case.

I wondered if there was information "out there" about my being one of Michael's victims. Christina was probably the one who tipped off the reporters about Michael being a rapist. I doubted she would have tipped them off about me being one of the victims. If that was known, I doubted I could maneuver how I wanted to on this case.

Rina and Abby were there with Sophia. Rina was watching television and didn't make a move towards me when I walked through the door. Abby came up and hugged me. "Aunt Harper, it's almost tomorrow. I can't wait to get that flute! I just can't wait!"

I laughed. "I never thought you'd be so excited to play a musical instrument, but I'm very proud of you."

Rina snorted. "Abby's just excited because James finally spoke a word to her. He bumped into her in the hallway and he said 'watch yourself.' As if Abby bumped into him. He's a jerk, Aunt Harper. You shouldn't be encouraging this."

Abby's face got red and she looked embarrassed. "He's not a jerk," she said. "I think I did bump into him. I don't know. The hallways are so crowded in between classes."

I sighed. I was with these girls. I was 11 years old once, and madly in love with different boys in my classes, none of whom knew I was alive. One crush after another, and I watched all kinds of girls in my class "go steady" with different boys. I never was asked to "go steady" with anyone. I was never the girl who got all the boys.

Nobody asked me to dance at the school dances, and nobody asked me to go to the movies or hang out at the mall. It was a painful, invisible existence for me in middle school and high school, and I hoped Abby and Rina would have a better time of it.

It sounded like this James guy was a jerk, but I didn't want to make a judgment on it. I certainly didn't want to discourage Abby's interest in playing the flute because of it. Maybe she genuinely wanted to learn how to play the instrument and James was just a side concern. I didn't know. I did know that I was in the band and I had great fun. We took a trip to Florida and that was one of the best trips of my life.

I was also crushing on somebody in band. A tuba player by the name of Bryce McNeil. He was dark-headed and blue-eyed and he played on the football team. I remembered coming to band practice early in the morning – I was in marching band, which Abby probably wouldn't be for awhile – and I looked forward to these practices just because I wanted to see Bryce. He was way out of my league, but I didn't care. I imagined he liked me as much as I liked him.

He didn't, of course. He was in some of my other classes, even though he was a grade ahead of me, and I day-dreamed about him constantly. He was even on my same bus on that trip, which was a good 22-hour ride, and I watched him the entire time.

"Well, okay, come on girls. It's Friday night, let's do something fun. What do you say we go and get some spaghetti at Cascone's and go see a movie. I'll even invite Axel. He's coming over tonight, anyhow, I'll just drag him along. What do you say?"

Abby jumped up and down with joy and Rina managed to drag herself off the floor, where she was perched in front of the television. I looked at her face and saw she was happy to be going out, too, even though she was trying to hide it. Her arms were crossed in front of her and her face was turned down, but I could see a slight smile.

Things would be okay. It might take some time for Rina to truly get over it, but I knew things would be okay.

. . .

That night, Axel and I curled up on the love seat under a blanket. We each had a cup of hot tea and a fire was burning in the fireplace. He had his arm around me and my head was on his shoulder. "I had fun tonight," Axel said. "That restaurant was amazing, mate."

"It is," I said. "I've always loved their food." I loved that the restaurant also had a little band playing, with a clarinet player and a drummer and a guitar player. They played standards, which bored the girls but got me going. I told Abby that she should pay attention to the band, because they were playing the kinds of music she would playing, so she tried to pay attention to what they were doing.

Axel kissed me on the forehead and then kissed me on the lips. I sighed, feeling a tingle go through my body, but still feeling terrified.

He smiled. "So, how are things going with that murder case?"

I shrugged. "I can't talk about that too much, but I think I'm going in the right direction."

"What's the right direction in this case?"

"The direction towards showing my client did it." I was lying about that. Actually, with the deposition of Christina and the talk I had with Anita, I was further away from proving to myself that Michael did it. I was being increasingly led in the direction that either Christina or Ava Sanders did it. I didn't want that to be the case, but it was certainly looking that way.

"What will you do if you decide he did it?"

"I don't know yet." That was a lie, because I did know. If I figured out what really happened, if the evidence started to point towards Michael, I would give what I had to the prosecutor, even if they didn't ask for it formally. I would do that anonymously. That was what I decided to do.

But I could only do that if I got the evidence I needed to sabotage him. Thus far, I wasn't getting that at all.

He stroked my hair and pulled me closer to him. "This fire is nice," he said.

"It is." I felt my heart pounding as I put my hand on his firm abdomen. He might have been forty, but he was in amazing shape. I guess it came with the territory of him being a detective. I bowed my head, still feeling frustrated that I was so afraid of going too far with him. Maybe my therapist was right – maybe the reason why I took Michael's case was that I would get some closure from what he did. If I could have a hand in making sure he fried, I could finally bury what happened to me at that fraternity house and I could move on.

But, at the moment, I wasn't anywhere near moving on.

"Harper," he said, taking my hand, his fingers interlacing with mine. "Maybe I better leave. I don't want to, but being near you is driving me wild. Don't worry, though, lass, I'll be back as often as you need me to come back."

He smiled and I nodded. I knew that he would back as often I wanted him to come back. I knew that.

We were falling in love. I hoped that I could get over my issues and allow myself to truly love him the way that he deserved.

Eighteen

"So, my wife came in here and spoke with you, didn't she?" Michael asked me. We were meeting in my office to go over Christina's testimony as well as Anita's answers to my questions. I wanted to go over everything with him because I didn't want him to suspect what I was really doing. As far as he was concerned, I was working on his case in a legitimate way.

"She did."

"And? What did she say? I need to see those deposition transcripts."

I leaned back in my chair as I watched him. I wasn't quite sure what I wanted him to know about what Christina said to me. "The deposition transcripts are with the court reporter," I said.

He got up and paced around. "She tried to throw me under the bus, didn't she? Didn't she? That little bitch."

"No," I said, knowing he would find out the truth if he got the transcripts and saw that she did just that – throw him under the bus. "But I'd like to know about something she told me. She told me you were in the best position to poison your father-in-law because you refilled his pills. Is that true?"

His face showed a great deal of anger when I said that, and he shook his head. "So, that's why she wanted me to refill those pills every week. I wondered why."

"I'm sorry?"

"Christina. When her father had to go on medications for his blood pressure and diabetes, about a year ago, my wife put me in charge of giving him his pills. She nagged me about it. Now I see why." He shook his head. "She wanted me to do that so she could frame me when *she* poisoned Robert. She wanted to say that only I had access to Robert's drink and food because I was the only one who went into his kitchen on a regular basis. I fell for that, too. Goddamn her. Goddamn her."

I sighed. "Are you saying Christina killed your father?"

"I wouldn't have thought that before, but now that I know that he was poisoned and my wife is pointing her finger at me, I do. I think she did it. She poisoned him and then hired somebody to shoot him. Guess he wasn't dying fast enough for her."

"Why do you think she did it?"

"It's obvious, isn't it? Robert was abusing her, he had a different family, and her mother was wanting to divorce him but that would mean giving him half her fortune. And she hates me, too. She hates me, so she did all this and then framed me."

I narrowed my eyes. "Why didn't you tell me about your father's different family? About your wife's sexual abuse? Why did I have to hear all of this from Anita?"

"I don't know. I guess I didn't think it was relevant. I thought some random intruder killed Robert, so I didn't think you needed to know that. I didn't want to drag Robert's name through the mud like that. I really loved that man."

I leaned forward. *Bastard is lying to me again.* There was something else up his sleeve. I didn't believe, for one second, that he neglected to tell me about the other family because he cared about his father-in-law and didn't want to drag his good name through the mud. He probably never did anything altruistically in his life – why start now?

"You have to start telling me the truth," I said. I wanted to threaten him with withdrawing from his case. That was my usual method of dealing with lying clients. That made them straighten up and fly right. But I wouldn't dangle that particular stick over this guy – I was too afraid he would just say "okay" and I'd have to withdraw. I had to see this through.

"Why would I lie about something like that?"

"I don't know. I just think you're lying."

He looked pained. "All right, yes, I'm lying. The fact of the matter is, I didn't know about all that until I read about it in the paper. My wife never told me. I didn't want you to know just how bad our marriage has been. I mean, this was a huge thing, and I was completely out of the loop about it."

"Why did you care what I think about your marriage?"

He shrugged. "I guess I thought you might've suspected me more if you knew my wife and I barely spoke to one another and have barely spoken to one another for years. We've gone to the weekly dinners with her parents and..."

"You insulted her right in front of her father. I've been told that by two different people. I was also told that Judge Sanders had you followed and found evidence you were sleeping with Ariel Winthrop. I know you were also sleeping with Kayla Stone. I'm sure there were others you were sleeping with, too. I was told Judge Sanders and you had words about that, and he threatened to tell Christina all about it."

I didn't quite tell him that Christina knew all about the affairs, anyhow. She knew everything about him. I guessed he didn't know how much she knew.

He furrowed his brow. "Yes, that was true. He threatened me. But so what? I wouldn't kill him for that."

"Maybe you wanted to kill him. If Christina divorced you, you'd lose everything. I'm subpoenaing your bank accounts and all your other accounts, and I think I'll see a pattern – she's worth a lot, and you're not worth squat. She told me she had an air-tight prenup. I'll get a copy of that, too. You had motive to kill your father-in-law if you thought he'd tell Christina about your affairs and you didn't want that to happen."

He stood up. "Go ahead. Get the prenup and our records. I've got nothing to hide."

"You don't? Are you telling me I'm wrong? That she doesn't hold the purse strings? Where will you be if she divorces you?"

"I don't have to put up with this," he said. "You work for me, lady. Let's get this straight."

Oh, no, he didn't. He didn't just disrespect me like that. "You *do* have to put up with this because the prosecutor will ask you that question. She'll ask you about your relationship with your father-in-law and she'll ask you about whether or not your father-in-law was threatening you with telling your wife about your affairs. That gives you motive to kill him."

He rolled his eyes. "If I killed him, why would I call the police when I found my father? I mean, really. Think about that."

"Reverse psychology. That's simple enough to explain away."

"You think I did it. You're my attorney and you think I'm guilty."

Actually, that wasn't true. I still had it in my head that either Christina or Ava did it. Maybe they were in cahoots and they did it together. But it was still in the back of my mind that Michael might've done it.

"No," I said. "I don't believe you did it. But you have to realize one thing – the prosecutor will present arguments that show you're guilty. You need to know what those arguments will be. That's why I need to prepare you and I need straight answers."

"Well, I didn't do it. I think we should show Christina did it. Or Ava. I think they did it, anyhow, especially since Christina screwed me by pointing the finger at me. That makes me suspicious, to say the very least. Show she had motive to kill Robert, and Ava *really* had motive to kill Robert, and that will put doubt into the jury's mind."

This guy was making me sick. Here he was, trying to get me to blame the murder on his wife and mother-in-law. Maybe he was right about that, but it still made me sick. I didn't want to do that.

"Well, I need to do my due diligence," I said. "I need to get your mistress, Kayla Stone, in here next. I need to speak with her."

He stood up. "No. I forbid you to do that."

"What do you mean? As I said, she's your alibi. You were with her at the time of the murder. She's the only person who can testify you were nowhere near the house when your father was shot."

"No. No means no. I won't let you speak with her."

The wheels started to turn in my head. "I *am* going to speak with her. I *am* going to get her on the record. She *will* appear for a deposition. I might work for you, but the trial strategy will be all me. I'm the lawyer, you're the client, and I call every shot. Every.shot. I hope I've made myself perfectly clear."

"If you call her in for a deposition, then I swear to God, I will fire you." He crossed his arms and glared at me. I felt a chill. I felt the same type of chill I felt way back when. Every time I saw him on campus after the rape, I felt a chill running up and down my spine. Now, the way he looked at me, I felt that same type of cold, prickly feeling.

Like I was looking into the eyes of evil.

I stood up. "You go right ahead." I raised my eyebrows, knowing he was stuck. He was broke and Christina was paying my fee. She also probably paid his bond, which meant she could call it in at any time. He'd spend the pre-trial process in jail and would have to get a Public Defender to take his case.

The Public Defender attorneys were excellent attorneys – they were dedicated to their jobs. They were knowledgeable and experienced. I knew this about the PD office, but I doubted Michael did. He probably had the same view of the PD's office that many people did – that those attorneys were overworked, underpaid and didn't do a good job. This was a common misperception and Michael probably shared it.

He stormed out the door.

"Pearl," I said, calling her into the office. "I need for you do something for me. And I need it ASAP."

She popped her head in. "What's that, Harper?"

"Get Kayla Stone in here for a deposition. You need to get that subpoena out for her today. Get it out and have it served, before something happens and she disappears."

"On it," she said.

I suddenly felt out of sorts. Something about Kayla Stone made Michael nervous. I didn't know what it was, but I sure as hell would find out. I was nervous because I was afraid Michael would make her somehow disappear from the jurisdiction.

Maybe that was the missing piece of the puzzle.

I hoped I was getting close.

Nineteen

That night, I started to feel weird again. Not quite as weird as before, but I had a sudden burst of energy. I lay in my bed, tossing and turning, not feeling tired, even though it was 3 AM. My thoughts weren't jumbled, but I had a sudden clarity.

I'd win this case, and by winning, I'd really lose it. I would have to figure out what was going on, and I had to do it before the case was tried.

I sat up straight in my bed and heard a voice. "You're missing a case pending in front of Judge Sanders," the voice said. "A very important case."

I was hallucinating. I knew I was. But I knew this voice was coming from inside my own head. Something in my subconscious was shouting at me. I was missing something.

I didn't know what it was, though. Something told me the missing puzzle piece would be found in all the pending cases before the judge.

But I didn't want to let go of my belief that Michael did it, so I didn't want to go that route. If the person who killed the judge was involved in a case before him, that would point the evidence away from Michael.

I sighed and went back over all the pending cases. I'd repeatedly reviewed these cases, and nothing was popping out at me. Some companies stood to lose quite a bit in front of the judge, which was a good place to go, but I didn't have a good hunch about any of them. None of them.

"What case?" I asked nobody in particular. "What case? Please tell me. I need to know which case? There are so many of them. I don't know how I'm supposed to prove anybody on this list would've killed him."

"Environmental issues," said the voice. "Lots of people getting sick. Follow the money."

Environmental issues. Lots of people getting sick. Follow the money.

I sighed. What did any of this mean? The only possible case I saw pending in front of the judge that had to do with the environment was the case of a plant that exploded. That case had nothing to do with making people sick, though.

There obviously was something else.

I sighed. I would have to do research on this issue. I might as well. I certainly wasn't tired. I was feeling strange, too. I got frightened that I would get as weird as before. That day when I felt out of sorts, I wanted to do nothing more than spend, spend, spend on stupid things I'd never spent money on before. I'd have to see a doctor if I felt this way for a long period.

I sat down in front of my computer. I'd have to look for information about environmental issues and people getting sick. There were companies all over the country doing this. I knew this to be true. *Erin Brockovich* was a true story, after all. But I would have to find out a company that was doing this and also based in the Kansas City area.

Or not. Maybe a subsidiary company was poisoning people. The parent company might be based in Kansas City. That would make things much more complicated.

This would be a needle in the haystack. A case was brewing out there, yet to be filed, but brewing. It could be a class action, which took a long time to be brought to court. It was a lot of work getting a class together, certified and then finding victims flung around the country and even the world.

I got up to make myself a cup of tea, and, for some odd reason, my mind drifted to Elmer. I had no idea why I thought about him at that point. He just popped into my head for some odd reason.

I decided to get on my coat and hat and head downstairs. I had an overnight sitter named Lauren who stayed the night because I needed reassurance that Rina wouldn't just up and leave. She still hadn't forgiven me for the John Robinson thing. She was slightly friendlier with me but was up to no good. So, I had Lauren sleep over just in case something happened and I had to look for Rina in the middle of the night.

Because Lauren was spending the night, I felt comfortable leaving the house. I would go down to the jail and see Elmer. I knew he was sleeping, but I'd wake him up. The jail would let me see him because I was a professional. Therefore I could visit the jail 24 hours. The jail personnel wouldn't be happy I was there, but I didn't care.

I didn't even know why I wanted to see him. I only knew he had some clue for me about this whole Michael Reynolds case.

What would I ask him? And who would I see when I got there? Would it be crazy Elmer or the charming one? The charming one wasn't charming for long, so I probably would be up against the raging bull. That was okay, though. I felt invincible for some odd reason.

Like nobody could touch me. I could take him if he tried to kill me again. I could beat him up with my bare hands. Tear him limb from limb.

Why was I feeling this way again? My brain was going haywire.

I thought about Axel's mother. She locked herself in her room and painted picture after picture after picture. 20 pictures in a week, he said. I never thought about it, but my mother's brother, my Uncle Patrick, was the same way. He was a heavy drinker and had attempted suicide several times, but I also knew there were times when he went completely off the rails. He would call my mother at all hours of the night, telling her about some novel he was writing or some painting he was working on. It got to the point where she had to turn off her phone when he was like that.

He also went out and gambled for long periods. He'd come over for dinner and talk the entire time about nonsense. His speech during these times was almost stream of consciousness – he'd go from one topic to another to another. He'd also fight anybody for any reason. He would start screaming at my mother, sisters, and brothers for no reason.

He went into psychiatric facilities several different times. I was a kid at that time, so my mom didn't talk to me about what was really wrong with him.

Nowadays, it seemed he had it all together. I guess he managed to finally figure things out because he had a decent job and, to my knowledge, hadn't had any more incidents where he started to act crazy.

I'd have to ask my mother about Uncle Patrick the next time I saw her. I was scheduled to have dinner at her house this coming Sunday. I'd have to ask her to confide in me because I was acting just like Uncle Patrick.

I saw the Jackson County jail come into focus. I went through the doors and went right up to the windows. "I need to see an inmate," I said. "His name is Elmer Harris."

She looked at me strangely. "Miss, do you know it's 4 AM.?"

"I know. I need to see him. I need to talk to him."

She shook her head and called on the phone. "Go on up," she said. "Do you know where he is?"

"I do."

As I headed to Elmer's pod, I didn't know what I was doing or why I wanted to see him. I felt like I was being led to him by some unknown force. I assumed this force was my gut instinct, but I had the mental clarity I never had before. Because of this extreme mental clarity, I knew Elmer had some clue about Michael's case.

I got to the meeting area and sat down. Within minutes, Elmer approached me. His wrists were shackled, and so were his ankles. He looked like somebody had just woken him up, which was undoubtedly the case.

"What do you want, darlin'?" he asked me.

I cleared my throat, not knowing what to say at first.

He just stared at me, and I noticed something I never really noticed before - his left eye drooped. "I wanted to know a few things," I said. "About you."

"Why are you here in the middle of the night?"

I shook my head. "I just had a hunch about something. I admit, I didn't get to know you very well."

"No, you didn't." He continued staring at me, and his left eye, which drooped only subtly, haunted me. I didn't even know why. I only knew the whole thing was a clue to proving Michael was guilty.

Come on, Harper, you're not making a lick of sense. So his left eye is drooping. What does that have to do with Michael's case? It has nothing to do with it, that's what.

Yet my gut was nagging at me. "Elmer," I began. "When did you first start to exhibit violent behavior?"

He shrugged. "I don't think I exhibit violent behavior, Ms. Ross."

"Are you medicated now?"

"Yes, I am. I have been ever since that day in the courtroom. They give me the good drugs now, so I don't feel like I want to kill everyone I see anymore."

I shifted in my seat. "You don't see your behavior as violent?"

"No. I see it as a reaction to bullshit. That's all it is. Nothing more and nothing less."

"But, Elmer, you killed your crime partner and almost killed me. You don't see anything wrong?"

He shrugged. "I guess there is. But why are you asking me these questions?"

"I don't know." I shook my head. "Were you ever diagnosed with any kind of brain condition? Any kind of brain damage?"

He nodded his head. "Yeah. I was. I apparently was born this way. Born bad."

"Born bad? What do you mean?"

"My mother was exposed to something before I got born." His jaw started to go back and forth, back and forth, as if he was trying to chew something. "She got money for it."

"What were you exposed to? Do you know?"

He shook his head. "No. I don't know. You're gonna have to get my records."

"Can you sign a waiver for me to get those records?"

"No, ma'am." He stared at me, and I got a chill, but I tamped it down.

"Why not? You just said I'd need to get your records. I can't get your records unless you sign a waiver for me to obtain them."

"You'll just have to figure it out yourself."

I sighed. Anna would have to get on this one. It wouldn't be difficult. I still had copies of his criminal records, so I knew his date of birth and things like that about him.

Still, I always felt intrusive doing this. It was necessary, usually, but I always felt dirty when I did things without knowledge or consent.

"Is that all you want to know from me?" he asked.

"Yes," I said. "I needed to see you and talk to you. I don't know why, but I think it'll become extremely clear to me at some point."

He shrugged. "I guess. By the way, my new attorney got a real good plea deal. Life in prison. It sure beats being on death row. They don't feed you real good on death row, and you don't get out in the yard and the library and things. If I'm in prison, I don't want to be on death row."

I smiled, wondering how his new attorney got him to take something. I guessed that his being calmed down with "good drugs" had something to do with it.

I left the jail wondering how Elmer's case would tie in with Michael. I just knew it would. I had an unbelievable amount of insight and clarity. I had so much energy, and I felt invincible. I'd figure out why Elmer was significant and would do that soon.

Twenty

The first thing I did that day, after I got the girls up, fed and dropped them off at school, was get on the computer. I also called Anna and had her look for Elmer's medical records.

I remembered that a drug used in the 1960s caused severe birth defects. It was used to treat morning sickness, and then kids came out without limbs. I did a Google search and quickly found the name of the drug – Thalidomide. I went through the images on the page and saw kids with no arms – their hands were attached to their shoulders, or they had extremely short and useless arms. I shook my head, reading on. The drug was not readily available in America, as only 17 babies were born in the 1960s with Thalidomide birth defects.

So what? Elmer had his limbs. And he was American. There was very little chance he was affected by this drug. Brain damage was another side effect of this drug, but the main birth defect seen was the missing limbs.

Nevertheless, I was on the right track. He was exposed to something that caused brain damage. He said he'd been "born bad." I wondered if that meant he'd been born with brain damage that affected his impulse control and moods and caused rage. I had enough clients to know that certain aspects of the brain modulated different things. Damage to the prefrontal cortex, for instance, generally meant a loss of impulse control and increased aggression. I didn't necessarily know if that would cause his left eye drooping, but I had a feeling it was a piece of the puzzle.

I was itching to get a hold of his medical records. Itching to find out what he was exposed to *in utero* that might've caused his problems. A voice inside me told me that I was missing something important, and once I figured out what had happened to Elmer, I'd be led on the right path.

Anna called me. "Harper, can I come in? When you asked me to research Elmer's history, I discovered some interesting things. I think you probably need to see this stuff in person."

"Sure," I said. "Come on in."

Pearl came into my office. "I got that lady scheduled. Kayla Stone. I had to subpoena her, though, because she didn't want to come in on her own."

"Yeah," I said. "Sit down, Pearl. I need to brainstorm with you."

She sat down, a pad of paper and pen in her hand. "What you need?"

"It's weird that Kayla Stone doesn't want to come in," I said. "Don't you think?"

"Why is that weird? Who is she? What role does she have to play in this case?"

"She's my client's lover. The other woman, as it were. But one of many. She's important, however, because she was with my client when his father-in-law was shot. She'd be his alibi."

Pearl nodded. "His alibi. Well, then, she should be eager to come in and talk to you. She could get him off the hook for the murder, right?"

"Yeah. But Michael, my client, was adamant that I not involve her. He doesn't want me even to speak with her. Why? Why do you think he'd be like that about her? She would be key to his case."

Pearl thought about it for a few seconds. "Maybe she has

damning information about him. Maybe he really did it, and she knows it."

"That's what I'm wondering. That's what I'm hoping."

Pearl narrowed her eyes. "Wait, what? You're hoping she has damning information about your client? Come again?"

"Yes." That was all I said. Not that I didn't trust Pearl. I did, implicitly. But I could never be too careful. I regretted even opening my mouth at all.

She pursed her lips and looked at me skeptically. "All right. You don't have to tell me why you want your own client to go down. I guess you have your reasons."

"I never said that," I said calmly. "I never said I want him to go down."

"I guess." She still looked suspicious. "You'll find out what's going on with Kayla Stone soon. She's coming in tomorrow."

Just then, the phone rang. I knew who it was, even before I picked up the phone.

"Harper Ross," I said.

"Harper, you bitch," Michael said, his voice full of rage. "I told you not to bring Kayla into this mess. You disobeyed me."

"Okay, then. Fire me. Go ahead."

He was quiet. I knew I had him. He couldn't fire me. Not when Christina was paying my fee. "Why don't I file a Bar Complaint against you instead?"

I shrugged my shoulders. "You're going to file a Bar Complaint against me for scheduling your girlfriend in for a deposition? Knock yourself out." I rolled my eyes. I *hated* clients who filed Bar Complaints against me because they didn't like how I did my job.

Then he started to yell. Loudly. I held the phone away from my ear and then sat it on my desk. While he screamed into the phone, I calmly looked at my computer for information I'd need to know to answer my questions. I was excited about Anna coming over and telling me what she'd discovered. There was something there. I knew it. I could feel it.

Pearl was still sitting across the desk from me. She looked at the phone and shook her head. He was yelling and screaming, although I had no idea exactly what he was yelling and screaming about. It was unintelligible. I had no interest in what exactly he was screaming about. *Let him scream.* I wasn't interested in anything he had to say, and he was stuck with me. I knew that. Christina told me as much.

It was me or nobody.

"Do you hear me? Are you listening, you little cunt?"

I picked up the phone. "I have to go. Goodbye." At that, I hung up.

"Girl," Pearl said. "What's up with that dude?"

"He hates me, obviously."

"That's Michael? No wonder you want to send him up the river."

"Now, Pearl, no, I don't. He's just another client. I don't want you to ever think I won't meet my ethical obligations to him or any other client just because I don't like them. I've had many clients over the years I've not been fond of. He's no different."

"Um-hm," she said. "I guess." She rolled her eyes. "You need anything else from me?"

"No. Thanks for brainstorming with me, though."

Anna soon appeared in my office. "Hey," she said.

"What do you have for me?"

"Here," she said. "Here are the records I have for Elmer. I have birth records, medical records and school records. He's had problems his whole life. He's gone from one school to the next and got kicked out for the last time when he was only in the 10th grade. That last school was an alternative school for behaviorally challenged kids."

I nodded my head. That sounded about right. "What else did you find?"

"Well," she said. "It seems like his mother could afford to send him to that last school, which was a full-time residential treatment school, because she won $5 million as part of a class-action suit against a chemical company that buried toxic waste that seeped into the groundwater. It caused problems in her community. The kids were born with severe birth defects, including brain damage, and the adults got sick. The adults just had a range of problems, including memory loss, confusion, nausea and loss of appetite. Apparently, the real problem was the effect on the unborn babies, including Elmer."

"$5 million. What did you find out about his medical issues?"

"The doctors established his prefrontal cortex was severely damaged at birth, and they traced it to the toxic seepage of this chemical called Toluene. This nasty chemical is associated with paint thinners, cement, and glue. It causes neurological harm, but it generally just makes people feel really sick. It's also been established to cause brain damage in fetuses. Elmer's mother, Jolene, gathered enough experts to show that Elmer's issues were caused by this chemical. She was awarded $5 million for Elmer's brain damage."

Toluene. I bit my lower lip. I made a mental note to do more research on this chemical, but perhaps more importantly, I'd have to find out if any companies in the area had recently been accused of dumping this chemical. I suddenly realized why Elmer was so important to me. I needed to speak with him because his problems would lead me to the right company. Something was lodged in my subconscious, something I couldn't acknowledge until recently. With my sudden ultra-clarity and burst of insight, I knew I was missing something. Elmer provided it.

Why was this important? This chemical?

"Thanks, Anna," I said. "You did great, as usual."

She nodded. "You need anything else?"

"No. You brought me what I need, so I appreciate that."

After Anna left, I brought my pen out and tapped it on the desk. I would have to do more research on Toluene. I booted up my computer and immediately started to Google the issue. I read about it, and Anna was right – the chemical was nasty. It caused a lot of sickness, and it caused brain damage in fetuses. It caused birth defects mainly when the mother huffed it, as they huff glue. But, in the case of Jolene and Elmer Harris, the exposure was caused when the chemical seeped into the groundwater and made everybody sick.

Then I went and Googled whether or not a company was accused in the Kansas City area of dumping this chemical.

It took me a short time to find what I was looking for. The company's name was Dowling Chemicals, and the news articles I found indicated the company had been accused of allowing Toluene into the groundwater in Raytown, Missouri, a Kansas City suburb. The Raytown community had suffered for years with a disproportionate incidence of birth defects, cancer and low-level sickness. Toluene had not yet been certified as a carcinogen, yet the Kansas City Star articles indicated that lawyers planned to demonstrate that the high cancer levels were caused by the Toluene dumping.

The Toluene dumping was caused when the Dowling Chemical Company put the waste products into large barrels buried in the ground. The barrels disintegrated, which caused the chemicals to go through the porous containers and contaminate the groundwater. This, in turn, made the community sick.

I nodded and immediately went through the list of pending cases in front of Judge Sanders, looking for whether the class action suit had yet been filed in the District Court. I found nothing that indicated that Dowling Chemicals was on Judge Sanders's docket. Not that that meant anything - class action suits weren't always filed immediately. It took some time to get these lawsuits together, although I knew this suit was coming.

But how would the Dowling Chemical Company know Judge Sanders would oversee the case? In this case, they'd have the motive to kill the judge because Judge Sanders would probably slap them down hard. This kind of class-action suit would cost a company millions, especially if punitive damages were involved. The punitive damages would come if the lawyers could show that some kind of criminal act was involved or if the conduct was willful, wanton or malicious. If Dowling was found merely negligent, they wouldn't have to pay punitive damages.

After carefully reading the article in the Kansas City Star, I knew punitive damages would most likely be awarded in this case – especially by a judge like Judge Sanders, who habitually ordered severe punitive damages, much more than any other judge in the Western District of Missouri. The company wasn't just careless in how they disposed of these chemicals – they flat-out broke the law. Although most of the chemicals were buried in barrels, the barrels were not rated for the kinds of chemicals Dowling buried. In some cases, the chemicals weren't in barrels at all. The newspaper article, quoting whistle-blowers' testimonies, indicated that thousands of pounds of paint thinner were simply thrown out and spread on the ground. In these cases, they didn't even bother to put the stuff into barrels.

Punitive damages, in this case, could very well soar into the hundreds of millions before everything was said and done – but only if the "wrong" judge heard the case. Judge Sanders would definitely be considered, by the defendant, to be the "wrong" judge.

Again, though, how would Dowling know for sure that Judge Sanders would be assigned to the case? It still wasn't filed.

A quick search gave me the answer. Cases may be assigned to judges according to areas of expertise. That wasn't a guarantee since cases were typically randomly assigned, but when a judge has a certain expertise area, the judge typically will get cases that correspond with this expertise. After reading about Judge Sanders' background – he was an EPA attorney for twenty years before he came to the bench – it stood to reason that he could get this Dowling Chemical case.

I then reviewed the list of cases brought before the judge over the years and found he'd tried hundreds of cases involving environmental concerns.

Judge Sanders would've probably gotten that Dowling Chemical case and would've hammered them.

I nodded. This was promising, although I almost hated to go down this lane. I still wanted to make Michael pay for the murder of his father-in-law. I hated to find some alternative explanation for the judge's murder.

Yet a nagging voice still told me that finding the Dowling Chemical case information was getting me *closer* to proving that Michael had done it, not further away. I didn't know why that was. I only knew there were still some missing pieces of the puzzle that I was determined to find.

TWENTY-ONE

The next day, I'd have Kayla Stone in for her deposition. I didn't know what to expect, but I knew what questions to ask. I'd get to the bottom of her relationship with my client, find out if she was really with him when the judge was killed, and ask her whether or not her husband would cut her off if he found out about her relationship with Michael.

She came in right at 1 PM, just after lunch. She was just how I pictured her in my head. She was about 5'7", with long brown hair, big green eyes, and a fake rack. At least, I assumed that her rack was fake, as it was extremely large, too perfect, and too big for the rest of her frame. She looked like money, just like Christina Sanders, but I thought she'd be much more demure than Christina. I didn't know why I thought that, but I did.

She was dressed head to toe in winter white – her tightly-fitting dress was that color, and so was her coat. Her shoes were colorful, though, as was her purse. Everything on her was designer, including her enormous sunglasses with the trademark Chanel logo on the arms.

"Hello," she said, her voice light and breathy, like Jackie Kennedy. She lifted her hand, and I shook it. "I'm Kayla Stone. This is my lawyer, Arnold Vogel."

Arnold also shook my hand. He was tall, about 6'3", with a completely bald head and glasses. He looked around 65 years old, and I could tell that, as a younger and thinner man, he was quite a looker. He had large dimples and brown eyes, which looked like he laughed easily. He had a twinkle I usually saw in good-natured people.

"Hello, Ms. Ross," Arnold said. "Where are we doing this deposition?"

"Right this way." I led them into the conference room and offered them iced tea or bottled water. Kayla opted for bottled water while Arnold joked.

"I'll take some scotch neat, please," he said with a smile. "Or a glass of iced tea if I can't have the scotch."

I smiled. "I'd love to offer you some scotch, believe me. I know why you want it, too." Just being an attorney was enough to drive sane men to drink.

I got the water and tea, and we all sat down while the court reporter got her machine ready to go. I was fascinated by court reporters – I had no clue how they could take those chicken scratches and, somehow, make heads or tails from them. I also admired how they transcribed everything. If it were me, I'd have problems focusing for such a long period, my mind would wander, and I'd miss a ton of words.

One thing was for sure – court reporters earned every penny they were paid.

We went through the preliminary questions – her name and her address – before I started with the substantive questions.

"Ms. Stone, are you aware of why I'm deposing you today?"

"Yes."

"What is your understanding of why I'm deposing you?"

She shifted uncomfortably in her chair. "Because Michael Reynolds is my, uh, boyfriend." She shrugged her shoulders. "I don't know what else to call him."

"Mr. Reynolds is your boyfriend. How long has he been your boyfriend?"

"For the past six months."

"And you're married, is that correct?"

She looked uncomfortable. "Yes." Her face flushed red. "I know what you must be thinking."

"No, you don't," I said. "No judgments."

She nodded, looking relieved.

"Where were you on the evening of October 19?"

"I was with Michael."

"Were you with him the entire evening?"

"Yes."

"What did you and Michael do that evening?"

"We went out to dinner and a movie and got a hotel room downtown. The downtown Marriott. We planned on spending the night, and Michael would return home the next day."

"What was Michael supposed to be doing?"

She sighed. "He was supposed to be looking after his father-in-law, who had been very sick. Very bad health problems. Nobody could figure out why." She hung her head and then started to bite her nails. That was one thing I noticed about her – she was very well-groomed, with her hair perfect and her makeup just as perfect – but her nails were short and plain. She didn't have a decent manicure because she had an issue with biting her nails. I noted that she was most likely nervous because nail-biting was generally a nervous habit.

"So, he was with you the entire night?"

She nodded.

"Please verbally answer the question," I said.

"Yes." Her voice was weak when she said that word. I raised an eyebrow, knowing she was lying.

"Were you present when Michael got a phone call from his wife, Christina Sanders?"

"Yes."

"What happened after he got that phone call?"

"He rushed to the judge's home."

"Why did he rush to the judge's home?"

"Because Christina told him over the phone that she couldn't contact her father."

"What time did Michael get that phone call from Christina?"

"Around 11 or so."

"And then he rushed out the door?"

"Yes."

"Did he try to tell Christina that maybe she couldn't get in touch with the judge because he was sleeping? Why did he think it was such an emergency?"

She cleared her throat. "I don't know. He just told me it sounded bad."

"Was there chicken involved that night?"

"I'm sorry?"

"Did he pick up fried chicken that night?"

"No." She shook her head. "Why?"

"He told the police he was getting fried chicken when his father was killed. He obviously didn't tell them he was with you."

"Oh, okay. No, he didn't pick up fried chicken that night."

"Are you aware he showed the police on the scene he had fried chicken?"

"No."

"Let me pivot some. Tell me about your marriage to Gerald Stone."

At that, her face got red. "I was told I should plead The Fifth on this one."

"Who told you that?"

"Michael told me that."

"Why would testifying to the facts about your marriage cause you to self-incriminate?" All at once, I was suspicious. What about her marriage would cause her to plead the Fifth?

She shrugged. "I plead the Fifth. I don't have to answer these questions, do I, Mr. Vogel?"

"No," he said. "Not if you think that answering that question would incriminate yourself."

"Thank you. I plead the Fifth."

I bit my lower lip. That was so weird, and it made me suspicious. Was something about her marriage significant in this case? Pleading the Fifth meant she'd say something that would implicate her. Was she involved with the murder? What motive did she have to murder this judge? I suddenly had about a million unanswered questions that I needed to answer.

I would have to answer these questions on my own, though.

"Thank you for coming in," I said to Kayla.

"We're done with our deposition?"

"Yes. We're done." I stood up and gathered my things. I walked out the conference room door without shaking her hand or the hand of her attorney.

She was playing games, and I'd have to figure out why.

"Anna," I said, calling Anna on the phone. "I need something from you."

"What do you need, Harper?"

"I need a copy of the prenup filed between Kayla and Gerald Stone." I didn't know if it was filed or online, but I hoped it was. Attorneys often put their documents on the cloud, which was secure. But Anna could get past any security mechanisms, so if that prenuptial agreement was somewhere on the cloud, she'd find it. I had faith in her.

"Okay," she said. "Is there anything else?"

I bit my lower lip. "No," I said, the wheels suddenly turning in my head. "That's all I need from you."

"I'll have that for you in an hour," she said. "I'll put it in a PDF and email it to you."

"Great."

I tapped my fingers on my desk as Tammy came into my office. There was a kernel forming in my brain. It was nascent, though, unformed.

I booted up my computer and read about Stone Enterprises.

Stone Enterprises was a chemical company founded by Gerald

Stone in 1991. I looked at the firm's financials and found the company's annual revenue was $100 billion. Gerald Stone was not only the CEO of this company but was also the largest shareholder and the founder – in 2016, he was paid a $30 million salary and was the largest shareholder, so his stocks were worth another $150 million a year. Stone Enterprises was an international conglomerate with sites located around the world. It also was a parent company to some 118 subsidiaries.

I nodded my head. This was something. I was on the right track.

As I read through the information on Stone Enterprises, I looked at my email and saw that Anna had sent me the PDF I was looking for. I downloaded the PDF and printed it out.

This document made one thing clear – Kayla Stone was in danger of being completely cut out of a fortune. She had one thing in common with Michael: both of them went into their marriage with very little. When Kayla married Gerald, she listed her property as a car. Just a car. Nothing else.

On the other hand, Gerald had already been established with Stone Enterprises, so he came into the marriage with millions. He'd also made millions more since the marriage occurred 12 years ago. I looked at his list of premarital property and saw that, in addition to $50 million in cash, he possessed four homes, paintings worth millions, and stock worth hundreds of millions. He even had his own private plane and island. An island!

Since the two married, the couple acquired several more homes and priceless paintings by Monet and Warhol.

The agreement stated that, in the event of a divorce, Kayla would be entitled to half of what the couple had accumulated during their marriage and 25% of what Gerald brought into the marriage. That would mean that, at this point, if Kayla and Gerald were divorced, Kayla would be entitled to property worth more than $200 million. The Monet alone would be worth almost that much. The couple acquired millions during the marriage, and Kayla would get half of that.

I nodded and then saw the clause Michael told me about.

Apparently, if Kayla was unfaithful to Gerald, she forfeited everything. Everything. The couple had no children, so this prenup would be valid. If they had kids together, Gerald would never be able to cut Kayla off with nothing – he'd have to pay support for his children. But that wasn't the case. There were no kids, so Kayla would be out on the street if she and Gerald divorced, provided Gerald could prove she was unfaithful.

I wondered if Gerald had definitive proof that Kayla was having an affair with Michael. I suddenly knew this was also why she refused to answer questions about her marriage in that deposition. She admitted Michael was her boyfriend, so she already incriminated herself. Her husband could use that deposition to cut her off completely if he divorced her.

So why was she so willing to tell the truth about Michael? Why didn't she lie about him and their relationship? She readily told me Michael was her boyfriend. She admitted she was with him in a hotel on the night Judge Sanders was killed.

Why? If that were me, I'd lie. I wouldn't even care if I was under oath. And, if I didn't lie, I'd quash the subpoena. I'd fight it every step of the way.

Yet she didn't do any of that. She came right out and said Michael was her boyfriend. She didn't try to get out of the deposition.

Michael had tried to intimidate me out of asking her these questions, and that was another odd thing.

I went back to my email and saw another PDF document was attached. I didn't even notice it before. I opened the second document and saw an amended prenuptial agreement. It clearly stated this was a new document and superseded any previous documents. Therefore, all previous documents were considered null and void.

It was dated October 20, the day after Judge Sanders had been murdered.

I raised my eyebrows, looking for how it differed from the previous prenup. The document itself was the same as the previous one – as in the previous one, Kayla Stone was entitled to 50% of the property acquired during the marriage and 25% of the property brought into the marriage by Gerald. That part was identical.

After I carefully read the document, I realized just what was different – in this document, there was not an addendum that indicated Kayla would forfeit any and all property if she was unfaithful to Gerald.

I blinked, not quite understanding what I was seeing and why. The day after the judge was killed, Gerald changed the prenup terms. I shook my head. Why? Why did he change the terms? What did Kayla do for Gerald to get him to make such a drastic change? That would explain why Kayla didn't care that she incriminated herself in her deposition by telling me Michael was her boyfriend.

It explained that much. But what else did it explain? Dammit, this was significant, but I was missing the puzzle piece. The piece that brought everything together.

I sat back in my chair, feeling completely frustrated. I pinched my nose with my thumb and forefinger, feeling nauseated.

I would have to walk away from this case for now. Walk away from it, and hopefully, when I was more relaxed, the missing puzzle piece would come to me. It could be a coincidence that Gerald changed the prenup terms the day after Judge Sanders was murdered. It could be.

It could be, but it wasn't. There was some level of involvement that I simply wasn't seeing.

I wasn't seeing it, but I would. I was determined to figure it out.

Twenty-Two

That night, I was home with the girls. Abby had her flute and was practicing in the living room. Rina was sitting on the floor next to Abby and kept howling like a dog.

"Rina," I said. "For the last time, let your sister practice her flute."

She crinkled up her face. "She sounds terrible, Aunt Harper. She sounds like one of those geese we see in the park."

Despite myself, I laughed. "No, she doesn't sound like that. If she was playing the oboe or the bassoon, you'd be absolutely correct. But a flute sounds nothing like that."

"Whatever. She sounds terrible, though."

Abby put down her flute and looked embarrassed. "Aunt Harper, I'd like to practice in my room if that's okay."

"No," I said. "I'll make sure your sister is quiet from now on. I really would like to hear you play."

Rina was right, in a way, because Abby couldn't play the flute very well. Of course – she'd just started learning to play the instrument. Rina couldn't expect much. Neither could I. Neither could Abby. When I first started learning to play the flute, I couldn't get the fingerings down for months. My flute wasn't as nice and expensive as Abby's. She and I went shopping, and we found her a top-of-the-line instrument.

"But Aunt Harper-"

"Play, Abby. Rina, be quiet. If you're not quiet, you'll be on restriction for the rest of the evening."

Rina gave me the stink-eye, got off the floor, and dramatically went to her room and slammed the door. I tried to suppress a smile. Anymore, Rina's histrionics were amusing me. I knew they shouldn't amuse me, but they did. She was always slamming doors and pouting and giving me dirty looks. I knew she wasn't over finding out I defended her mother's murderer. I hoped that, in time, she'd get over it, but if she didn't, I'd have to go to family therapy with her.

Abby sat down on the chair, her flute in her lap. Tears were in her eyes. "I'm not good, am I, Aunt Harper?"

I sat down next to her and put my arm around her shoulders. "Buttercup, you just got that flute last weekend. You just started to learn how to play. You have to walk before you can run, and right now, you're still mastering your fingerings and scales."

She nodded and then looked up at me. "James doesn't think I'm very good. He teases me every day when my teacher makes me stand up and do my scales in front of everyone. It seems like my teacher singles me out because I'm new. And I'm last chair."

"Buttercup, you're being too hard on yourself." I took her chin in my hand and looked into her pretty blue eyes. "And if James is teasing you, it's a good sign. It means he's noticing you and probably likes you too, but he just doesn't have a good way of showing it."

She seemed to brighten when I said that. "Really?" Her voice was hopeful. "You think he likes me too?"

"I do. Why else would he tease you? What does he say to you when you stand up and do your scales in front of everyone?"

"I don't know, he kinda dances around and screeches. Like this." Abby got up, danced a little jig, and screeched, her voice going up several octaves. "He says that's what I sound like. He's kinda goofy, I guess."

"He sounds like it. Tell you what, why don't we have a little party over here Friday night, and you can invite a bunch of your classmates, including James, and I can check him out? Do you think he'd come?"

She shrugged. "I don't know, but a party sounds nice. What will the occasion be? What will I tell them? Me and Rina don't turn 14 until December."

"Rina and I, Buttercup. Not me and Rina. And I know you two turn 14 in December, but you don't need an excuse to have a party, do you? What kind of things do today's kids do at parties, anyhow?"

"I don't know, Aunt Harper. I'd love to have a laser tag party for my 14th birthday. Rina's not up for that, though. She wants a DJ and a dance party. We could transform the backyard so that we both can have what we want.

I smiled. "Yes, those are really good ideas, but Abby, your birthdays are in December. I think you two should probably schedule a sledding party instead. I'm talking about now. What would you two like to do if I throw a party so you can have James at the house?"

She looked embarrassed. "Maybe have the birthday ideas? Since we can't do them for our birthdays, maybe do the laser tag and dance party now? Then when our birthday comes, we can hang out and watch movies or something."

"You got it." I tousled her hair. "I'll call Axel to have him come and help out. Will the kids come to this on such short notice?"

"I think so. Kids like parties, and they love laser tag. I'll let everyone know. How many kids can come?"

"What about ten for you and ten for Rina?"

She nodded and smiled. "I'll go up and tell Rina. I'm sure she'll be excited."

At that, she ran up to Rina's room, and I soon heard shrieking. Two seconds later, Rina came running down the stairs.

"You're gonna get a DJ, Aunt Harper? Or maybe a Karaoke

machine?" She wrapped her arms around my waist, and I squeezed her tightly.

"Let's have the Karaoke machine, Lady Bug. I don't think I can line up a DJ on this short notice."

"That's okay. My friends love Karaoke. I can have 10 kids, and Abby can too? Why are we having this party, Aunt Harper?"

I cleared my throat. "It's an early birthday party since you guys turn 14 in December, and there won't be much karaoking in the backyard, nor laser tag. But Rina, you have to be good. No more insulting your sister. She's trying to learn the flute and doesn't need your put-downs."

"I'll be good." She hugged me tighter. "I love you, Aunt Harper."

I laughed. Those words from Rina were music to my ears. I didn't know if that meant she forgave me for not telling her about John Robinson, but that's how I interpreted her words.

"I love you too, Ladybug."

That night, I suffered from yet another sleepless night. I tossed, turned, and looked at the clock and was frustrated that it was 4 AM, and I still wasn't close to sleep. In fact, I had no idea the last time I could sleep. It had been several days.

I decided to get on the computer and do some more digging. After all, since I was awake, I might as well get something done in the meantime.

I was still trying to figure out the connections between Kayla Stone, Gerald Stone, Michael and the murder of the judge. If there was any connection, that is.

The first thing I did was check and see if Stone Enterprises had any pending lawsuits in front of Judge Sanders. I booted up the computer and got on the Western District of Missouri website. I typed in the name "Stone Enterprises" and found nothing. I tapped my fingers on the desk and got up to get a glass of water.

As I was standing at the sink, filling my water glass, I heard Rina. "Aunt Harper," she said. "What are you doing up?"

I spun around, startled. "I could ask the same about you. What's wrong, Lady Bug? Can't you sleep?"

She shook her head. "I had a bad dream. Aunt Harper, I don't like what you do. I don't like you having those bad dudes as your clients." She started to cry. "I don't want to lose you, Aunt Harper."

I put my arms around her. "Now, why would you lose me?"

"Because. You have all these murderers around you all the time. I'm afraid one of them will come after you, and you'll end up like our mom." She cried harder, and I stroked her hair.

"Shhhh," I said. "Tell me about your dream."

She shook her head. "I just dreamed you were killed like my mom."

"Oh, Ladybug," I said. "I've done this job for years and years. I've never had a problem with any of my clients." That was a big, fat lie. Elmer threatened me and put me in the hospital. That gangbanger years ago, Randall Thompson, almost strangled me.

But somehow, Michael threatened me even more than Elmer and the gangbanger did. He was sociopathic. I knew that. I could feel it. I was getting closer to proving it.

If anybody would try to kill me, it would be him. That thought popped into my brain, and it startled me.

If anybody would try to kill me, it would be him.

I shuddered.

"I don't believe that, Aunt Harper. You've had clients like John Robinson. Look what he did. He could've done that to you too. He couldn't control himself. He got angry, and he just couldn't control himself. You're around men like that all the time, Aunt Harper. All the time. I just wish you'd get out of it. Get out of having these bad men as your clients."

Her words were stabbing me like daggers, but I couldn't let on. In a way, she was right – I *was* representing bad dudes. Bad dudes who threatened me. She was also right to worry. "Ladybug, please stop worrying. Now, go on back to bed. Try to get some sleep. 7 AM comes early."

She hung her head, hugged me again, and ran back up the stairs.

I sighed and returned to my computer.

Stone Enterprises didn't have lawsuits pending in front of the judge. I decided to go ahead and Google it to find out if it had any major environmental violations, violations like Dowling Chemicals did, and I didn't find anything about that, either.

Was there something else? Some other violations that would cause it to be sued? I shook my head. None of that made sense. Number one, if a lawsuit was pending on some other issue, like a labor or safety issue, it wouldn't be specially assigned to Judge Sanders. It probably would be randomly assigned. Number two, my gut was telling me loudly that the entire case would turn on environmental issues. Issues like Dowling Chemicals.

I put my head down, trying to think. It was difficult to think right at that moment, though, because of my encounter with Rina. She always seemed unbothered by the fact her mother was murdered. Abby was much more transparent – I often saw her cry, and she would tell me she was thinking of her mother. But Rina, aside from her getting angry with me and teasing Abby, always seemed okay. I now knew she wasn't.

Being a parent was tougher than I thought it would be. Not that I thought that my parents had it so easy, but-

With a shot, my head was off that table.

A parent. A parent. That was it! That was the part of the puzzle I was missing!

I immediately got on the internet to find out who was the parent company of Dowling Chemicals. And then gasped when I found out this information.

Stone Enterprises was the parent company of Dowling Chemicals.

TWENTY-THREE

I felt my heart pounding, and my breathing went faster and faster. That was another piece of the puzzle, and I'd figure out the rest of it. But Stone Enterprises, as the parent company of Dowling Chemicals, stood to lose millions of dollars when this class action went into effect. When this class action was filed, they'd go down hard if they got the "wrong" judge. Punitive damages alone could be in the hundreds of millions of dollars, and since thousands of people were hurt by the contaminated groundwater, the actual damages would be millions more.

On the other hand, they could limit their liability if this company could draw a different judge – a judge who wasn't known to be a bleeding heart plaintiff's judge.

I was suddenly excited. I was onto something but would have to do even more digging. Who would replace Judge Sanders? Whomever it was, he or she would be a lot more of a defendant's judge than Judge Sanders. That was safe to say, as our Republican President would appoint this judge. The Senate was also Republican. Judge Sanders was a Clinton appointee. Guys like him wouldn't be on the bench in today's climate. That was clear.

But what about the other issue? The lawsuit had yet to be filed, so there wasn't ever a guarantee that Stone Enterprises would be assigned to Judge Sanders. They might've been assigned a different judge. Why would they choose Judge Sanders, out of all the judges, to knock off? Was it just because he was the most liberal judge in terms of siding with the plaintiffs, the little guys, against the large corporations?

I'd have to answer those questions before I became more confident that Stone Enterprises would've done something like this. Because knocking off Judge Sanders would be pointless if Stone Enterprises would've just drawn a different judge.

After all, why wouldn't Stone Enterprises just have filed the case and then knocked off the judge once they figured out he would be hearing it? Wouldn't that have been more logical?

I'd have to go down to the courthouse when it opened and investigate more. Maybe speak with the chief judge and see if she had any insight on whether or not the Dowling case would come before Judge Sanders. In my opinion, that would be the smoking gun on whether Stone Enterprises was behind Judge Sanders' murder.

At 8 AM, I went to the courthouse and spoke with the clerk behind the glass in the lobby. "Hello," I said. "It's me again. I need to speak with Chief Judge Sally Haynes, please. It's important."

The clerk grimaced. "She has some time right now. She doesn't get on the bench until 9 AM. She ordinarily doesn't like to be ambushed by attorneys, so can I ask what this is regarding?"

I drew a breath. "I'm in the middle of a murder case, and I really need to find out about a case that will be filed. A major class-action lawsuit will be coming down the pike. Soon."

She raised an eyebrow. "Are you talking about the Dowling Chemical case?" she asked.

"Yes. The Dowling Chemical case. That's right. The Dowling Chemical case." I was repeating myself, and I knew it. I felt funny again as if my thoughts were racing 100 MPH. I had energy like I'd never had before, even though I didn't sleep a wink and hadn't slept a wink in several days.

"And what do you need to know?"

"What judge would be assigned to that case?"

"Well, it was actually filed late last night. It's been assigned to Judge Perez."

Judge Perez. He was a well-known defendant's judge. He was known to be skeptical of plaintiffs' claims and almost always bent over backward to ensure corporations either won their cases or, at the very least, their liability was severely limited. I thought about how convenient it was that Dowling would draw that judge, but then again, Dowling would've been better off under *any* other judge besides Judge Sanders. Judge Sanders was, by far, the most liberal judge on the District Court bench. He was, by far, the most likely of any of the Western District judges to find for the plaintiff and slap huge punitive damages on the defendant.

"Thank you," I said. "But could I still speak with Judge Haynes?"

"Just a second. I'll call up there and make sure she has a minute." She got on the phone, said a few words and then nodded at me. "She has about ten minutes to speak with you right now. Go on up."

"Thank you."

At that, I ran to the elevator.

I got to the Chief Judge's suite and talked to her personal clerk. "Hello," I said. "The clerk downstairs called. My name is Harper Ross, and I need to speak with Judge Haynes." My speech was rapid, as rapid as my thoughts. I couldn't help it, though – I was amped.

"Yes," she said. "She's expecting you. This way."

I followed the clerk to the Chief Judge's chambers, which was twice as large as ordinary judicial chambers, which were large enough, and even more ornate. I felt almost like I was walking into a museum room when I walked into the chambers because of the high ceilings, the wood paneling and the floor-to-ceiling windows that looked over the expanse of the city.

She stood up, an imposing woman who stood over 6 feet tall. At 5'9" myself, I was very tall for a woman, but I felt like a midget compared to her. "Your honor," I began, "Thank you very much for seeing me."

She nodded. "Have a seat," she said. "I have a few minutes to speak with you. I understand you were asking questions about Dowling Chemicals?"

"Yes. I was. That will likely be one of your largest cases this year."

"You're not kidding about that." She shook her head. "But what do you need to know about it?"

"It's been assigned to Judge Perez, I see. I wanted to know if the case would've been assigned to Judge Sanders."

She nodded her head. "Yes, it was, as a matter of fact." She looked sad. "You're right. That will be one of our biggest cases this year. As a former EPA attorney, Judge Sanders had the expertise to handle a large case like this with very complex issues. He's handled some of our largest class-action suits in the past, too. So, yes. This would've been Judge Sanders' case. Ordinarily, the cases are randomly assigned, as you know, but once in a while, when there's a large case like this one, I try to assign them to judges who really know an issue inside and out. Judge Sanders was that man."

I felt excited as I spoke with her. "Can I ask if Dowling Chemicals was informed they would be in front of Judge Sanders?"

"Yes. The attorney for Dowling Chemicals was informed about this months ago when he asked who would most likely be trying their case. I told him I'd assign it to Judge Sanders."

Months ago. That was about when everything was blowing up in this case. That was about when the Kansas City Star had run their story about the people being sickened by those chemicals. I was sure that was when the attorneys for the plaintiffs were interviewing potential victims and trying to get people into the class.

"And how did it end up with Judge Perez?"

"Well, when Judge Sanders was murdered, I decided it was best to be randomly assigned. After all, all the other judges on the bench are equal as far as this case goes. None of them have particular expertise in environmental concerns. I only wanted Judge Sanders to have that case because he was an environmental lawyer for so many years before he was appointed to the bench, so he knew those issues inside and out. Once he was murdered, I knew the case should be randomly assigned."

I nodded. "Thank you, your honor. You don't know how much you've helped me out here."

She smiled. "I'm happy to help." She looked at the clock. "I have to prepare for my 9 AM docket, so is there anything else I can help you with?"

"No, thank you very much."

We shook hands, and I left her chambers and exited the suite, saying goodbye to the clerk on the way out. Judge Haynes was immensely helpful because she answered the one nagging question – how did Dowling Chemical know that Judge Sanders would be their judge? Judge Haynes answered that question for me.

Now, I would just have to piece the rest of the puzzle together. I still hadn't tied Michael into the crime. Yet I knew there were only a few more pieces to fit together until I could prove he was in on the murder, if not the actual murderer.

Then I would have to prove it.

Twenty-Four

After I saw the judge, I knew what I had to do. I went over to the prosecutor's office to tell her my suspicions. I violated every ethical duty in doing this because I would point her toward a possible motive. The motive was only possible because I still hadn't figured it out.

What I did figure out was that, as far as I could see, Stone Enterprises was probably behind Judge Sanders's murder. And it seemed like Kayla Stone was also in on it. That suddenly seemed the most likely and logical explanation for why the prenuptial agreement was changed in her favor.

Might she have agreed to kill the judge in exchange for Gerald Stone changing the prenup? She had special access to the judge, after all, through Michael. That was how I started to think it went down. Michael killed the judge for Kayla.

But how would the prosecutor prove it? The connections were tenuous and circumstantial. Worse, the connections could've been all in my mind. My imagination was too active, and this whole thing was shaping up like a bad pulp novel. A really bad pulp novel. One that was unbelievable.

The prosecutor would probably laugh me out of the office, but I was determined to put my theory out there for her. April Todd would hear my story. She would bite or not, but I was determined to give her food for thought.

I went to the prosecutor's office, hoping to see her. I knew she would be in her office because she didn't have an early docket. April Todd didn't have a docket until 1:30, when she did her probation violation dockets.

"Hey," I said, entering the prosecutor suite where the clerk, Mika Coulter, was sitting. "Is April in?"

"She is. Do you want to speak with her?"

"Yes, I do. I need to speak with her about the Michael Reynolds' case."

She nodded. "Go on back. I think she was going to call you about it, too, so I'm sure she'll make some time for you."

"Thanks."

I went back to the office and knocked on the open door. April turned around, her face somewhat startled, but she smiled when she saw me. "Hey, Harper," she said. "I was just going to call you. Where are we on the Reynolds' case?"

I sat down. I would have to handle this deftly so she didn't suspect what I was doing. I wanted to help her, but I didn't want her to openly know this. "I don't know, where are we? I did some depositions, so I'll send you those transcripts. However, that's been the only discovery I've done so far."

She nodded. "I'll be honest with you, I haven't been doing as much on this case as I should be. I'll get you my discovery by the end of next week. The results of our investigations and reports and deposition transcripts. I'm so sorry, I'm very behind on this."

I leaned back in my chair and regarded the frazzled prosecutor. I knew how she felt. I was a Public Defender once and knew what it was like to have case upon case piling up on you. I looked at her desk and saw the files piled up, and looked around her tiny office and saw white file boxes filled to the brim. I knew she would need a lifeline on this. I doubted she had many trials scheduled because prosecutors never tried too many cases, but she had probation violations to attend, plea agreements to figure out and victims to speak with. Her work was never done, and somehow, in the middle of all she had going on, she would have to prepare for this enormous trial.

I didn't envy her.

"Is there anything in particular you need to speak with me about on the Reynolds' case?" she asked.

"No. I was just wondering what you were thinking about regarding my clients' motive. Where is your head on this?"

"I'm in the process of figuring that out," she said. "I need to speak more with the investigators on this case. They're trying to piece that together. And, by the way, I have an offer for you to take to your client. Life in prison without a possibility of parole. It beats the death penalty, and you know your client will get the death penalty if he takes this to trial and loses. Food for thought."

"I'll be sure and get to that. I mean, I'll tell him about this offer. I'm sure he doesn't want to take it, but I'll tell him about it."

"It's not nothing, the offer. I don't think I need to tell you that life in prison is much better than spending years on death row, waiting for the needle. You should probably tell your client as much."

"I know." *How would I put the bug about the judge and the Stone case in her ear? All I need to do is point her in the right direction and hope she picks up the ball and runs with it.*

I felt frustrated because I didn't know how to screw Michael over. I didn't want April to have suspicions about my motivations for being on this case because I didn't know if she'd gossip about me. She might tell other prosecutors that I was in the office helping her out, which would mean my career could be in trouble.

I rose to my feet. I'd have to figure something else out. Some way of letting April know that she needed to look into the Stone case and see how it tied in with everything happening.

I was still determining what was going on. I was getting close to proving I was correct about my hunch. Not getting closer to letting the prosecutor know what I knew, though.

"Thank you, April, for seeing me on such a short notice."

"Of course. I'll be in touch with my discovery within the next week or so."

I left the office, frustrated with my inability to figure out how to tell the prosecutor what I knew. I wanted to throw the case, just like Christina Sanders hoped.

But how?

Friday night and the girls' party would go on. I had the laser tag company bring over the laser tags, a tent was set up in the backyard, and a karaoke machine was set up. Rina and Abby invited 5 boys and 5 girls, and everything was ready to go. Axel had even taken off work early, so he was over at my house at 5 PM to help me with whatever I needed.

"Hey, lass," he said, coming in the door with five 2-liter bottles of various soft drinks. "Tell me what I need to do. Put me to work."

I handed him an apron, and he readily put it on. He put his hands out and smiled, and I grinned at him back. "That suits you. It really does." The apron had little cherries on it, and it was too small for him, but I liked seeing him in it.

"I've always wanted to wear an apron," he said. "So, what are you serving these rugrats?"

"I have some stuff I bought from Costco. I picked up some pizzas and some frozen buffalo wings. Some chip and dip. And a cake. Look at this cake."

I opened up the ice cream cake I bought from Baskin Robbins, and it was decorated to say "Happy Early Birthday Rina and Abby."

He smiled. "Now remind me again why you're having this party now, in the first part of November, instead of when their actual birthdays are?"

"Well, two reasons. One, their birthdays are in December, so there's not much we can do outdoors at that time. It'll be cold, but I have outdoor heaters, and they'll be running around, so they won't really feel the cold. But there's bound to be snow in December, so I don't anticipate they can do much outdoors on their birthdays."

"Okay. That makes sense. But this party came on suddenly. Why did you decide to do it so quickly?"

"Well, actually, Abby likes a boy. I told her she could have a party over here and invite him. She's too shy to come out and ask him to go out with her. I know girls do that now, but Abby doesn't. She's way too insecure. But she wasn't too shy to ask him to come to a party, so I decided to have this party for them."

His smile broadened, and I melted just a little. I felt like this ice cream cake after it had been left out in the sun. "Mate, that's brilliant," he said. "Having a party so her little crush can come over."

"Yes. So, I need somebody to make this spinach dip while I set everything up outside. And I don't know how to set that heater up outside, and you're a guy, so I assume you probably know how to set up heaters and things like that. I hope I'm not wrong about that."

"You're not wrong. I am well-versed in bloke things like putting up outdoor heaters, so I'll be happy to help you out there."

Axel and I worked together for the next hour to ensure everything was set up, and Abby and Rina did the same. They were totally excited about their party, and so was I, in a way. It was an excellent distraction for me, and it was a healthy way for me to direct my excess energy. I still hadn't slept, except for about two hours the night before last, so I didn't know why I was still so energetic. I only knew I was, and I felt like I could do anything at all. It was a weird feeling.

"So, who's on the guest list?" I asked Rina.

She rattled off a bunch of names, and, for some odd reason, one of the names caught my attention: Amelia Stone.

"Wait a second. Amelia Stone. You mentioned her before. You said that she'd broken up with her little boyfriend and that all the kids were talking about it. Right? That's the same girl, right?"

She shrugged. "That was like a million years ago. She likes this other boy now, but he won't be here. Why do you care?"

I furrowed my brows. "Who are her parents?"

She dipped a chip into some dip and forced it into her mouth. "I don't know. Her dad is some really rich dude. Her mom is somebody. I don't really know. Why do you care?"

I remembered reading on the prenup that the Stones had no children. I had a feeling Amelia Stone was Gerald Stone's child. I didn't know why I thought that, but that was the first thought that popped into my head.

Kayla Stone and Gerald Stone had been married for 13 years. Amelia Stone was in the same grade as Rina and Abby, meaning she was 11 going on 12. Might Amelia have been born to a different mother? And, if so, how was that significant to this case? *Was* it significant?

I shook my head. "Nothing, nothing. But what do you know about her? Who does she live with?"

Rina rolled her eyes. "She lives with her mother. They live in Hallbrook. Her mother stays home with her and doesn't work. That's all I know. Her mother doesn't have the father around anymore. I don't know if the father has ever been around. I only know he's some really rich dude that gives Amelia's mother a lot of money. That's all I know. Why? Do you want to meet her parents?"

"Actually, I do. I'd love to meet her mother."

"Okay. Her mother will bring her here, so you can meet her."

"Thanks."

Axel came in after Rina left the kitchen. "I overheard you talking to Rina," he said. "What's going on?"

I sighed. "Oh, Axel, I haven't spoken with you about the Michael Reynolds case. I'm getting so close to breaking it wide open. I have to investigate more, but I think things are going my way."

"What do you mean? Are you saying you're finding evidence that will solidly exonerate your client? Or are you saying something else?"

"I'm saying something else." I sighed. "I know you won't like what I'm doing. Hell, *I* don't even like what I'm doing. I'm happy about it, but I don't like it."

He sat down at the table and pulled me down on his lap. I threw my arms around his neck and put my head on his shoulder. "Harper," he said. "Tell me what's going on? Are you trying to undermine your own client?"

I nodded my head. "I'm a horrible person, aren't I?"

He laughed. "No, of course not. I've never heard of an attorney doing that, but I don't blame you. That's a bad bloke you got there. Are you sure it should be you who sinks him, though?"

"Yes," I said. "I spoke with the prosecutor and know she won't figure out what happened in this case. She's a good prosecutor, but she's busy. She has investigators out there looking at the facts of this case, but I don't think they'll figure out what really happened. I know the cops won't figure it out. So it falls on me."

"Why won't the cops figure it out? I'm a cop. A detective. My brothers in blue will be all over this case. After all, the media's all over it, so they're under a lot of pressure to perform."

I shook my head. "I spoke with the first responder cop. I wasn't encouraged. I got the feeling they stopped looking after my client was arrested. Which is fine, but they're not looking hard enough. They aren't looking at the big picture."

"What is the big picture in this case?"

"The big picture is there's a conspiracy going on. I can't say anything, but it involves a large corporation that can lose hundreds of millions if the case goes wrong. And the case would go the wrong way under Judge Sanders. The ironic thing is that the person involved, Gerald Stone, has a daughter I didn't know about, and she'll be at this party tonight. So is her mother, who's bringing her here. I'll get to speak with her, but probably only briefly. I don't even know if I can say much to her. I don't even know what I'll ask her."

Axel looked skeptical. "Lass, tell me what you think happened in this case. And how does it tie into your client?"

"I'll tell you later. Believe me, it's a long and sordid tale. One that can't be told in a short period, which is what we have right now. The kids will be here in a half hour. We have to get moving on this."

Axel and I put the finishing touches for the party. The outdoor tables were set up with snacks, and Axel checked the outdoor heaters to ensure they worked properly. We also set up stations for the laser tag, and I tested the karaoke machine.

Axel laughed as I sang an Adele song on the machine. "Your voice is very nice," he said. "You should be a lounge singer."

"Ha ha."

"No, really, you should. You're very good."

I blushed. "I can't carry a tune to save my life."

He joined me, and we sang a duet, looking into each other's eyes. Rina came out, saw us singing to each other, and she rolled her eyes. "Gross. Get a room."

We both giggled. "We're only trying it out, Ladybug."

She came up to me and whispered. "Don't call me that around my friends. It's embarrassing."

"Okay."

As she walked away, Axel put his arm around me. "Don't feel bad. She'll get to the age where you'll be embarrassing to her no matter what you do. Trust me. In a year or two, she won't even know you if you're out in public with her. Fair warning."

"Yeah, I know. I did the same thing to my parents. We used to go to the mall, and if I saw some kids from my class, I hid from them. I didn't want them to see me with my parents. I know Rina will be the same way. Abby maybe won't, though. She's just a little doll."

"Oh, Abby will disown you too one day, mate. Just trust me on this." He kissed my forehead. "I think everything is good to go."

I looked around and knew Axel was right. Everything was in place, and I didn't need anything else. The kids would have fun.

The doorbell rang, and about three kids, and their mothers, came in the door after I answered it. I greeted all the mothers, shook their hands and made small talk while their daughters ran into the living room. They were energetic and bouncing around excitedly, and I heard more than one shriek.

Over the next half hour, all the kids came in with their mothers. Amelia Stone was the last to come through the door with her mother.

Amelia was a pretty girl - tall, thin, blonde and somewhat awkward. She had the slightly slouched posture of a young Taylor Swift and was gangly like her. She looked, for all the world, like a young lady who would blossom into supermodel status at any moment, but, at present, she just looked like an awkward teen girl. Complete with braces.

Her mother, whose name I didn't yet know, looked like an older version of Amelia. Tall, long blonde hair, sophisticated. Carried a designer purse, wore designer shoes, and was tanned. Since it was November in Kansas City, the only way she could've attained a tan was through a tanning bed or a long vacation in a sunny place.

I guessed the latter was the case.

"Hello," she said. "My name is Megan Baker. I'm Amelia's mom."

I nodded and shook her hand. "Harper Ross. This is Axel Springer. He's my right-hand man in this. My partner in crime."

She nodded at Axel appreciatively, and they shook hands.

Amelia reluctantly joined the melee happening in the living room. Somebody had turned on a music video station, and the girls were dancing and singing along while the boys stood around awkwardly.

James was one of the boys, and I thought Abby had decent taste. He was a cute, skinny kid with floppy copper-colored hair and freckles. I saw him look over at Abby more than once and go over to her as she stood off to the side. Abby looked embarrassed because her face was turned down towards the floor, and I saw him lightly punch her in the arm as she giggled.

No doubt about it. He was digging her too.

I wished the best for her.

"Well," Megan said. "I'll pick up Amelia around 11. Would that be okay?"

"Yes." I hesitated. "But I'd like to discuss something with you if you don't mind."

She looked perplexed but nodded her head. "Okay, sure."

She followed me into the sunroom, and I beckoned her to sit next to me. "Would you like something to drink?"

"No," she said. "I really can't stay long. I'm meeting a guy at McCormick and Schmick's on The Plaza at 8."

"I won't keep you long. I just wanted to ask you something. I hope I'm not prying."

She looked uncomfortable when I said that. Her eyes didn't meet mine, and she looked around the room. "This is a cute room," she said. "I love the colors you chose. The yellow walls are very bright and sunny, and the green curtains go very well with the walls. The rug pulls it all together. Very nice." She picked up her purse and clutched it to her chest.

"Yes, this room wasn't me, unfortunately. I don't have a good eye for such things. I hired an interior decorator. I think she did a pretty good job of making my house not look like a color-blind person lives here."

She smiled weakly and nodded her head. "Yes. I'll have to get her name from you."

I took a deep breath, knowing there was a time limit on what I would ask her. She indicated that her date was at 8, and it was presently 7:30. The Plaza was pretty close, but it was a Friday night, and parking was always hard to find at this time. "Yes, I'll give you one of her cards before you leave." I hesitated. "But I didn't want to talk about the decoration of my house. I wanted to..."

She looked at me, her eyes quizzical.

"I wanted to ask you about Amelia's father. Her father is Gerald Stone, isn't it?"

The color drained away from her face, and she clutched her purse tighter. "I don't see how that's your business. I just met you. Why are you asking me these questions?"

I leaned back in my chair. "I'm an attorney. I'm working a murder case."

"What does that have to do with me?"

"I'm working on a theory. It involves Amelia's father. I know you don't have to answer my questions now, but if you don't, I'll have you subpoenaed to answer questions under oath. I don't really want to do that. Amelia and Rina are friends, and I don't want to drive a wedge between them. If Rina gets wind that I'm grilling her friend's mother, she'll surely hate me."

"You're grilling me now." Her fingers on her purse were quivering, and her leg started to twitch. "What's the difference between grilling me now and subpoenaing me to come into your office for a deposition?"

"You've done depositions before?"

"Of course. Gerald didn't want to acknowledge Amelia as his own. I had to have a DNA test ordered and paternity established, and then I had to drag him into court to get support."

"I see." I raised an eyebrow. "Tell me about Gerald. What's he like?"

"I won't answer these intrusive questions."

"I'll find out anyway. I have ways of finding things like restraining orders you might have filed against him and court records regarding your custody case. So you might as well speak with me so you have a chance to defend yourself."

She looked at her watch. "I have to go. I have to be on The Plaza at 8. You know how parking is."

"I do. But I want to ask you one question."

She rolled her eyes. "What is that question?"

"You don't work, is that right?"

"I do. I'm a homemaker. I raise my daughter. Believe me, that's work."

"Oh, I know. I have a nanny to help me raise my two girls, but children are a lot of work. But that wasn't what I wanted to know."

"What are you getting at?"

"You don't work outside the home, but Rina told me you live in Hallbrook. You just told me you had to drag Gerald into court for him to even acknowledge Amelia is his child. He strikes me as the type of guy who'd give you what's owed for child support under the law and not a penny more. That means you couldn't afford a house in Hallbrook. Not unless you somehow got a nice settlement from Gerald."

I raised an eyebrow at her. She looked furious, but at the same time, I saw in her eyes that she wanted to tell me the whole story.

"How do you know that I didn't inherit money from my parents?"

"Did you?"

She shook her head. "No. My parents live east of Troost if that tells you anything."

"It does."

She sighed. "I really have to go. I'll meet you in your office on Monday if you like. I don't want to be put under oath, however. But I'll tell you anything you need to know."

"Thank you. I'm very sorry to ask these questions. I'm just trying to get to the bottom of something."

She nodded. "It's okay. Gerald...is not a good man. I found that out too late. But that's all I'll say for now."

"Let me walk you out."

The two of us walked to my front door, and I put my hand on her shoulder. "Thank you. How about 2 PM on Monday? Here's my card, so you know the address."

"Yes, I see." She looked at my card. "Looks like you're in one of those high-rises on The Plaza. Do you like working there?"

"Oh, I love it. Thanksgiving is around the corner, so the lights will be coming on. My absolute favorite time of year."

She laughed softly. "Mine too. Well, I'll be seeing you Monday at 2."

"Monday at 2."

Twenty-Five

Monday rolled around, and I went to my office in anticipation of meeting with Megan Baker.

The party with the girls went well. Everybody seemed to have fun, and there weren't any major fights, so I counted that as a success. Best of all, Abby and James seemed to bond that evening. He seemed to like her as much as she liked him, so she was anxious about seeing him at school.

"What if he doesn't talk to me?" she asked me anxiously over breakfast.

"He will. Be positive. I think he really likes you."

Abby shook her head. "I don't know, Aunt Harper. I think he still doesn't know I'm alive."

"Don't be silly, Buttercup. I saw the two of you at your party. I think he's really digging you."

She smiled. "If you say so."

For once, Rina said nothing nasty to her sister. In fact, she said something nice. "I think he likes you, Abby. But if he ignores you in school, I'll get Axel to punch him in the mouth."

I laughed. "I don't think he'll do that, Rina. But you never know."

. . .

Pearl poked her head through the door. "Megan Baker is here to see you."

"Please send her in."

At that, Megan came into my office, looking unsure and a bit lost. "Hello," I said, standing up and shaking her hand. "Come on in. Thank you for making time for this."

She nodded her head and said nothing. "I'm very nervous," she finally said. "If Gerald knew I was here..." She shook her head. "I worry about what he would do."

"Have a seat," I said, gesturing to the chair in front of my desk. "Would you like something to drink? Bottled water, raspberry iced tea, or pop?"

"I'll have bottled water."

I then buzzed Pearl and asked her to bring Megan water. She popped in a few seconds later, handing Megan the drink. Megan opened the water and took a nervous sip. Her hand on the bottle shook, and I felt bad for her.

"It'll be okay," I said. I'd done some basic research before Megan came to my office and found she'd filed three restraining orders against Gerald. In these orders, she wrote he had threatened her life, had attempted to strangle her, and had beaten her so badly that she ended up in the hospital. I hated that he'd gotten away with this. I imagined the only reason he wasn't in prison for assault was because he was wealthy enough to buy his way out of his problems.

Maybe. But I had a feeling his luck was about to run out. If he was behind murdering Judge Sanders, he'd spend the rest of his life behind bars. Where he belonged.

"That's easy for you to say. Gerald has had me followed more than once. I, uh, did some research on you before coming here. I learned you're on the case involving Judge Sanders's murder. How is that coming along?"

"It's coming along fine. But that's why I need to speak with you."

She looked confused. "Okay. I don't understand why you need

to speak with me. I've been trying to figure out the connection, or at least how you're connecting me to this murder. Or maybe you need to speak with me for some other reason?"

"No. I don't think you're mixed up with Judge Sanders' murder. Not at all. But I have to ask you some more questions about Gerald."

She shifted uncomfortably in her seat. "What do you need to know?"

"Tell me about your relationship with him. I take it he was already married to Kayla when you and he met?"

"Yes." She sighed. "I didn't know that, of course." She bit her lower lip. "I was working then. At a club. Bazookas. I was a dancer there."

Bazookas was a strip club in midtown that featured totally nude dancing. It was a juice bar, which meant it didn't serve alcohol – this was a requirement because a local ordinance stated that if girls were dancing nude, the men could not be drunk. I thought it was a good ordinance because it somewhat protected the girls from pushy men.

"You were a dancer. Did you meet Gerald at Bazookas?"

"I did. He was a regular there. He came in at least once a week. He paid for a lap dance from me, only from me, every time he came in. He told me he wanted me to give him lap dances because he found me beautiful." She shrugged. "I believed him. I didn't know who he was. I didn't know he was rich. I only knew that, at least at first, he made me feel like I was the only woman in that club. He could be very charming."

She started to cry, and I wordlessly gave her a box of Kleenex. She took one, dabbed her eyes and blew her nose.

I made notes as she spoke. I had a feeling she'd be one of my most important witnesses.

"So, yeah. I was a dancer, and he was one of my most important clients. He always tipped extremely well. I mean, extremely well. He would tip me $1,000 for a lap dance, so I was excited when he came in. All the other girls wanted him to choose them for a dance, too, but he was pretty well fixated on me."

I nodded along and didn't say anything. I wanted to draw her out, so I wanted to say as little as possible.

"Well, sooner or later, he asked me what I was doing after work. I worked the 2-10 PM shift three days a week. I would go to work and go home and watch television or something before returning the next day. In other words, I didn't have much going on, so I didn't mind having him take me out. Again, though, I didn't know who he was. If I did, I doubt I would've gone out with him. Then again, if I never went out with him, I wouldn't have Amelia, so, for that reason alone, I'm grateful to have met him. But that's the only reason I'm glad I met him, though."

"Okay," I said as I made notes. "So, you met him while you were working, and the two of you went out."

"Yes. But we only went out one time." She looked down at my desk. "He, uh. He did something. I still don't know what. But he did something. Put something in my drink or something. All I know is that I woke up on my couch the morning after he and I went out, and I had no idea how I got there. But I could tell we had sex. I could feel it - the tenderness you get when you've had sex after not having had sex for a long time."

I felt nervous when she spoke. It was safe to say I'd be *very* tender, probably in pain, the next time I had sex. It had been 17 years. I was practically a virgin again.

I also felt an affinity with her. Gerald raped her. There was no other word for it. He undoubtedly put GHB, the "date rape" drug, into her drink and then had his way with her while she was unconscious.

"I thought nothing of it at first," she continued. "I mean, I was angry, but I wasn't all that sure we did it. I couldn't accuse him of something like that. I had no proof. So I just moved on. Forget I ever went out with him. I was relieved, too, when I realized he wasn't coming into the club anymore. I didn't want to see him." She visibly shuddered. "I moved on. I forgot about him until about six weeks later when I started throwing up in the morning and realized I hadn't gotten my period in a while."

I nodded along. "So, you realized you were pregnant."

"I guess so. I mean, I didn't want to accept I was pregnant. I tried to pretend nothing was wrong. I'm a dancer, you know. A dancer. I couldn't be pregnant." Then she laughed. "And I wasn't sure Gerald and I had sex, either. People think we dancers have sex all the time, but the reality is much different. At least, for me, it was different. I didn't date all that much. And Gerald was my first sexual experience in over a year, and I didn't have sex with anyone else after him. So I thought my system was haywire, and I had the flu."

She looked sad, and she blew her nose again. Then she looked out the window. I carefully watched her as she looked out the window and took sips of water from time to time.

Finally, she spoke again. "I saw the doctor and discovered I was pregnant. I knew who the father was, of course. And I knew for sure that I'd been raped. So I was furious. And the first thing I wanted to do was go to Planned Parenthood and take care of it. I couldn't have a baby. I was a dancer, making great money, but I'd have to quit, so there wouldn't be money for a kid."

She sighed and, for a long time, she said nothing else. I saw the look on her face, and I knew that telling this story was difficult for her, to say the very least.

She flattened out her mouth as if she was trying to hold back tears again. "No money for a kid," she said softly. "I didn't even know how to get in touch with him. I never got his phone number. I didn't know where he lived. It was a disaster. I was pregnant by a man who raped me while I was unconscious, and I had no clue how to find him again."

"How did you find him?"

"Well, it was the weirdest thing. His company, Stone Enterprises, was in the newspaper. It lost a lot of money that year, yet Gerald was still pocketing millions of dollars a year as its CEO and founder. People were outraged, so the company was in the newspaper, and they showed a picture of Gerald there. I read the newspaper, saw the picture, and I was stunned. Absolutely stunned. You could've knocked me over with a feather."

I made notes furiously while she spoke. "So, you found out who he was. How did you get in touch with him?"

"It wasn't easy. I knew who he was, finally, but that did me little good. I couldn't just call Stone Enterprises and ask to speak with the CEO. That wouldn't work. I went to the headquarters and asked to see him, and they laughed at me. They said there was no way I could get a meeting with him. So, I was frustrated."

"How were you able to finally speak with him?"

"I had to have him served at his office. With a paternity petition." She shook her head. "To say that he wasn't happy would be an understatement. He called me the night he was served and cussed me up and down. He told me there was no way he was the father of my baby, and I was a stripper, so I probably had sex with a hundred men since him, so how did I know he was the father? He was completely different from the man I'd gotten to know at the club. But I was firm. I told him he was the only man I'd slept with in over a year, so I was positive he got me pregnant."

I had to smile. I imagined his face when he received that petition, which made me want to giggle just a little. Men like Gerald needed to be brought down to size, and I imagined that her petition did just that – brought him down to size.

"And then what happened?"

"He fought me the whole way. He had some powerful lawyer file a bunch of motions, and I didn't have a lawyer at all. I was doing it all myself. The lawyer tried to stop me from getting a DNA test, but the judge ordered it anyway, and, of course, the results came back that he was the father. He was the only one possible, so I wasn't surprised. He was, though, and furious. He was married, which made things more complicated."

To say the least.

"Did he lose his temper?"

"Oh, yeah. He did. He came over to my house three separate times. He strangled me one of those times. He had me down on the floor, his hands around my neck, and I thought I would die. The second time he came over, he kicked me in the stomach. I knew he was trying to get me to lose the baby, which scared me. The third time, he beat me up so badly that I was hospitalized. After each time he came over, I filed a restraining order against him. He obviously didn't care because he kept on coming over."

"The bastard," I muttered, and Megan laughed softly.

"To say the least," she said. "You can call him a sociopath. That would be the better term for him. I was very angry. I kept going to court because he kept violating the restraining order, and the judge would let him go every time. The cops refused to arrest him every time he came over. I felt pretty helpless. I had restraining orders against him, and he was beating on me and strangling me, and I couldn't get law enforcement to protect me. I thought he'd kill me next."

She put her fingers on my desk and drummed them while she looked out the window again for several minutes.

"Would you like another water?" I asked her.

"No," she said with a shake of her head. "I just want to get through this." She paused again. "I thought he'd kill me. But I got the upper hand on him and could make him do what I wanted."

My ears perked up when she said this. I was genuinely curious about how she got the upper hand on him. "What happened? What did you do to get the upper hand?"

"I got smart. I hired a private investigator to find out any information about him I could use. I needed to fight fire with fire. And that PI came through like a house on fire."

"In what way?"

"My PI, Manuel, discovered Gerald was stealing from the company. He had a forensic accountant go through the company's books. I guess he also had somebody hack the company's financial records, and they discovered Gerald had been stealing millions from his own company. I couldn't believe it. I mean, I read in the paper he was being paid $30 million per year and that his stock options brought him millions more, sometimes over a hundred million dollars a year, and that wasn't enough. He had to also steal millions more. I mean, how much does one person need? Truly. I guess for some people, they can never have enough money. It's some kind of psychological disorder."

I believed it. I believed people obsessed with acquiring millions upon millions by any means possible were suffering from a psychological disorder of some sort. That made sense to me. At any rate, Gerald sounded like a real piece of work.

A real piece of work.

She looked out the window again. "I told him I had the goods on him, and I'd go to the authorities to have him arrested."

"How did he react to that?"

"He blustered. He told me he had no clue what I was talking about. But he suddenly played ball. We went to court, and I got child support from him, but I wanted to really make him pay. So I continued to hold that information above his head. Also, I knew he wanted to literally kill me. He was desperate for me to keep my mouth shut. I knew he was the kind of guy who'd kill to protect himself, so I told him the information I had about him stealing was in a secure location. My mother knew where it was, and so did one other person. I didn't tell him who the other person was."

She was a smart cookie. If Gerald thought he could kill her to shut her up, she told him that plan wouldn't work. She also told him two people had that information without telling him who the second person was. Therefore, he wouldn't know who to kill to keep everything quiet. Very smart.

"So, then what happened?"

"I got what I wanted from him. He bought me that house in Hallbrook and agreed to pay me $100,000 a year in addition to the child support he was ordered to give me, which was $5,000 a month." She smiled. "And he hasn't harassed me since. In fact, I haven't seen him since. Thank God."

I leaned back in my chair as I regarded her. She was smart and tough. She also had the goods on Gerald. One thing was for sure – after speaking with her, I knew, with zero doubt, that Gerald could've ordered the murder of Judge Sanders.

"Let me ask you this. I wanted to speak with you because I'm hot on the trail of finding out who killed Judge Sanders. Gerald Stone is looking pretty good to me right now."

She furrowed her brow. "Gerald is? Why do you think he did it?"

"His company has a pending class action against Dowling Chemicals, a subsidiary of Stone Enterprises."

She nodded her head. "Yes. That chemical. Toluene or something like that."

"Toluene. Yes. That's exactly it."

"Those poor people. I mean, I know that community. It's pretty similar to the neighborhood where I grew up. Those people have very little to begin with. They certainly don't need some negligent company poisoning them. All those babies born with brain damage – it's heartbreaking. Absolutely heartbreaking."

I nodded my head. "It is. It breaks my heart, too. And you're right – those people have enough to worry about without worrying about getting sick because some idiotic company doesn't ensure they're disposing of chemicals correctly."

"Amen. So, that case is pending. Why do you think Gerald wanted to get rid of Judge Sanders?"

I raised my eyebrows. "If you knew about Judge Sanders, you'd know why. He was a plaintiff's attorney. By that, I mean he consistently ruled on behalf of plaintiffs against big corporations. He had no qualms slapping companies with large punitive damages when they were guilty of criminal wrongdoing. Here, there was the possibility of being assessed millions, perhaps even billions, in punitive damages. At any rate, the punitives would've probably been in the hundreds of millions if Judge Sanders was trying this case. I read through his opinions, and he *hated* criminally negligent corporations. Despised them. He slapped them down hard. And how Dowling got rid of those chemicals was criminally negligent. I mean, the employees were just pouring that stuff on the ground. They didn't even bother putting all the chemicals in barrels. And the barrels they did use weren't rated for those chemicals."

"Really? I didn't pay that much attention to that case. I saw it was Dowling Chemicals, but I didn't associate it with Gerald." She smiled. "If I associated it with Gerald, I probably would've thought the same thing you're thinking – that Gerald was behind Judge Sanders' murder. Because you're right – Gerald would have a judge killed. He'd do that without even thinking. The man's a straight-up sociopath."

I drummed my pen on the desk. "He is. I mean, he sounds like it." I bit my lower lip. I was fairly certain Gerald's fingerprints were all over this murder. But were Michael's fingerprints on it as well?

That would be the trick. I would somehow, someway, connect Michael to this whole murder. I didn't know how I'd do that, however. Gerald Stone had a motive to kill the judge. Gerald Stone had the right mentality to do it. Michael, however, didn't quite have the same motive.

It might've been a huge coincidence that Michael was involved with Kayla Stone, and Gerald Stone most likely ordered Judge Sanders killed. Yet Michael had the best access to the judge. He was in the best position to poison Judge Sanders.

Michael told me, however, that Christina was setting him up.

I was confused. After speaking with Megan, I thought I knew who did it – Gerald Stone. But I couldn't deny that Christina and Ava Sanders also had reason to do it. Michael was having an affair with Kayla Stone, and Kayla Stone's prenuptial agreement was changed the day after the judge was murdered. That would show Kayla Stone did something for Gerald in exchange for getting the terms she wanted in that agreement.

That something might've been killing the judge.

It might've been. But I needed to figure it out. And I was a long, long way from proving any of it. I wanted to go to the cops and tell them what I suspected about Gerald, but I feared they would take their attention away from Michael. I needed Michael to still be the focus of the investigation.

I needed to make sure Michael did the perp walk at the end of all of this. That was within my reach. I could feel it. I could taste it. It was coming. I just had to prove it.

"Ms. Ross?" Megan asked me. "Are you okay?"

"Yes," I said, coming out of my reverie. "I am. Why do you ask?"

She shrugged. "I don't know. I've been talking to you, and you haven't answered me back. I think I lost you somehow."

"Oh, I'm sorry. I just got lost in thought. What were you just trying to say to me?"

"I was asking you if you needed any other information from me."

"No, actually. You've given me all the information I need. You've gone above and beyond the call of duty, so I thank you."

She grimaced. "Well, if what I tell you helps you somehow put Gerald into jail, I'll be happy. He's a bad man, Ms. Ross. A terrible man. Once you told me your suspicions about him – that you think he was behind the murder of Judge Sanders – I knew what you were thinking was probably right. Gerald would do something like that without even thinking twice. By the way, who's the judge overseeing the case?"

I sighed. "Judge Perez. He's a hard-ass who is really stingy with plaintiffs. The plaintiffs will probably get very little out of it. Which is a shame, of course. They've been hurt. They need justice, but it will probably be denied to them. All because of Gerald. They're collateral damage, and it just isn't right."

"No, that's not right," Megan agreed. "It's not right that one judge will award millions and another judge won't. That doesn't seem like justice."

"It's not. It's the legal system, though. Powerful people are behind getting these judges seated. Powerful lobbying interests ensure they get their men and women on the bench. Because the President appoints federal judges, the justice system is run by whomever the current President chooses. That's why elections have consequences. People don't think about that, but it's true – if the people want to have their cases heard by judges who are sympathetic to them and not to the powerful, then they have to elect politicians who will put those types of judges on the bench. Nobody ever thinks about that angle until they attempt to sue somebody and find out, too late, that the judge who oversees their case is a total hard-ass. Like Judge Perez."

I was on my soapbox, and I knew it. As an attorney, I knew, for a fact, how important it was to get the right judge to hear your case. As far as plaintiffs were concerned, Judge Perez was the wrong judge. However, as far as wealthy special interests were concerned, Judge Perez was a golden boy. It made me sick.

Megan nodded. "Well, Ms. Ross, I hope you get your man. By your man, I mean I hope you get Gerald."

I shook her hand, and she left.

I sat down at my office, thinking Megan was right. Gerald sounded like a bad guy. The very worst kind of person. But he had good company because Michael was also a bad guy. They were in on it together. I knew it.

But how would I prove it?

The next day, I was sitting in my office, minding my own business, trying to go through my stacks of files and triage them somehow. I was consumed with Michael's murder trial, but even so, I also had other clients who needed attention. They were mostly low-level cases that would plead out – stealing clients, DWI clients, and the like. It wouldn't be a big deal, except I had a lot of them.

And then I heard Michael come storming into the office suite. "Where is she? Where is my fucking bitch attorney?"

I peeked my head out the door, and he saw me. Pearl stood up and put her hands out, but he ran past her and charged towards my office. My heart pounded loudly, and I saw him tear off his leather gloves and throw them on the floor. His fists were balled up, and I shut the door before he could enter.

"You open that door. You open it right now. Right fucking now."

A part of me wanted to call the police, but I thought better of it.

I wanted nothing to complicate my mission, and having Michael hauled into the police station would certainly slow his case down. I was close to finding all the puzzle pieces and wanted nothing to get in the way.

"I won't. Not until you calm down."

I heard him breathing heavily, so I waited. I waited until I heard his breathing slow down before I opened the door.

"Come in," I said, pointing to a chair. "And sit down."

“You...you...you...” He shook his head. "What are you doing on this case? Where are you going with it?"

"Come again? If you're referring to the fact that I had Megan Baker in here for a deposition, you should thank me. She told me some information that was very interesting to me about Kayla's husband." I nodded, never letting on that I suspected Michael himself was also somehow behind the judge's murder.

"You lay off Gerald Stone. Do you hear me? You lay off him. That's an order."

I sat down. "Now, why would you ask me to lay off of him?"

He shook his head. "Listen, Kayla and Gerald are on their last tether. Gerald is ready to divorce her and leave her with nothing at all. I have to hear from Kayla that her husband is harassing her because he found out you're looking at him for this murder. Gerald is ready to cut her out. Do you hear me? He's ready to cut her down to size."

I narrowed my eyes, wondering what his game was. Why he was so upset. After all, Gerald changed that prenuptial agreement to take out the infidelity clause.

Or was he getting ready to change it back? To put that infidelity clause right back in? That would make sense. I was closing in on Michael. I was putting him in a vise. It was a vise of his own making, to be sure, but a vise nonetheless.

"Michael," I said, my voice calm and measured. "What happens to Kayla Stone is not my concern, and it shouldn't be yours, either. Your concern should be laser-focused on my finding an alternative person who did this murder. If we go before the jury, at this moment, you'll fry. Do you know why the jury will fry you? I'll tell you why. Because there's nobody else to pin this murder on. Somebody will go down for it, and you're the only candidate. The only one. Now, my job is to turn over every stone, no pun intended, and find alternative explanations for the murder. I'd like it if you would back off and let me do your job, or else you'll be as fried as that chicken you bought the night of the murder."

"Lay off Gerald. This is your last warning."

I raised an eyebrow. "Or what?"

"Or you're a dead woman."

In spite of myself, I laughed out loud. "Oh, really. Really. Listen, if you don't like how I'm preparing for this case, I suggest you find a different attorney to threaten. And that's not even a suggestion at this point. That's an ultimatum. Either stop telling me how to do my job or fire me." I crossed my arms, sat back in my chair, and stared at him.

We engaged in a staring contest for a few minutes before he looked away. I could see his wheels turning, and I knew I had him. I knew it. He couldn't fire me. I had all the cards, and he knew it.

But was there something else? Some other reason he refused to fire me? Christina told him he had to hire me or get a Public Defender, but I thought he'd rather go with the Public Defender. After all, the Public Defender might not put together who did this crime. They might, but they might not have looked at the Stone Enterprises angle. If I were Michael, I'd go with that gamble.

Ah, but then again, Christina would call in the bond if he did that. He would end up in jail, awaiting trial. That would be motivation enough to stick with me. For that reason alone, I was confident I would remain on his case.

"I told you who did this," he said. "It was my wife."

"You never told me that. You told me you suspected her. You never told me definitively that she did it." I glared at him, appalled that he would try to bury his own wife. Christina was the mother of his five children, too. Was he really willing to let her take the blame for this? That made me sick.

His left eye twitched. He looked like a monster to me, so I turned my head.

"She did it. You get her in here and ask her one question, which will tell you everything you need to know."

"What's that one question?"

"You ask her who fathered our oldest child, Lindsay."

Twenty-Six

Oh, God. I was going to be sick. Really, really sick.

Michael had left the office in a huff and left more breadcrumbs for me. The trouble was that these were breadcrumbs I didn't want to have left for me. His implication was clear – Judge Sanders fathered Christina's oldest child, who was 13 years old. That very thought made me sick. I knew he had raped his daughter, which was awful enough. But to father a child with her? That was seriously outer limits.

Was Christina angry enough to kill her father?

Or was her father crazy enough to threaten to tell the child the truth?

That was the only thing that made sense to me about why Christina would do something like that to her father. But why now? The child was 13 years old.

Why indeed? I could think of at least two reasons Christina might've gone outer limits and killed her father now, as opposed to 14 years ago, when the child was conceived. Number one, Christina just found out her father had another family, so she killed him as a favor to her mother. Number two, the judge might've threatened Christina with telling the child the truth. Or, door number three was that Christina might not have known for sure, until recently, who the child's father was.

Sitting back in my chair and looking out the window, I thought it was probably the third option. It made little sense that the judge would threaten to tell Lindsay about her parentage. That made zero sense. After all, if that ever got out, his career would be finished, and he could spend some time in prison.

No, he wouldn't threaten Christina with doing that. It wouldn't be a credible threat.

I decided to get to the bottom of it. I called Christina on her cell phone.

"Yeah," she said. "This is Christina. Who is this?"

"Christina, this is Harper Ross."

"Oh, hey, Harper. How are things cooking over there? You figure out the motive yet?"

"I'm working on it. Listen, I need you to come into the office again. At your earliest possible convenience."

"I'll be there at 5. I hope that's not too late. I must pick up my kids from school, take them home, and get a sitter. Don't ask, but suffice to say, the school where my kids are going has asked that only I pick them up."

"I'll see you at 5."

I hung up the phone, my wheels turning in my head. This was likely a smoke screen Michael had thrown up before me so I'd stop looking at Gerald. The equivalent of screaming "squirrel!"

Or it could be Michael was telling the truth. But why now? Why would he bring this up now and not during his initial meeting with me?

Christina came in right at five, looking harried. "Oh, crap," she said. "I'm so sorry, I have to call my babysitter. I forgot to tell her something." She got out her phone, her hand shaking. "Yeah, Teresa, this Christina. Don't forget to give Lindsay her medication...okay, goodbye." She hung up. "It's not been a good day."

"Tell me about it," I said, beckoning her into my office. "Have a seat. I'll get you water."

"No water," she said, taking a metal flask out of her purse. "I'm really sorry to have to do this, but I can't take a second longer of this bullshit." She took the cap off the flask and put it to her lips. Her hand was still shaking.

I took a deep breath and watched her drink whatever was in the flask. I could smell it. It was some kind of bourbon. My drink of choice. I wanted her to hand me the flask so that I, too, could take a drink.

I wanted that more than life itself.

But I couldn't do that. If I did that, I would be in the bar right after work and wouldn't stop. I knew that, so I couldn't ask her to share her alcohol.

She shook her head wildly and made a face. "Eeeyah," she said. "That hit the spot. You want some?"

"No. I mean, yes. I'm dying for some. But I can't."

"I see. You're a recovering alkie, huh? I guess I should be, too, but I'm not. I'm a raging alcoholic, and I don't give a shit who knows it. I don't give a crap who cares about it. Harper, they can all kiss my ass. My mother, my kids, my husband, everyone. They all are on me to stop drinking, but I never will. Never."

Her words were slurred, so I could only assume this wasn't her first drink of the day. "I hear you," I said. "I was there once, too. For many years, I was there. I'm not there anymore, of course. But I struggle, every minute of every day, not to take a drink."

"Oh, I suppose seeing me drink in front of you isn't doing you any favors, huh? I'm sorry about that. But I've had a rough day. A very rough day."

I sighed. "Your rough day is about to get worse." I picked up my paperweight and looked at it closely.

"How can it possibly get worse? The reporters are up in my grill, night and day, trying to get information. Somehow, what my father did to me was splashed in the papers. I don't know who leaked that wonderful information to the media, but I have a good idea. And now my daughter's school has informed me that only I can pick her up because somebody tried to pick her up from school, and that person wasn't authorized. Yet he insisted. The school had to call the police to get him to leave."

I furrowed my brow. "Who tried to pick up your daughter from school?"

Christina burped lightly and pounded her chest with her fist. I noticed her blonde hair, which was ordinarily perfectly coiffed, was slightly messed up in the front. She looked worse for the wear, but I didn't blame her. She was going through hell.

"I don't know. But I have a pretty good idea. It's the same person trying to get me to fall on the sword for my father's murder the entire time. I won't let him get away with it, though. Nope, never. He'll never get away with it."

"Who's been trying to get you to fall on the sword?"

She pointed at me and closed her eyes. "I'll tell you, but you must first tell me why you wanted me to come here. You wanted to ask me some more questions, so go ahead. I won't bite."

"Well, okay. Michael told me something very interesting. Very interesting. I wanted to ask you about it."

"Okay, go ahead. Ask your question. I won't bite." She growled a little, batted her hand at me like a lion, and smiled and laughed. "Of course, I sometimes would like to bite you because you're a really gorgeous woman." Then she laughed again. "Yeah, I swing that way. Not always, but sometimes."

She made me feel slightly uncomfortable, but not really. I'd been hit on by women before. I never swung that way, though, so nothing ever happened. But it was slightly flattering because Christina was a beautiful woman. "Christina, your husband told me something about your father. He gave me another motive you might have for killing Judge Sanders."

"For the last time, I didn't kill my father. Get that through your goddamn head. I didn't kill him. I didn't kill him. I didn't kill him, I didn't kill him, I didn't kill him. Ahhhhhhhhhh!!!!!" She was screaming wildly. "Why does everybody want me to take the fall for this? Goddammit. Now they're threatening my children. Why? Just because I'm a boozer? That hardly seems fair."

I didn't know what she was talking about. "Wait, wait, wait. Back up. You're not making sense. What do you mean, everybody wants you to take the fall for this? What does that mean?"

"I mean everybody. My husband wants me to take the fall. His girlfriend wants me to take the fall. But they're not the ones I'm worried about. And I am worried. Very worried. I can't tell you who else wants me to go down because they're powerful people who can do a lot to harm me and my family. So, I'm keeping my mouth shut."

That pointed to Gerald. He was powerful.

But she said "people." She didn't say "person." She distinctly said the word "people."

"Go ahead," she said. "Ask me the questions you were going to ask me. I have to get home to my freaked-out daughter Elise, who is only 6 years old and terrified someone will kidnap her. If I were you, I'd watch my back, too. You have daughters, right? Well, not daughters, but they're your charges. Don't let anybody get to them. Because they can. They can, and they will. Mark my words about that."

I swallowed hard, feeling a cold tendril of fear. I would call Axel and see what he could do about finding somebody to protect Rina and Abby. If I got too close to discovering what was happening, those two girls' lives could be in danger.

I suddenly had the urgency to see the two of them. Hold them and make sure they were safe. But I had to ask Christina some more questions.

"Excuse me," I said. "I have to make a phone call."

At that, I called Axel. "Yeah, Harper, what's up?" he asked me.

"Are you in the middle of something?"

"Not really. I mean, I'm kinda always in the middle of something, but I'm not more than usual right now. What do you need?"

"Please go to my house and check on Rina and Abby. Sophia is there with them, but I'm freaked out right now. I'll be home, too, as soon as I can, but..."

"I'll be at your house in fifteen minutes."

"Thank you."

I hung up and looked at Christina, who hung her head like really drunk people do. "You have a good guy there," she said. "If he's going to look after your kids right now, he's a good guy. Good guys are hard to find. You need to not drive him away."

"I won't. Now, Christina, about the questions I need to ask you. Michael told me something I wanted to clear up with you."

"Oh? What was that question?"

I cleared my throat and fidgeted. I didn't want to ask her this question. It was a sickening question, but I needed to get to the bottom of it. "He told me Robert is the father of your oldest child, Lindsay."

She rolled her eyes, which was the last reaction I was expecting. "Oh, brother, this again. He'll never get off that, will he? Well, okay, here's the deal. As I told you, my father raped me when I was 15 years old, but it was only one time, and it was only because he was drunk. Okay? Okay? That wasn't an ongoing thing. Anita told you it was, though, didn't she? And my husband? He told you that too?"

I nodded. "Yes. They both told me that."

"Well, don't believe either of them. They both want me to fry for the murder of my father, so they're all about making me look guilty. And that's the best way to make me look guilty, isn't it? By telling you my daddy was raping me all the time? That's the best way to drag my skinny ass fifty miles over dirt roads."

She shook her head rapidly. "That damned Anita. I never trusted her. I always knew she had it bad for Michael. I'll never know why anybody finds that man attractive, but women do. You've seen Kayla Stone. She's a knock-out. So is Willow Cass. So is Ariel Winthrop. So is..." She hung her head. "Oh, I could sit here and recount his mistresses to you, but we don't have all night. We both need to get home to our kids. But women find

Michael catnip. I can't understand that, and I'm married to the guy."

I had to get her back on track. "So it's not true? Your father is not the father of Lindsay?"

She gave me a look. "Oh, hell no. Hell no. But I'll be goddamned if that Judge Perez didn't make a finding that way. That made me sick, too."

What? Judge Perez made a finding that way? What in the hell did that mean? "Wait, wait, wait, whoa. Back up. Judge Perez made a finding of what? That your father was the father of Lindsay?"

"Yes, that's what I'm saying. But I'm here to tell you my father didn't father Lindsay. Period, end of story."

At that, she picked up my trash can and threw up in it. "Oh, God, I need to go home," she said. "I mean, really. I have to go home."

"No, wait. Wait. You can't just leave and not tell me the entire story."

"I'm sick. I mean, I'm really sick. I need to go home."

"You can't drive."

"Oh, yes, I can. I mean, no, I can't. I have a cab waiting outside for me with his meter running. I'm sure I owe him a shit-ton, but that's okay. It's better than me getting a DWI. Of course."

"No, wait. Answer me. What did you mean, Judge Perez made a finding that way? What did you mean?"

She just shook her head. "I'll have to answer your questions later. Right now, I can't do anything. I've said too much as it is. Today, it's Elise being threatened. Tomorrow it might be Tommy. The next day it'll be Maddy. It'll never stop. That's the whole problem with having five kids. You have five targets of some powerful people. You do the math."

I wanted to put my head down on the desk and just cry. Every time I turned around, something else was thrown in front of me. Something else got me twisted around like a pretzel. Some other squirrel distracted me.

As Christina stumbled out the door, I suddenly felt I knew less today than I did yesterday. I was so sure yesterday that I was on the right track.

But somehow, someway, Christina put more doubt in my head.

Judge Perez made a finding that way.

What did that mean?

Twenty-Seven

I got home and, to my relief, Rina and Abby were there, playing cards with Axel on the floor. "Beautiful lass," he said, coming up to me. "I'm showing your girls how to play three-card Monte. It's a well-known con game from the dawn of time. They're really taking to it."

I nodded and said nothing. I felt like the energy was finally draining away. Finally. I had a lot of energy for a week, and I was still not sleeping. I slept maybe two hours every night, and it had been like that for a week. Now, after seeing Christina, right after seeing Michael, and having both of them confuse me, I felt like I just needed to go upstairs, hit the sack, and not wake up for a week.

"I'm kidding," he said. "I'm actually teaching them Hearts. They really like it."

"Oh, that's nice." I had zero energy to pretend that I was interested in Axel teaching Rina and Abby cards. None.

He looked at me and immediately looked concerned. "Harper, what's going on?"

"Nothing. I just have gotten little sleep lately. It's finally catching up with me."

He grimaced and looked over at Rina and Abby, who were lying on the floor. They both looked up at me, concern in their eyes.

"Tell you what. Why don't I call Grubhub, and they can bring us all some food? That way, you don't have to cook. I'd cook a meal here, but you'd not like what I serve. My kitchen skills are limited to boiling hot dogs, maybe putting some sauerkraut over the hot dogs and warming up the buns."

I smiled weakly. Axel was trying to cheer me up, but I was suddenly so damned tired and depressed I couldn't engage him in his banter.

"That's good. Just order me a hamburger from somewhere, and I'm good." I was dying for a hamburger. I didn't even know why. I only knew a burger sounded amazing at that point.

"Okay. Let me get the orders from the girls, and I'll call."

He went over to Rina and Abby, who excitedly told him what they wanted and what restaurant they wanted it from. "PF Chang's," they both said. "I want the orange chicken, and Abby gets the sweet and sour chicken. And lettuce wraps. Yum, yum, yum," Rina said, her little voice getting higher and higher pitched as she spoke.

"Harper wants a burger," Axel said.

I shrugged. "I'm not married to the burger idea. Just get me some Sesame Chicken, and we'll call it good."

At that, Axel called on the phone, and I flopped down on the couch. I felt a blinding headache coming on. I rarely got headaches, but when I did, they were doozies. This one felt no different.

"Okay," Axel said. "They'll be here in about a half hour." He took off my shoes and rubbed my feet. "Do you want to tell me what's going on, lass?" he asked me as he slowly rubbed my heels and soles and finally worked his way up to rub each of my toes.

"That feels amazing," I said. "Just amazing. You should do this professionally. No joke."

"I missed my calling. But you still need to answer my question. What happened today? You seem...out of sorts."

"I'm just confused. Yesterday, I thought I was on the right track. I thought I knew what happened in Judge Sanders' murder. And now..." I shook my head. "To say I'm not sure would put it mildly. I suddenly am questioning everything. Perhaps that was the plan all along. Throw up a million roadblocks, a million red herrings, so I can never figure out what happened. But I don't know why Michael would do that. I mean, if I can't figure out what end is up on this case, how the hell am I supposed to try it?"

"Wait," Axel said. "Slow down. Now, what happened?"

"I don't know. My client is trying to nail his wife for this. He started out telling me he didn't know who did it, and now that I'm getting closer to who really did it, he's stepped up his efforts to point the finger at Christina. But Christina is singing a different tune, and somehow, someway, she dragged Judge Perez into this mess."

"Who is Judge Perez?"

"He's a judge. He was a state court judge until recently. He just got on the federal bench with our current Republican President." My head hurt. "And now he's the judge overseeing the Dowling Chemical case, and the parent company is Stone Enterprises. That was the direction I was going, that Gerald Stone was behind this murder, then Michael threw something up in front of me, and then Christina did, and now I'm just confused."

"Well, let's see. Let's do this. Let's have our dinner, and then, after dinner, I'll watch the girls while you go upstairs to your office and try to figure out what's going on. I know you want to do that. Unless you're not in the mood to do that."

"Oh, I'm in the mood, even though I'm nauseated, my head's splitting open, and I have a big, empty pit right here." I pointed to my stomach. "And a knot that won't go away. But I need to do some more research on this. I have to figure out exactly what happened, and I need to figure that out soon because if I don't, Rina and Abby might be in danger."

Axel looked perplexed. "Why would they be in danger?"

"Because Christina Sanders' child is in danger. She said powerful people were behind Judge Sanders' murder and that these powerful people would stop at nothing to ensure she took the fall. I finally have gotten it through my head that Christina

Sanders probably didn't do it. But somebody did. Several somebodies did."

"And how do you know it was more than one person?"

"Because Christina kept saying 'they.' She kept saying 'they' were threatening her and 'they' were out to get her. I don't know who the 'they' are in this case, but I'm determined to find out."

The food came about half an hour later, and Axel paid and tipped the guy, even though I insisted I would pay. "It's my idea," Axel said. "So I'll pay. I insist."

I simply nodded, as I had no energy to fight. "I'll get it next time. I insist."

Axel just shrugged and brought the food to the table. "Now, let's all eat this stuff family style like you're supposed to with Chinese food." He spooned a little of everything on everybody's dish, and we all dug in.

The girls started in about their day, and I smiled and nodded along, even though I wasn't hearing a word of it. Axel was right. I'd have to go to my office and figure out a few things. I would right this ship and put it in a better direction. If I didn't, I would lose.

By losing, it meant Michael would win. I was still determined he was a part of the conspiracy.

But I also had to understand everything happening in this case.

I ate everything on my plate and got up from the table. "I hope you guys don't mind if I retire early."

"Of course not," Axel said. "I told you, you probably need to go upstairs to your office and try to sort things out. I'll hang out with the girls and ensure they get to bed by a decent hour. By midnight at least." He smiled and winked to let me know he was joking, and I smiled back.

"Thanks." I hugged the two girls and went upstairs.

I entered my bedroom, intending to change into my pajamas and then get on the computer, but I lay down on my bed and promptly fell asleep.

Twenty-Eight

The next day, I was refreshed, and when I looked at my clock, I knew why. It was 10 AM.

I ran down the stairs, frantic I'd overslept and needed to get the girls off to school. But they were nowhere to be found.

"Rina, Abby!" I called. I went into both of their rooms, and they weren't there.

Oh, God. Where were they? Why didn't they wake me up to take them to school? I couldn't think straight. The stress was getting to me, but I was also frantic because I remembered Christina Sanders' warning. Powerful forces were behind the murder of her father, and these powerful forces would stop at nothing to intimidate me.

She also warned me to make sure Rina and Abby were safe.

My heart was pounding. I was still wearing the suit I was wearing the day before as I fell asleep on my bed, fully clothed. My head was pounding, my hands were shaking, and my mouth was dry.

With shaking hands, I called Axel, thinking he might have spent the night and taken the girls to school. I got his voicemail, and I left a frantic message. "Axel, this is Harper. I can't find the girls. I hope you know where they are."

I hung up the phone, got my keys, started my car, and drove off. I would go to the girls' school and find out if they were there.

But, of course, the best-laid plans...traffic was horrendous, and I hit every red light. I hated hitting red lights on the best days, but on days like today, when I was experiencing sheer panic, the red lights seemed to just taunt me. *You'll never see your girls again,* the red lights seem to say to me. *Never again.*

"Shut up, shut up, shut up," I screamed at the lights. "I will see them again. I will. They're safe and sound. They are safe and sound. Axel took them to school this morning, and he forgot to leave me a note. But he should have left me a note, the jerk. But he didn't. He didn't, and they're in school, safe and sound. Safe and sound. Safe and sound."

I finally made it to their school, and I ran in there. "Hello," I said to the headmaster, storming into her office without even knocking. "Are Rina and Abby here today?" I was breathless, and, unfortunately, the headmaster had a mirror in her office. I looked in the mirror and saw a woman with wild red hair and streaked makeup.

She looked like a dangerous loon.

"Yes, of course," she said. "They're in their homeroom. Are you okay?"

"No. No, I'm not okay. I'm not. Okay. I haven't been sleeping well, and I slept last night, but then I overslept. And, I don't know..." The adrenaline that coursed through my veins, as I panicked over whether Rina and Abby were kidnapped, drained away. All I could feel was a deep pool of sadness. That was how it felt. My entire body was made of a large pool of tears, which ran infinitely deep.

I sat on the chair across from Ms. Hayden, knowing I was on the verge of crying. She silently pushed the box of Kleenex my way, and I took one out of the box and dabbed my right eye. "I'm sorry," I said. "I must have scared the living daylights out of you. I look a fright, I know. I'm really not out of my mind. It's just..."

She nodded. "I know. Sometimes we all get to the end of our rope. I'm sure it's hard for you, juggling your job of defending criminals and caring for two young girls. It's hard enough to care for two young girls, even if you don't have a demanding job. You don't have to explain how much stress you're under. I can just imagine it."

"Yes, but it's more than that. I can't explain it, except that my biological clock has been going haywire lately. It's almost like..." I closed my eyes, getting the insight I'd been trying to avoid. Trying to avoid for way too long.

"It's almost like I've been manic. Manic. Bipolar disorder. That was what my Uncle Patrick had. I mean, I was very young when he was institutionalized, but my mother always talked about his symptoms, and his symptoms are my symptoms. I've had problems with depression my entire life but never had a manic episode. But that's it. That's what's been wrong with me this whole time."

I opened my eyes. "But I can't do anything about it right now. I need mental focus, and I have to admit, I've been focused like a laser beam this past week. Things have been coming to me that I never would've thought of before. I need to keep this high, this rush, until the end of the trial. Now is not the time to try new medicines that might dull my senses. I need to do something about this problem after the trial."

Ms. Hayden sighed. "Harper, I know something about bipolar disorder. My sister has had bipolar disorder for most of her life. And you might think that you have amazing insight. Amazing clarity. But it's most likely a delusion. Your mind is playing tricks on you. If I were you, I'd see a doctor right away. Right away. Because you might end up thinking you cracked your murder case when you haven't even come close."

I shook my head, not wanting to hear what she told me. "No. You don't understand. I'm solving this case. I am." But, deep down, I was afraid of what she was telling me. Was this whole Gerald Stone tie-in a ruse? Was it something my brain was making up from whole cloth? I mean, whoever heard of a company CEO putting a hit on a judge? I'd never heard of such a thing. It was a crazy idea, and I didn't know if it was a crazy idea that was true or a crazy idea that my crazy mind had cooked up. Because I was crazy.

Ms. Hayden shook her head. "Do what you think is right. But I'd see a doctor straight away. You don't want to ignore this issue because you'll eventually break. I've seen it happen way too many times with my sister. She ends up in the hospital if she doesn't take her meds. I don't want to see that happen to you. You have that adoption pending with the girls. Just please think of that."

I sighed. The girls. The adoption. She was right. If I was going crazy...no, bipolar disorder didn't mean you were going crazy. It simply meant the chemicals in the brain were going haywire. That was all it meant. And medicine could fix that.

"Thank you, Ms. Hayden. The girls will be picked up today at the usual time, but I will be the one to pick them up. I'll take off work early to do it."

"Okay. Please, Harper, think of the girls. And see your doctor."

"I will."

I walked out of the office feeling dazed and confused. She was right. I'd have to see a doctor. I was heading for a total breakdown if I didn't see a doctor.

And one thing I couldn't afford was a total breakdown.

Twenty-Nine

I got into my office and shut the door. I'd tried calling my doctor in my car on the way over but couldn't contact anybody. I left a message for them to call me.

I'd have to do the research I was going to do last night. I had to find out what Christina Sanders meant when she told me about Judge Perez finding that Judge Sanders was the father of her baby. Unfortunately, the court records for that case would be sealed, as it was a paternity case. So, Anna would have to come to the rescue once again.

"Anna," I said, calling her on the phone. "I need your help. Stat."

"I'll be right there."

"Thanks."

I could barely keep my head up at that point. All the manic energy coursing through my veins had emptied, and I felt hollow and alone. I hated that feeling. I wasn't alone. That was clear. I had the girls; I had Axel; I had my family. I even had Tammy, even though she hadn't been around that much lately. She'd taken a much-needed vacation and had been gone for two weeks.

But that feeling of loneliness was the feeling I got when I was about to go into a deep depression. I had to will that away. I now knew the anti-depressants I took probably didn't work as well as they should have because I probably didn't have unipolar depression. I probably had bipolar depression, which was a different beast and demanded different meds.

I wanted my doctor to call me back. I needed to see her. I needed her to change my meds. I couldn't afford to lose my mind. Not now. Not when I was in the middle of a case that was threatening to consume me. I either had to let the case consume me so I'd go blissfully under, or I had to pop my head up and fight with everything in my arsenal.

That was what I chose to do. I always chose to fight. And I'd choose that here, too. This damn case wouldn't consume me. I'd figure it out.

I went into the suite where Pearl was sitting at her desk. "Harper," she said. "I found these on the floor."

I cocked my head and looked at what was in her hands. It was a pair of leather gloves.

"Thanks," I said. "Michael must have left these. I appreciate your giving these to me. I'll put them in my desk drawer, and when I see him again, I'll give them to him."

"Sure." She looked at me. "You okay?"

"Oh, right." I suddenly remembered looking in the mirror at the headmaster's office. I looked like a truck had dragged me through the mud. "I guess I have to comb my hair, wash my face, and reapply my makeup, don't I?"

She nodded, a deeply skeptical look on her face. "You sure do. Here, take some of these." She handed me baby wipes stored in her purse, and I took them from her.

"Thanks."

I returned to my office, took the wipes, and washed my face. I then got some makeup out of my purse and applied it. I took out a brush and brushed my hair, and put it in a high pony. I looked in the mirror again and saw I looked presentable, so I sighed with relief. I had court appearances in the afternoon. I couldn't go in there looking like something the cat dragged in. People would talk.

Anna came into my office just as I was applying some lipstick. "Hey, Harper," she said. "What's up?"

"Yes. I need you to get some closed paternity records for me. Here's the name of the mother - it's Christina Sanders. The child's name is Lindsay Reynolds. Find me everything that you can. I need the petition, and I need all the attachments. Especially the DNA test result."

"Okay," she said. "Not a problem. It was filed here?"

"Yes. The judge's name is Judge Perez. He was a judge here in the state court, but he's sitting on the federal bench right now. There's something rotten, and I'll find out what it is."

She nodded and brought out her laptop. "Do you mind if I do my work right here?"

"No, no. That's fine. You can keep me company. I need that right now."

She talked to me a little as she clacked along on her laptop. "Harper," she said. "I didn't want to say anything, but I need to. You've seemed out of sorts. Not quite yourself. Are you feeling okay?"

"Yes. I'm feeling fine. I mean, I'm not entirely fine. I need to see my psychiatrist and get my meds adjusted. I think I might be manic, or I was manic, and now I'm just depressed. But I need to figure out what's happening with this case. If I can get a handle on it, I'll proceed. But right now, there are too many loose ends. Too many threads. Every time I pull on a thread, another thread gets loose. I just don't know..."

She nodded. "I'm sending you the paternity case," she said. "With the attachments. Look at your email."

"That was fast."

She shrugged. "Getting into sealed state court records is a snap. I mean, come on, Harper. I could hack into the Department of Defense if I wanted to. Do you think it would be a problem for me to get a simple sealed paternity record?"

"No, of course not." I booted up my email and found Anna's message to me. I clicked on the attachment and read.

I shook my head. The court order was that Judge Sanders was found to be the father of Lindsay Reynolds. Just like Christina told me. That wasn't surprising – Christina told me this happened, so I only would've been surprised if Judge Sanders *wasn't* found to be the father of Lindsay Reynolds.

I clicked on the attachments and found the one I wanted.

"Well, I'll be goddamned," I said. "The DNA test results are attached to this order, and they clearly say Michael Reynolds is the father of Lindsay Reynolds. Clearly." I shook my head.

What the hell was going on? Seriously. What was going on?

"What? What are you seeing?"

I shook my head. I didn't know what I was seeing. It was another layer, another damned layer, to this entire thing.

"Judge Perez can't try this case," I said. "He can't."

"What case?"

"The Dowling Chemical case. He can't do it. He can't get away with it."

"He can't get away with what?"

"He's part of the conspiracy. He is. The conspiracy to get rid of Judge Sanders." It suddenly became clear to me. This paternity order was probably used as a blackmail device to Judge Sanders. He would either play ball and find for Dowling Chemicals or have this paternity order leaked to the world.

I leaned back in my chair. A part of me was questioning my logic. Was this all a fever dream my brain was cooking up? Or was this real? Would I go over to the Chief Judge and tell her my suspicions, only to have her throw me out of her chambers? And how did Michael fit in with any of this?

Something at the back of my brain told me I had a smoking gun. The smoking gun that would tie Michael, at the very least, to the murder of Judge Sanders. But I couldn't quite figure out what my brain was trying to tell me.

"I need to speak with the Chief Judge of the Western District," I said. "I need to tell her what I know about Judge Perez. He can't try that Dowling case. If he does, he'll find for the defendant, and all those plaintiffs, who had been hurt, won't get a thin dime. I know it. It's not right. It's not right. He can't try it. Those plaintiffs need compensation. They need medical care. The babies will need a lot of medical care, and they'll be special needs children, and they'll need special education. That community was hurt. The justice they thirst for will be denied. That's not right. That's not right. It's not right. It's not right. It's not right."

"Harper, you're scaring me." I could barely see Anna, even though she was standing right before me. She was hazy, and then it seemed she was multi-colored, like in those psychedelic movies. I knew vaguely that I was going into some other zone, some other reality, and I couldn't stop it. I couldn't stop it. I felt like I was about to take off flying. I closed my eyes, and I felt like I was flying over to the Federal Courthouse. Flying into the chamber of Chief Judge Haynes and bursting in there with my evidence that Judge Perez was as corrupt as the day was long.

My breathing came faster and faster, and everything around me looked like it was speeding up. Like that scene in Willy Wonka, where everybody was going through the terrifying tunnel while the maniacal Willy Wonka sang a song. What was wrong with me?

The next thing I knew, I was in the hospital. I looked at a man in a white coat, my senses dulled. "Where am I?" I asked the man.

"Just lay back," he said. "The doctor will come and meet with you soon."

I looked at the door and saw Axel coming through the door, along with Albany. I didn't know what was going on. I really couldn't figure out what had happened.

"Mate," Axel said, coming over to me and smoothing my hair. "I guess you're conscious now."

"Yes. I was always conscious, wasn't I?"

"No. Anna brought you over here from your office. She said you started speaking, well, she used the word 'gibberish,' but she said the words coming out of your mouth were unintelligible. And you kept talking about flying. She was afraid you'd somehow open the window to your office and jump. So she called 911, the ambulance came, and the men gave you a sedative and brought you here. Don't be angry with Anna. She was only trying to help."

"Oh, God. Am I on a 72-hour psychiatric hold?" A 72-hour psychiatric hold referred to the length of time that somebody judged to be a danger to herself or others can be held in a psychiatric facility against his or her will. After 72 hours, the facility can't hold the person without consent. If they want to hold the person without consent, they must seek a court order.

"Yes," Albany said. "That's what's happening. You'll be here for 72 hours, but hopefully they can get everything straightened out with your meds before then, and you can leave."

I grimaced. "What do you mean, hopefully? I mean, I can't be in here for longer than three days. I have that case to pursue." I looked around. "Where are the girls? Where are they? They're safe, aren't they?"

"Relax. Sophia picked them up from school. They don't know you're here. Sophia will watch them until you get out of here."

I groaned. "How will we explain this away?"

Albany looked embarrassed. "We told them you're taking a short vacation. That you needed some time away. They seemed to understand, believe it or not."

"Okay, then."

Albany came over and put her hand on my shoulder. "Emma is here, too," she said, referring to my little sister. "And Mom and Brad." Brad was my brother. "We're all worried about you. We think you need to take a vacation."

"Maybe after this case is over."

"I think you need to get off that case. It's literally driving you over the bend," Albany said.

"Oh, don't be so dramatic. That case has nothing to do with why I'm here. I don't know, the psychiatrist will have to talk to me, but I suspect I've been dealing with undiagnosed bipolar disorder. I've been manic, off and on, for weeks. Not sleeping, staying up all night on the computer, just generally feeling I want to crawl out of my skin. But if you knew anything about bipolar disorder, you'd realize I'd have these same symptoms no matter what was happening. Whether I was working a huge murder case or sitting around on a beach tanning my ass, I'd feel the same way." That wasn't entirely true - bipolar disorder, like all mental illnesses, was exacerbated by external stress. But I didn't want to tell Albany this. I didn't want her to lecture me about slowing down for the sake of my mental health.

Albany looked skeptical. "Okay. But sis, I don't want-"

I shook my head. "I know. I know. I know. But you don't understand. I have to get out of this place and tell the Chief Judge of the Western District about what I know. I have to get out of here."

The doctor came in with his chart. "I need to speak with you privately," he said. "Unless you're fine with your sister and friend hearing. Either way."

"Go ahead," I said. "Tell me what you need to tell me. I'm sure my sister and...Axel... don't mind." I still didn't know what to call Axel. Was he my boyfriend? We hadn't discussed that yet.

"Okay. You had a manic episode. I strongly suspect you're suffering from bipolar 1 disorder."

I nodded my head. "Bipolar 1. I know something about the difference between bipolar 1 and bipolar 2. Bipolar 1 is the more severe one. Am I correct about that?"

"Yes. But it's manageable with the right medication. I'll start you on a course of medicine called Geodon. That will be added to your usual course of Prozac, which is, as I understand it, the anti-depressant you are currently taking. The Geodon should even out your polarities so you feel a better sense of equilibrium. Of course, it's not fool-proof, so when you leave this hospital, you must constantly monitor your feelings when taking this new drug."

I nodded. "I know the drill. Okay, Dr. Wilson," I said, reading his name tag. "Put me on this drug."

We talked a bit more, but I was eager for him to leave. I was embarrassed I ended up here, even though I always felt I'd end up here eventually. I also consciously knew I shouldn't feel embarrassed. Bipolar disorder wasn't something to be ashamed of. It was a disorder, just like any other disorder. Just like diabetics shouldn't feel ashamed of taking insulin, I knew I shouldn't feel ashamed of taking this Geodon. Or whatever drug that would be tried in the coming weeks and months. I hoped the Geodon could help me, but I also knew that it was hit or miss with these antipsychotic drugs.

Dr. Wilson finally left, as did Albany and Axel. My mother then came in with Emma in tow. "Hi, Mom. Hi Emma."

Mom shook her head. "Harper, you're doing too much. You know how I worry about you. Imagine how I felt when I got this phone call telling me you're here."

I looked over at Emma. She was my little sister, only 22 years old and still in college. She was a pretty girl, red-headed like we all were, but didn't have as many freckles as I did. In fact, she didn't have any freckles. She was the only one of us who could tan, too. "Are you going to lecture me, too, Emma?"

"No," she said. "You don't need a lecture. Mom will take over that role, as usual. But I'd like to help more. If you need a babysitter or anything like that, when Sophia needs a break, I'll be more than happy to come over."

"Thanks." I looked over at my mother. "Emma knows how to talk to me. She offers to help. She doesn't just lecture me."

"I'm trying not to just lecture you," Mom said. "But Harper, you're doing too much. All these murder cases and having those two little girls at your home. You're burning the candle at both ends."

"But what a glorious light, huh, Mom?" Edna St. Vincent Millay was one of my favorite poets, and she wrote about how burning the candle at both ends meant it wouldn't last the night, but would give out a lovely light.

"I don't consider what you're doing to be a glorious light." Mom always disapproved of what I did. She hated that I defended hardened criminals. It wasn't just that she worried about me, but also because she didn't think that people who committed violent crimes deserved representation, period. She thought they all should fry. I tried to tell her that the United States Constitution guarantees that anybody accused of committing a felony is entitled to representation. She always told me that might be true, but that representation didn't have to be me.

"Mom, I won't listen to this. Now, I need to get out of here to get right back on this case I'm working. I'm close, Mom, to finding out what happened to Judge Sanders. I'm itching to get back to it."

Mom just shook her head and left the room. Emma and I looked at each, and we both laughed. "I understand, Harper," she said. "I know why you enjoy your job."

I sighed. "I sometimes wonder what I'm doing, though, Emma. Why do I represent these people? Sometimes they're innocent, like poor Heather, but usually, they're pretty bad guys. I guess I feel sorry for a lot of them. Most of my clients have had awful lives. The current guy, however, the one I'm currently representing – he's just a bad seed. He's a rich boy, a golden boy, somebody who has been given everything and continues to be given everything on a silver platter. And yet he's just a bad guy."

I thought about Elmer, who, even though he was a bad guy, too, had an excuse – he was poisoned *in utero*, so he never had a chance. But Michael had no excuse. Well, maybe he could plead a fancy disorder like Affluenza or some nonsense like that, but he really had no excuse for being a scumbag.

Brad came in next. "Hey, sis," he said. "I never thought we'd be meeting here." His tone was teasing, and I smiled.

"Oh, Brad, it's okay. It'll be much better now, really. I'm finally getting the right meds because I have a correct diagnosis. I mean, you know I've always had depression and anxiety, but I've never been manic until now. But now that I have the right diagnosis, I think I can get the right meds, maybe for the first time."

"Well," Brad said. "The right meds have worked for Uncle Patrick, so hopefully, they'll work for you, too."

"Yeah, I hope so too."

For the rest of the day, the people who loved and cared about me shuffled in and out of my room, two by two, and I felt better than I had for a long time. It wasn't just that I enjoyed the company. I also felt hopeful that I'd be on a more even keel. That was necessary because, if it was the last thing I did, I would get to the bottom of Judge Sanders' murder, and I had to be mentally sharp to do that.

THIRTY

When I got out of the psychiatric facility, I got right back into it. When I was in the hospital, and I was alone in my room, I spent my time trying to make a flow chart of everything that I knew thus far. My mind was clearer than it had been in some time, and, unlike before, I didn't have super clarity, but I felt more normal than I had been feeling. I was sleeping normally, too. I felt hopeful that maybe these new meds were just what I needed to stabilize my emotions and brain.

On my flow chart, I put the names Gerald Stone, Kayla Stone, Michael Reynolds and Judge Perez. I was working on a theory, but I had no way to prove any of it. I figured the best way to prove it would be to get one of the people on the list to flip on everyone else. Kayla, to me, seemed like the most likely candidate for that. I met her and she seemed to be a decent person. She also struck me as somebody who was a bit weak-minded.

I hadn't met Gerald Stone, but, from what Megan Baker told me, Gerald Stone was a total bastard. As for Judge Perez – I'd tried cases in front of him, so I knew him, but he was pretty high up the food chain as far as this conspiracy went, in my mind. I would have to concentrate on the low-hanging fruit.

I called Kayla when I got out of the hospital.

"Hello," she said. "This is Kayla."

"Kayla, this is Harper Ross. I need to speak with you at your earliest possible convenience."

She was silent for a few minutes. "What do you need to speak with me about?"

"I need to speak to you about your husband."

"I'm very sorry, but I'm busy."

I was expecting this. "I'll subpoena you for another deposition. You can either come and speak with me off the record, or you can come and speak with me on the record. It's your choice, but, either way, I need to speak with you."

She sighed. "I can come in this afternoon. Three o'clock?"

"Three o'clock is perfect." I had an afternoon DWI to take care of at 1:30, so I knew that I would be back at the office by 3, so meeting her then wouldn't be a problem at all.

I hung up and called Anna. "Anna, I need something from you."

"Sure. Just tell me what you need, and I'll get it for you."

"I need for you to find something out for me. Judge Perez was randomly assigned, by the computer, the case of Dowling Chemicals down at the federal courthouse. I need for you to find out if it wasn't random after all. Can you do that? Can you find out if somebody hacked into the database to make sure Judge Perez would be assigned that case?"

"I can do that," she said. "I'll have that information for you in about fifteen minutes."

"Thanks."

I had to get my ducks in a row before I presented the Chief Judge with what I had found out. There was just no way I would just let him get away with trying that case. I would connect him to this whole rotten enterprise if it was the last thing I did. I already knew what would happen, because that judge was rotten as the day was long – he would find in favor of Dowling, and all the people hurt by Dowling wouldn't get a dime. Not a dime.

Fifteen minutes later, Anna called back. "You're good," she said.

"You were right. Somebody hacked into the system to make sure Judge Perez was assigned to that Dowling Chemical case. What does that mean?"

I sighed. "It means that the judge is dirty and in the pocket of Gerald Stone." The evidence was circumstantial, but I put the pieces together and figured out what was going on. "Thanks, Anna. You're the best."

"Not a problem."

I hung up the phone and put that issue on the backburner. I would have to prepare for my meeting with Kayla. The low-hanging fruit that she was, I knew her testimony would be key. The dominoes were going to fall, starting with her.

Kayla arrived right at 3, looking nervous. She was very pale and, when she sat down to speak with me, she kept looking around. Specifically, she kept looking at the front door. "I'm sorry," she said. "But I'm just a little bit freaked out. I don't trust Gerald. I think he might've bugged me." She shook her head rapidly. "I hired this guy to sweep my car and my house. He even swept my purse. So far, nothing has been found."

I raised my eyebrow. "*Your* house. Does that mean you're no longer living with Gerald?"

"That's right." Her blue eyes were wide and she looked towards the front door again. "I moved out two weeks ago. I'm not seeing Michael anymore, either."

"I see. Any particular reason why you and Michael aren't together anymore?"

She shrugged. "It just ran its course."

This was good. This was very good. If Kayla wasn't emotionally attached to either of the men who I suspected were behind this whole mess, then perhaps she'd be willing to roll on both of them. That is, if she wasn't scared of doing that.

"Okay. Well, I don't want to beat around the bush here. I need some information about your husband and your ex-boyfriend."

"Ms. Ross, I think I told you I'll plead the fifth on that."

"There's no pleading the fifth right now. You're not under oath. I'm not making a record. You can't take the fifth. You can refuse just to answer me, but I need to tell you one thing – I know what happened. I know who killed Judge Sanders. I know you were involved with it, and I know Gerald was too." I was bluffing. I didn't know any of these things, but I had to make her believe I had the goods. That was the only way this whole gambit would work.

She rapidly shook her head. "What do you mean? What do you mean? I don't know anything about that murder. I wasn't involved with it."

"Oh, but you were. You were. Here's what happened. Your husband, Gerald Stone, is the CEO of Stone Enterprises. Stone Enterprises is the parent company of Dowling Chemicals. Dowling Chemicals has been criminally negligent in the handling of a particular chemical, known at Toluene. This chemical has affected thousands of people. It has made them very sick and it has caused fetuses to suffer brain damage *in utero*. Because of the way Dowling Chemicals has handled the Toluene, they were going to be found liable. Under Judge Sanders, they would've been slapped down with hundreds of millions of dollars in punitive damages. Gerald Stone didn't want that, so he had Judge Sanders killed. But, before he had Judge Sanders killed, he first tried to blackmail Judge Sanders with a bogus paternity case that purportedly showed Judge Sanders impregnated his own daughter. Personally, I think that's the most disgusting part of this whole sorry scenario."

I watched as Kayla's face got whiter and whiter, and she started to bite her nails. I knew then that I had put this whole thing together perfectly. The only question was how Michael fit in with it.

"What do you need from me?" Her voice was tiny and fearful.

"I need you to tell me what happened. In your own words. How exactly the judge was murdered, who did it, and who poisoned him."

"What will happen to me? I mean, if I tell you everything, what will happen to me?"

I almost felt sorry for her. Almost. I mean, I had a feeling Kayla was heavily involved in the murder because she would be cut out of her prenuptial agreement. Therefore, she was just doing it for greed. But I also had the feeling she was intimidated into doing it by the two men squeezing her on her right and her left – Gerald and Michael.

"I have enough evidence to go to the police," I said, knowing that was a big, fat lie. "And the three of you will be hung out to dry. But if you tell me the truth, I'll ask the prosecutor to not only go easy on you, but offer you immunity in exchange for your testimony. Believe me, getting somebody like Gerald and Judge Perez would be worth it to an enterprising prosecutor. If Gerald could do this to a judge, he could do it to anybody. As for Judge Perez, a corrupt judge does not need to be hearing federal cases that potentially involve millions of dollars. You can be a hero, Kayla. You only need to tell me what happened."

She continued to bite her nails as she nervously looked to the door and then back at me. I saw her shaking and then she lowered her head and started to cry.

I wordlessly handed her a box of Kleenex. She took the box and brought one of the Kleenexes to her nose and blew it. "Oh, God," she said. "I knew we wouldn't get away with this. I knew it. I told them."

I nodded my head. "You told them? Who was involved besides Gerald? I mean, who was involved in the murder?" I doubted Judge Perez was involved in the murder, but I knew he was involved in possibly blackmailing Judge Sanders and I knew he was involved in making sure he'd try the Dowling case. I wondered if money had changed hands there. I was quite sure it did.

She sighed. "Ms. Ross, I know you'll think horribly of me. But I need to tell you the story. The whole story. Please, when you go to the prosecutor, please ask her to go easy on me. Please ask her to offer me immunity. I'll tell them anything they want to know. But I might have to go into the witness protection program too." She looked at the door again, looked back at me, and went back to biting her nails.

"That's why you're here."

"I know." She hung her head. "Okay. I'll just start from the beginning. Gerald and I were having marital problems, and I met Michael. I met him on-line. On one of those dating sites. The one that caters to married people looking for affairs. I know, I know, it's really sleazy. I don't think that site is even around anymore."

"Ashley Madison," I said. "Actually, it is still around, believe it or not." That site was hacked and thousands of names were divulged, but it somehow managed to survive.

"Yes. Ashley Madison. I was unhappy, Ms. Ross, with Gerald. He was never at home, and I mean never. He practically lives at the office. I wanted children when we got married. He promised me we could have a family. But after we got married, he told me he didn't want children, so he forced me to have my tubes tied. So, he lied when he told me we could start a family."

"When you came into the marriage, you didn't have any assets or property, did you?"

She sighed. "No. I didn't. I've worked my whole life, and I was working as a nurse when I met him. But I could never hold onto money. I always just lived in small apartments, I leased my cars, and I never opened up any financial accounts. So, yeah, when we got married, I came into the marriage with nothing. Literally nothing."

"And Gerald was already wealthy."

"Yes. Very wealthy." She sighed again and shook her head. "And he made me sign a pre-nuptial agreement before we got married. Basically, if we ever divorced, I would get 25% of the property Gerald brought into the marriage and 50% of the property acquired during the marriage. I thought that was very fair. But he put in a clause that said I wouldn't get a dime of property if it was found I'd been unfaithful during the marriage."

I tried to act surprised about what she was saying, but I was a terrible actress. I was afraid she'd see right through me. However, she was so distraught by this whole situation that she didn't even look at me, so I relaxed.

She stopped talking and then looked out the window. She looked past me and started to bite her nails again. "Gerald found out about Michael. He had a private investigator and had all the pictures he needed. He threatened to divorce me and leave me penniless."

"Okay. Kayla, can I ask you a personal question?"

She nodded.

"What would be the harm in Gerald leaving you penniless, as you say? I mean, you were a nurse before you met him. You were living in a small apartment. Couldn't you just go back to nursing and living in another small apartment and just start over?"

I couldn't quite understand her mentality. If she got involved with the murder of the judge so she could get a nice settlement from Gerald, why would she do that? Was it really so worth it to her to make sure she remained wealthy after she was divorced from Gerald that she would do anything, even get involved with murdering somebody?

"Yes. In hindsight, I should've just broken away from him. Let him cut me out. I haven't worked in 15 years, though. That's how long we've been married."

I bit my tongue, but I wanted to ask her another question, and that was why did she quit her job? She didn't have children with Gerald. She told me she never saw the guy. I had no idea how she spent her time, but, if it were me, I'd still be working, even if I was married to a wealthy guy. I couldn't imagine living a life of leisure.

I leaned back in my chair and put my pen in my mouth. Kayla could probably see the judgment in my eyes, although I hoped she didn't.

"Well, as I said, he threatened to divorce me and leave me with nothing. But he made me an offer."

"An offer. Tell me about the offer."

"He told me he needed me to help him kill Judge Sanders. He told me it was almost perfect that I was having an affair with

Michael, because he was Judge Sanders son-in-law, so Michael had perfect access to Judge Sanders. He told me that if I got Michael to kill Judge Sanders that he'd take the clause out of our prenuptial agreement that said I wouldn't get anything if I was unfaithful."

I nodded. This was good. This was very good. "And you got Michael to do this?"

"Yes. I got Michael to put poison into the judge's orange juice. Arsenic. Michael went over to Judge Sanders' house every Sunday, and he refilled the judge's pills every week. When he went into the judge's kitchen to refill his pills, he put some poison into the judge's orange juice too. Just enough poison to kill Judge Sanders slowly."

Kayla started to cry. "Oh, I just can't believe I did that. I mean, what kind of person am I? That I would do that just because I wanted to make sure that I left my marriage with millions of dollars. I just don't know what I've become. I know you don't believe me, but I never cared about money before I met Gerald. But you don't know what it's like to go from living in a small apartment with a cat to going to a life where you're eating at 5-star restaurants all the time, and you're going around the world staying in the best hotels. All of a sudden, you have personal chefs and personal trainers and an indoor pool and maids. You're spending your winters in Belize and Costa Rica, when you're not skiing in Switzerland. Your summers are spent in the South of France. You can go to any department store and just pick up anything you want and never have to worry about the price tag. That's not an excuse, but you just don't know what it's like."

"I know I don't know what that's like," I said. "I've always worked for a living. I've worked for everything I have. I don't spend my winters in Belize and my summers in the South of France, and I probably never will. But I can look at myself in the mirror. I know I'd never get involved with a murder just to keep my lifestyle. I guess that makes me different from you."

"You're judging me, and I don't blame you. I'd judge me too if I were in your shoes. But, truly, you simply don't know how being really wealthy changes you. You don't know until it happens to you." She paused again and rubbed her eyes. "Anyhow, I got Michael to do that."

"And what did Michael get out of this deal? I see what you got out of it, but what did he get out of it?"

She shook her head. "Michael did something to Gerald's sister. It was really sick, but Gerald's a wily one. He found out Michael was a serial rapist. I didn't know this, of course, otherwise I never would've gotten involved with him. But Gerald wanted to trap Michael, so he set his sister up with him. He didn't tell his sister, whose name is Emily, about Michael's violent tendencies. But Gerald was pretty certain Michael would attack her. She's very beautiful and she's just Michael's type, but she doesn't sleep around, so Michael would have to force her to have sex with him. And he did. He did, and Gerald had it all recorded without Michael or Emily's knowledge."

"He had it recorded?"

"Yes. Recorded. He videoed it all with a hidden camera and hidden microphone. Then he showed Michael the videotape, which showed Emily clearly saying no, and him clearly holding her down and raping her while she screamed no, over and over again." She shuddered. "He showed me the video, as well, and it made me sick. Literally."

"Oh, I see. Gerald blackmailed Michael into going along."

"Yes. He bribed me and blackmailed him. Michael didn't want to do it, because obviously murder is worse than rape, but he rolled the dice. He figured Gerald could prove the rape beyond a shadow of a doubt, but if he murdered somebody, perhaps he could get out of it by showing it wasn't him. In other words, if Michael didn't go along with murdering the judge, he would for sure serve time in prison for the rape. If he went along with it, he had the chance to go free."

"But why involve you? Why didn't Gerald just deal with Michael and cut out the middle-man?"

"He needed both of us working hand in hand. I was Gerald's eyes and ears and Michael actually did the poisoning. I basically made sure Michael did what he was supposed to." She looked down. "I was the one who made sure Michael was poisoning poor Robert Sanders."

"I need to back up a bit. How did Gerald know Michael was a serial rapist?"

She cleared her throat. "The PI Gerald hired knew Michael was a serial rapist. The PI knew two different women who recognized Michael as being the man who raped them. So Gerald knew Michael had that in him, so he knew he could blackmail him if he could get him on video raping Gerald's sister. Gerald's own sister was used as bait. That's how sick Gerald is."

"I see. Go on with your story."

She shrugged. "Michael poisoned Judge Sanders, but Gerald was getting impatient. The judge was getting sicker and sicker, and Gerald started to freak because he thought that sooner or later a doctor would find out what was going on and possibly could treat the judge and bring him back to health. So, Gerald told Michael that he needed to end it completely. He told Michael he had to shoot Judge Sanders."

I started to feel excited. It was all coming together. The only problem was, how would I prove it? I could tell the prosecutor about Kayla, tell them what I found out from her, and suggest to the prosecutor that she should give Kayla immunity from prosecution in exchange for her testimony, but how could I do that ethically? Michael was my client. I couldn't just tell the prosecutor about this without violating my ethical duty to represent Michael zealously. I'd have to figure something out.

"What did you understand happened with Michael when he shot the judge? I mean, why did he do things the way he did them? Why did he go to the scene and call the police? When he did that, he became the prime suspect."

"We talked about that, Michael and me. We agreed that if he did that, he wouldn't look guilty. If he was the one who shot the judge, why would he call the police? Wouldn't he do a better job of covering it up? That was our thought. We knew if the judge was found dead by Ava Sanders that the spotlight would probably shine on Michael anyhow, because the prosecutor was bound to find out Michael was running around on Christina and the judge had threatened him with turning him into his daughter. Michael stood to lose a lot in a divorce. He was like me, in that, individually, he's broke. Michael knew this was the motive an investigator would give to him, and he knew he would become the prime suspect. So, we decided that if he was the one who called the police, it would make him look innocent. That backfired, of course, because the police settled on him immediately, just because he was the one on the scene. We didn't know it would've backfired, though. We thought we were being clever."

"Well, 20/20 hindsight," I said. "Well, okay, then. I thank you for this. I needed this information."

Kayla had a Kleenex in her hand, and she was wringing it over and over as she looked down at my desk. "What's going to happen now? I mean, I'm very sorry for my role, but I really didn't do anything. I was just the go-between in the middle of Michael and Gerald. I know I'm not innocent, but I'm the least guilty. You can get me a deal, can't you? I mean, you can encourage the prosecutor to give me a deal, right?"

I didn't want to tell her the truth, and that was that I didn't have the power to do much of anything. I had the satisfaction of her telling me her story, but her testimony was incriminating for my client, so I had to pretty much sit on this information if I wanted to keep my bar license. The only way I could divulge what Kayla just told me would be if it was in a deposition and the prosecutor specifically asked for the information in a discovery request. I didn't depose Kayla and, thus far, the prosecutor hadn't asked for witness testimony in a discovery request, so I couldn't just volunteer it.

I sighed. I had to figure something out. Some way to point the prosecutor in the right direction, without the prosecutor knowing that it was me doing that.

"I'll see what I can do."

She nodded. "Thank you. I'll testify at court, but only if I get immunity."

Again, that wasn't my call. That would be the prosecutor's call. How would I get this information to April?

"Thank you for coming in," I said. "I'll see what I can do."

She hesitated. "You don't sound very sure about that."

"I'll see what I can do. That's all I can promise."

She stood up, realizing she'd been played. "That's really a dirty trick you played," she said. "A really dirty trick."

I sighed. "No, really, you've been helpful, much more than you know. I just have to figure out how to put these puzzle pieces together so that they fit. I mean, I need to figure out how to get information to the prosecutor's office about what you've told me."

She looked unconvinced. "I want you to get me a deal."

"I can't possibly. Michael's my client. You're the co-conspirator. I obviously can't represent both of you. You'll have to lawyer up, but not with me." I was breaking every ethical rule just having her in my office, rolling on my client, asking to cut a deal in exchange for her testimony against my client. Every ethical rule was being broken.

"You lied to me."

I nodded. "I did. I'll admit it. But you need to lawyer up. I can give you some referrals."

"The Missouri Bar will be hearing about this." She turned and dramatically left my office and I shook my head. She could easily have my bar license for this dirty trick I played on her. Easily. I'd get a complaint from her, no doubt about it. And, after I did what I needed to do with respect to Michael, he, too, would have reason to make a complaint against me. If the two of them teamed up, I could be doing dishes for a living.

Even so, I felt good. I felt good because I finally had the whole story.

The only problem was, I had no idea what to do with it.

. . .

That night, I had a dream. Again, my subconscious was trying to tell me how to successfully bring my client down. There was a way of doing it, a way that wouldn't necessarily be traced back to me.

I sat up straight in bed. I suddenly knew what I had to do.

I tiptoed into Rina's room and saw her sleeping. I went into Abby's room and saw her sleeping, too. I sighed, feeling antsy and anxious. I wanted to get on with my plan, and I wanted to do it right away. I couldn't do anything, however, until it was morning and I got the girls off to school. Before the girls came to live with me, I often went to the office in the middle of the night. I'd get wild hairs in the witching hour and go down to the office and work. But I couldn't do that here. I had to stay in the house.

I could do one thing, though. I could take a better look at my discovery requests from the prosecutor and see if I could find the request that would suit the piece of evidence I'd send April.

I looked at the request for documents and saw what I was looking for. I nodded my head, knowing that I could find a way to ethically give the prosecutor what she needed to nail Michael. Granted, I didn't get this particular item above-board. I didn't even know if it was something that would bear fruit. But I had to try.

"Girls, come on," I said right at 6:30. I went into both Rina and Abby's rooms. "Rise and shine." I took the blanket off Rina, who was lying in her bed, curled up with a stuffed animal. She rubbed her eyes and looked out the window.

"It's the middle of the night," she complained.

"No it's not. The time changed, so it's darker out than before. It's time for you to get your pretty little butt out of this bed and into your shower."

"Why are you so full of unicorn farts this morning?" She reluctantly got out of bed and trudged into her bathroom.

"No reason. I have to get your sister up now, too."

I went into Abby's room and did the same ritual. She, too,

complained it was the middle of the night, and I had to remind her the time had changed.

I ran down the stairs and got breakfast ready for them. They appeared in a matter of minutes, and we all ate breakfast and then they got their backpacks. We all went to my car, and I found myself singing to the radio.

"Man, you're being weird this morning," Rina said. "What's up with that?"

"No reason. I'm just dying to get to the office this morning. There's something there that will crack my case wide open. Wide open."

"The murder case?" Abby asked. "Did you find the thing that will prove your client is innocent?"

I took a deep breath. I didn't want to lie to her, but I needed to. She wouldn't understand my desire to sink my own client. "Something like that."

I got to their school and let them off. They waved at me and joined the other kids at the front door of the school.

I then sped off to my office.

I got to my office and opened up my desk drawer. I put on a pair of plastic gloves and picked up the leather gloves Pearl had found on the floor after Michael was here. I then called the laboratory where I sent items for forensic analysis. "I need for you to do some glove analysis," I said. "On a gun."

Thirty-One

When I got the forensic analysis back on the gun, and found the glove prints on the gun were matched with Michael's gloves, I was pleased but not surprised. I knew these gloves would be the smoking gun. I knew it. Now, how would I get this information over to the prosecutor?

I decided to put the forensic analysis documents into the document dump I was giving April. Then, when Michael inevitably brought his bar complaint against me for sinking this case, I could give some kind of plausible deniability about how that document got to the prosecutor. I could simply say I gave that information to the prosecutor accidentally. April hadn't asked for the information, specifically, and she apparently wasn't doing her own analysis, nor was she asking for any and all gloves owned by my client. Therefore, I not only wasn't obligated to give her this information, I'd possibly be in trouble for giving it to her. I was giving her incriminating evidence that wasn't demanded. That was a no-no.

More complicated was what I would do with the information Kayla had given me about Gerald. I wanted to bring down Gerald. I wanted to bring down Judge Perez. I didn't care if I brought down Kayla, because she was more or less a patsy in the this entire sick scenario.

The problem with using Michael to bring down Gerald was that there would be the chance, a very slight chance, but still a chance, that the prosecutor would offer him complete immunity in exchange for his testimony against Gerald. The more I thought about that angle, the more I realized I didn't want Michael to even know I knew the whole truth about what had happened. I didn't want Michael to walk. I needed him to go down. He was guilty of this murder, but, more importantly, he was guilty of raping multiple women. He told me five women, but I had a feeling it was more. Much more. After all, Michael raped Gerald's sister, and that was just recently.

No doubt about it, Michael needed to fry. He needed to go down hard. The prosecutor's offer was life in prison without possibility of parole, so I knew I'd try this case, come hell or high water.

I was risking a lot in this strategy. For one, there was not a guarantee that Kayla wouldn't go right to Michael and tell him she told me everything. That would lead to the two of them plotting, maybe behind my back. But if Kayla told Michael that the jig was up, then Michael would probably tell me that he wanted to testify against Gerald in exchange for immunity. Rats will always turn on each other when the ship's going down, and I knew this situation was no different.

For another, if Michael ever figured out I had information up my sleeve when I tried this case, and I didn't tell him what I knew, then he could have my license for not telling him about it. My thought was that I would go ahead and try Michael's case, make sure he got what was coming to him, and then give an anonymous tip to the police to look at Kayla and Gerald. Kayla would roll on Gerald faster than her head could swim, and that would be that for Gerald. Hopefully. He would lawyer up, but hopefully Kayla had the goods on him and she could sink him.

If I did things that way, though, and it ever came back on me... That wouldn't be pretty. And it very well could come back on me, because Kayla knew that I'd be the most likely source of the "anonymous tip."

No matter. Gerald would get his, too. I had to make sure of that. But I wouldn't touch that information about Gerald and Kayla until I made sure Michael was in prison. I couldn't have Michael rolling on Gerald in exchange for him getting off scot-free.

I was open to tremendous liability, but I didn't care. The only thing I cared about was seeing Michael get his. I also really wanted to see Gerald get his, as well. And Judge Perez, too.

I sighed as I realized I didn't quite know how to bring Judge Perez down. He was dirty. That much was obvious. But how would I prove that? What could I do about it? I didn't really know. That was beyond my capabilities at the moment.

I'd figure that one out, and soon. But the first thing I needed to do, along those lines, was to talk to the plaintiff's attorney for the Dowling case and see if there was any way I could give him a heads-up on what was going on. Maybe the two of us could put our heads together and figure out how to get rid of that judge. At the very least, I could maybe get him to ask for a change of venue or a change of judge.

I called up the plaintiff's attorney for Judge Perez. His name was George Peale, and he was one of the most prominent personal injury attorneys in the Kansas City area. I knew he'd do well, but I needed him to know just how biased Judge Perez would be against his client.

"Hello," George said when I called his cell phone. I had his cell phone number because he and I had a case together several years back. "This is George Peale."

"George, this is Harper Ross," I said. "I need to see you."

"What's this about, Harper?"

"It's about your Dowling Chemical case," I said. "I have some information for you that's pretty important."

"Can you meet me in my office at 4?" He asked. "I've got depositions today, but I should be back by then."

"See you then."

I hung up the phone, seeing that everything was carefully falling into place. Granted, I was taking on a great deal of risk by doing things the way that I chose to do them. That was fine with me, however. If the whole thing ended up with Michael serving life in prison, my purpose would have been served.

I went to George's office right at 4. His office was close to my own. In fact, it was in the same building, which was convenient. His suite was much nicer than mine, because he was a partner in a mid-size firm of 20 attorneys, all of whom were more or less experts on personal injury cases.

The receptionist let George know I was there, and, within minutes, I found myself following her back to George's office, which was an enormous corner office with floor-to-ceiling windows and a little golf hole in the middle. When I walked in, George had his putter out and he was practicing sinking golf balls. He looked up at me and smiled.

"Harper Ross," he said, shaking my hand. "You're looking well. How the hell are you?"

"I'm doing great," I said. "I see you're practicing your putting here."

"I am. It relaxes me." George was a handsome older guy, around 65 years old, and was an absolute expert in his field. He knew his way around expert witnesses and doctors and had an absolute arsenal of hired guns who were willing to testify on his behalf about anything and everything. He usually got the job done and typically won most of his cases.

"Have a seat," he said, pointing to a chair next to a large couch.

I sat down and he sat on the couch and leaned back. "So, Harper, tell me what's going on. What information do you have for me about my Dowling case?"

"Well," I said, knowing that I'd sound like a paranoid loon. "I think Judge Perez is dirty."

"No doubt," he said. "I mean, everyone knows Judge Perez is a tight-ass who hates plaintiffs and will excuse all manner of corporate malfeasance. Tell me what else is new."

"You don't understand." I cleared my throat. "Can I become your client? I need to make sure that what I tell you stays in this room."

"Sure," he said. "Give me a dollar, and you're my client."

I gave him a dollar and he shook my hand.

"You're my lawyer now," I said. "And I might really need your services in the future on this case for real. I'll let you know. But here's what I know about Judge Perez. He's dirty as the day is long, and I don't mean he's a hard-ass. I mean he's corrupt."

George looked at me quizzically. "What do you mean? And how do you know this?"

"I have a client. His name is Michael Reynolds. He's being charged with the murder of Judge Sanders."

"Yeah, I read about that in the paper. But what does that have to do with Judge Perez?:"

"Gerald Stone was involved in murdering Judge Sanders. And I have proof that Judge Perez was involved in a blackmail scheme involving Judge Sanders. I don't have proof that this blackmailing scheme was directly connected to Gerald Stone, but I think it would be easy enough to find that out."

George looked like he was skeptical but interested in what I had to say. "I think I understand," he said. "You're saying Gerald Stone murdered Judge Sanders, because Judge Sanders would've awarded my clients millions of dollars and would've ordered hundreds of millions in punitive damages?"

"Yes. And I also have proof that Judge Perez wasn't randomly assigned to this case. Somebody hacked into the computer at the Western District of Missouri to make sure Judge Perez was assigned to this case. That, combined with the murder of Judge Sanders and the fact that Judge Perez was involved with finding a bogus paternity finding that showed that Judge Sanders fathered a child with his own daughter, and I think it's pretty easy to show that Judge Perez is dirty. You need to figure out a way to petition for a peremptory challenge to Judge Perez, so your clients don't have to face him."

"Hold on," George said. "What do you mean, Judge Perez

bogusly found that Judge Sanders fathered a child by his own daughter?"

At that, I showed him the proof. I had printed out the entire file that Anna found for me. It showed that Judge Perez signed an order finding that Judge Sanders fathered a child with Christina Sanders, despite the fact that the DNA tests showed that Michael Reynolds was actually the father.

George blinked his eyes, as if he didn't quite know what he was seeing. "This paternity case was when he was a state court judge," he said. "Which wasn't that long ago."

"No, it wasn't," I said. "Remember, he was a state court judge just six months ago. That was about when you were gathering your class and doing your investigations on this case. So, Gerald Stone knew, even then, this case was coming."

"But what would be the point in the blackmail then?"

"This is my theory. Gerald Stone has Judge Perez in his pocket. Gerald Stone knew that the Dowling Chemical case would be assigned to Judge Sanders, so he had Judge Perez rule on this bogus paternity case so that he, Gerald, could blackmail Judge Sanders into recusing himself from the case when it was assigned to him. When Judge Sanders refused, he was murdered."

George shook his head. "This sounds like a bad movie. But I'll look into it. In the meantime, I'll go ahead and try for a peremptory challenge against Judge Perez, but unless I can get some kind of hard evidence that Perez is in the tank for Gerald, I don't see that happening. But I will do my due diligence on the allegations you're making."

"Please do. Follow the money. Maybe you can find out if there were any secret payments made between Gerald and Judge Perez. Hopefully you can figure that out."

We chatted for several more minutes before I excused myself.

As I left his office, I knew that there was no guarantee that anything would come of this, but I knew that I did my part. That made me feel good.

THIRTY-TWO

EIGHT WEEKS LATER

"Michael Reynolds trial is today, isn't it?" Tammy was in my office, talking to me as I gathered together my files for my trial.

"It is. We picked a jury yesterday, and today's the day." I didn't tell Tammy this, but my jury selection was the worst I ever did. I made sure to get as many women on the jury as possible. I knew the prosecutor would try to introduce evidence that Michael had raped women in the past, and I wouldn't object to any of that, even though this evidence was not allowed, at all, in this context. But if I didn't object to her putting this evidence in, it would come in. I knew women would want to hang him once this evidence came in, so I loaded the jury up with 9 women. April didn't object to that, of course, and she admitted to me that she was surprised I'd do that.

"Method to my madness," I said. I hoped she'd accept that explanation and not question it.

I was still determined to bring down Gerald and Judge Perez. I hadn't yet figured out just how to do that, but I knew I'd have to do it after this case was over. Perhaps, at that point, I could go to the police and tell them my suspicions and ask them to look into it. I could've possibly gotten Kayla to speak with them, but she wasn't on their radar, so she'd been laying low.

That was so frustrating. I couldn't do anything with the information I had, because implicating Kayla and Gerald would also implicate my client, and I couldn't do anything to implicate him. At least, I couldn't do anything to implicate him at the moment. Once his case was over and he either had a guilty verdict or a not guilty verdict, and he was no longer my client, I could tell the police what I knew about Gerald and Kayla, and what I suspected about Judge Perez.

Gerald would be relatively easy. Kayla would roll on him in a heartbeat. But Judge Perez would be trickier. The evidence against him was circumstantial at best. But I'd show Chief Judge Haynes the evidence in the Christina Sanders paternity case and hopefully she could piece it together on her own. That was my hope, anyhow.

I got to the courthouse early and sat at my table. I'd have to make a show in defending Michael. I had to walk the line between total incompetence, which would get me in hot water, and basic incompetence, where I could tell the Missouri Bar that I simply was having a bad day. That would be a tough line to walk.

Michael soon arrived, along with April and her second chair, Ron Lankford. Michael sat down next to me at the table. "Were you harassed by the press outside?" he asked me.

He was referring to the fact that the media was outside the courtroom. This was a huge case, so there was media outlets from all over the nation sending their reporters to the courthouse. The cameras weren't allowed in the courtroom, but that didn't deter the satellite trucks and the hordes of press agents surrounding the perimeter of the Jackson County Courthouse.

"Of course. I can't tell them anything, of course."

Michael looked nervous. "Are you ready for this? I have to say, I thought you and I would have been meeting a lot more to go over trial strategy. I was disappointed that you haven't called me more to come in. I thought we'd go over cross-examination questions and would've gone over discovery and everything like that by now."

I shrugged. "I got this. There was no need for the two of us to get together."

"Do you treat all your clients like this?"

"Like what?"

"Ignore them before trial. I've been calling for weeks now, and I've come into your office to track you down, and I couldn't get in touch with you. This is my life, Harper. My life."

"I got this." I didn't have it, of course. I wasn't going to, either. By the end of this proceeding, Michael would do the perp walk.

And I would finally be free.

"Are your parents here?" I asked him.

"No. They're not. Why should they be?"

I shrugged. "I'm just curious."

"All rise," the bailiff announced. "God save the State of Missouri and this honorable court."

At that, Judge Graham took her place at the bench. "You may be seated," she said. "Ms. Todd, you may address the jury with your opening statement."

"Thank you, your honor." April walked over to the jury and began. "Ladies and gentlemen of the jury, I want to tell you the story about an honorable man, Judge Robert Sanders. He was an excellent judge and an excellent family man. During his time on the bench as a federal district court judge, he consistently was a man for the people. He delivered justice for the little guys, the Davids who were taking on the Goliaths. He always loved the Davids, because he was one of them. He knew them. He took his job very seriously and he loved what he did. He was about justice first, last and always."

April hung her head, walked away from the jury box and then came back. "Justice first, last and always. Ladies and gentlemen of the jury, the federal judiciary lost a shining light. A beacon of justice. On October 19 of this year, that light was cruelly snuffed by the defendant, Michael Reynolds. You will hear evidence in this case that Mr. Reynolds was found at the scene of the crime, standing over the body of his father-in-law. You will hear evidence that, prior to the actual murder, Judge Sanders was being slowly poisoned. His life drained away, agonizingly, day by day, hour by hour. You will hear evidence that Mr. Reynolds had special access to Judge Sanders, in that he, and he alone, filled Judge Sanders' pill boxes, which gave him opportunity to poison Judge Sanders' orange juice. You will hear evidence that Mr. Reynolds had motive to kill Judge Sanders, as Mr. Reynolds was carrying on multiple affairs, and Judge Sanders had threatened to tell his daughter, who Mr. Reynolds was married to, about these affairs. You will hear evidence that if Christina Sanders, the daughter of Judge Sanders, divorced Mr. Reynolds that Mr. Reynolds would have been left penniless. You will hear evidence that Mr. Reynolds has a violent past. Finally, you will hear evidence that directly ties Mr. Reynolds to the murder weapon."

As she spoke, she walked back and forth, looking each and every juror in the eye. "Mr. Reynolds murdered Judge Sanders in cold blood. In cold blood." She shook her head. "And, in so doing, he deprived this world of a generous and just man. Thank you."

She sat down.

"Ms. Ross," Judge Graham said to me. "Please present the jury with your opening statement."

I stood up. "Ladies and gentlemen of the jury, the prosecutor was absolutely right. Judge Sanders was a man of enormous stature. A generous man who found for the plaintiff against the defendant more often than any other judge in the Western District of Missouri. By an order of magnitude. If you were a plaintiff, you wanted to draw Judge Sanders, because he cared. He cared very much for the little guy."

I walked over to my table and then walked back to the jury box. "My client did not kill Judge Sanders. He called the police from the scene of the crime. He wouldn't have done that if he had killed the judge. Thank you very much."

At that, I sat down.

Michael put his hand on my arm. "That's it?" he hissed. "That's the only opening statement you're going to make? Why didn't you talk about what your evidence you'll show and all that?"

"Method to my madness," I whispered.

Actually, there was no method. I just had to go through the motions. I had to make some kind of showing for the Missouri Bar when the inevitable complaint came down the pike.

"There better be," he said. "And what's up with her calling me a violent guy? She can't say that."

I grimaced. "I'll object when she brings that in," I said.

"It's already in. It's in the opening statement. Why didn't you object?"

"I don't object to opening statements. It's bad form."

"It's worse form to allow something like that to go unchallenged."

Judge Graham was glaring at the two of us as we whispered back and forth to each other. "Ms. Ross, please. If you need to have a conference with your client, then I'll call a recess."

"No, your honor, that won't be necessary," I said. I turned to Michael. "Please be quiet."

I looked in his eyes and saw he was ready to blow a gasket. I smiled, knowing the jury was watching him, and, if I could get him to lose his temper, all the better.

"Call your first witness, Ms. Todd," she said.

"The state calls Officer Chris Murphy," she said.

Office Murphy was the cop on the scene. I sat up, because I had a feeling the case would fall apart right in front of my eyes. At least, I hoped it would. I really didn't want to sit next to my client any longer than I had to.

Then again, this guy probably wouldn't be the one to sink Michael. That would be up to the forensic guy who would testify that the gloves that belonged to Michael perfectly matched the glove print found on the gun. After I received the forensic analysis on Michael's gloves, which perfectly matched the glove print found on the murder weapon, I sent that analysis over to the prosecutor as a part of the discovery documents she'd requested.

Of course, if I cared to object to the prosecutor using that analysis, I certainly could've. I could object to lack of foundation. I could object to chain of evidence.

Yet, I knew the prosecutor would bring that evidence in, and I wouldn't object. I'd let her do it. And that smoking gun would reduce Michael's case to a rancid pile of rubble.

At least, that was the hope. And my prayer.

The bailiff swore Officer Murphy in and April asked the basic questions about his name, rank, etc.

"You were the first responder, is that correct?"

"Yes."

"Who called 911 in this case?"

"Mr. Reynolds," he said, pointing to Michael.

"Mr. Reynolds called 911," April said knowingly. "And please tell the ladies and gentlemen of the jury about what you found when you arrived at the scene."

"I found the deceased on the floor of the kitchen. He had been shot twice, once through the head and once through the chest. And Mr. Reynolds was sitting down on the couch, waiting for us to arrive."

"And what was Mr. Reynolds' demeanor at this time?"

"He was calm. In fact, when he called 911, he was calm then, too. That was what the dispatcher told me."

That was hearsay, full stop, but I let it pass. Because I let it pass, Michael nudged me, but I shrugged my shoulders.

"By calm, what do you mean? Explain to the ladies and gentlemen of the jury what you mean by that."

"He was sitting on the couch eating a piece of chicken," he said. "He had a piece of chicken on the coffee table in front of him. I asked him what he was doing, and he said he was having a snack while he waited for us to arrive."

I suppressed a smile. I hadn't heard this part yet. I knew somehow that chicken would make an appearance. I just didn't know it would make its appearance in quite this way.

"He's lying," Michael whispered. "Lying. I wasn't calmly eating a piece of chicken. He's making me look like a sociopath."

I realized then that Michael was right. The Officer *was* lying about Michael calmly eating a piece of chicken. He specifically told me that the only reason why he arrested Michael was because Michael was on the scene. Not that Michael was on the scene and acting like a sociopath by calmly eating chicken while his father-in-law's body was in the kitchen.

Still, it was an entertaining story, so I let it go.

"Sitting on the couch eating a piece of chicken. Sitting on the couch eating a piece of chicken," April said. She nodded her head. "What else caused you to believe that Mr. Reynolds was perfectly calm?"

"Just his body language. He was sitting on the couch, but he was slouched. As if he was getting ready to watch television or something. I had to ask him to stand up so I could question him, because he suggested to me that I should have a seat next to him to ask my questions. It was very odd."

"Lying, lying, lying," Michael whispered.

"Odd," April said. She nodded again and paced. "Odd. What happened when you questioned him?"

"He told me he was out getting fried chicken and he came back and found that Judge Sanders had been killed."

"I see. And was his story believable?"

Michael nudged me. "Object to that. It calls for speculation."

I just sat there and I heard Michael start to breathe heavily.

"No," Officer Murphy said in answer to April's question about whether Michael's story was believable.

"No. And why wasn't his story believable?"

"Because my partner, Howard Flynn, was outside speaking with the neighbors. There were neighbors on the street, because they heard the gunshots, and they all said that Mr. Reynolds car had been in the driveway for the past hour. That was unusual, because Mr. Reynolds said he'd been getting fried chicken, and that he called 911 immediately after he got into the house. That contradicted the witness statements."

I looked up at Judge Graham, who was staring right at me.

Michael, for his part, was nudging me hard the entire time that this witness was speaking. "Hearsay, hearsay, hearsay. Where are you? And he's lying about that. My car wasn't there in the driveway for an hour. Not at all."

Yeah, it was hearsay. It was double hearsay, really. This cop was quoting his partner, who, in turn, was reporting on what the neighbors were saying. I was sure April was delighted that I was allowing all this to come in, because it made her job that much easier.

As for the fact that the cop was lying...so be it. Let him lie. I wouldn't cross-examine him very hard. I knew the cop was lying, because he told me he arrested Michael simply because he was on the scene. I remembered that when I spoke with Officer Murphy. He certainly didn't say a word about the neighbors stating that Michael's car was parked in the driveway for an hour. That would've been significant, and it would've been in the police report. So, Michael was right - Officer Murphy was lying. But it was a good story, and this testimony made it look like they *really* had a reason to arrest Michael, so I let it pass.

The judge banged her gavel. "I need to call a recess," she said. "To speak with counsel. I'm very sorry, Officer Murphy. I'll have to excuse you, but I don't want you to go too far. Ladies and gentlemen of the jury, you are also excused. Thank you."

The jury left, as did the witness. I closed my eyes knowing what was coming.

"Ms. Ross, Ms. Todd," Judge Graham said to us. "Please come back to my chambers."

I sighed, knowing I was about to get my ass handed to me. I also knew I'd have to start trying just a little bit harder.

The three of us went back to her chambers.

"Sit down," she said to the two of us.

We both sat down.

"Ms. Todd, I don't know what you're doing," Judge Graham said. "You obviously didn't prep your witness before he sat down at that stand. He committed double hearsay and your question about whether his story was believable calls for a conclusion. Not to mention the fact that you brought up, in your opening statement, that Mr. Reynolds has a history of violence. This isn't your first rodeo, Ms. Todd, so I don't know why you are so unprepared."

April looked embarrassed. As for myself, I braced myself for the judge laying into me.

I didn't have to wait long.

"And Ms. Ross, you're not doing your job at all here. We're here in chambers discussing this for one reason – you aren't objecting when you're supposed to. I can't protect your client, Ms. Ross, from hearsay accusations and from character assassinations. You must do that. Now, this is a warning to the both of you – Ms. Todd, you need to rein in your witnesses. You know better than that. And Ms. Ross, you need to object. I won't stand for much more of this. If the two of you don't want me to call a mistrial, then I suggest you both start acting more professionally."

"I will your honor," I said. "I'm very sorry."

"I'm sorry too, your honor," April said.

At that, the three of us walked back into the courtroom.

I was slapped down, so I knew that I'd have to take a different tact.

Everybody filed back in, and the Officer Murphy was seated at the witness stand once again. "I'll remind you that you're still under oath," Judge Graham told Officer Murphy.

"Now, Officer Murphy, you said that you arrived at the scene, and the defendant was eating a piece of chicken and he calmly asked you to join him on the couch. Was there any other behavior that the defendant exhibited that seemed odd to you or out of place?"

"Well, just the fact that I asked him questions and he answered them in a calm voice the entire time seemed abnormal to me. I asked him about where he was that evening, and he calmly said he was getting fried chicken. And then he got up and got the cardboard container of chicken to show me and he smiled when he did that. He kept making jokes, too, about his father-in-law. Inappropriate jokes." Officer Jackson shook his head. "Mind you, all of this was happening as the body of his father-in-law was still in the kitchen."

"He's lying again," Michael said. "I wouldn't make jokes like that. You better cross-examine him hard."

"What kind of inappropriate jokes did Mr. Reynolds make in front of you?" April asked Officer Murphy.

"I don't remember exactly, I only remember thinking that it was odd that he was making jokes." He put his hand on his chin. "Oh, yes, I do remember one. He asked me what I would call 100 judges chained together at the bottom of the ocean. I told him I didn't know, and he said 'a good start.'"

I inwardly groaned. Of all the dumb jokes the Officer could've come up with, and he told that one. That particular one. That was the dumbest and oldest one in the book. Anyhow, he told it wrong. It was supposed to be 100 *lawyers* chained together at the bottom of the ocean, not judges. Everybody loved judges. Everybody hated lawyers. That was the whole point of the joke.

"Lying, lying, lying." Michael's voice sounded frantic and hysterical.

"So, Mr. Reynolds told you that he was out getting chicken and came home to find his father-in-law shot dead. Did you take him into custody right there at the home?" April asked.

"Yes."

"What gave you probable cause to make an arrest?"

"The fact that he was at the scene and acting odd. He wasn't acting like most people do who are in this situation."

I reluctantly stood up. "Motion to strike. Witness stated a conclusion."

"Sustained." Judge Graham smiled at me and nodded. Her eyes said *atta girl. Keep it up.*

I inwardly rolled my eyes. I didn't want to lift a damn finger in this case, but I'd have to. To avoid a mistrial, I'd have to.

"When you took him down to the police station, how was he acting in the transport over?"

"He kept making jokes to us in the backseat. And chatting to us about his day." He shook his head. "He didn't say a word to us about the fact that his father-in-law was murdered. Not a single word. He seemed to want to speak with us about anything else but what had happened to the deceased."

"Lying," Michael said.

"And how did he react when he was brought in for questioning?" April asked.

"He was smiling broadly and laughing. In fact, when his mug shot was taken, he was smiling in that photograph."

"That's really a lie. You can see in my mug-shot that I wasn't smiling at all."

That was true. I saw the mug-shot, and Michael really wasn't smiling. I inwardly shrugged and tried to let it go.

"One more thing. Did you recover the murder weapon at the scene?"

"I did not."

"Was the murder weapon recovered?"

"It was."

"Tell me, using your own knowledge, how you came to know that the murder weapon was recovered?"

"A gun was found in the city landfill. Our officers searched for it for three weeks. This gun was the weapon used in this murder, because it was matched with the bullets found in the judge."

I nodded my head, knowing the forensic guy who matched the gun with the bullet would be called. I could cross-examine that guy, but I wouldn't do that very hard. The forensic guys knew their stuff, so if that gun from the landfill was matched with the bullets found in the judge, then that was the gun, all right.

"I have nothing further," April said and sat down.

My heart was pounding, as I realized that I had to question this guy just enough to avoid a mistrial and a Bar complaint, and not so much that my client suddenly started looking sympathetic. I'd have to walk a fine line, which was made complicated by the fact that I wasn't prepared for this cop's testimony. He told me, when I went down to the station, that he arrested Michael simply because he was on the scene. I wasn't prepared for him to lie.

"Ms. Ross," Judge Graham said. "Your witness."

I walked towards the witness stand. Ordinarily, I would have ripped this guy apart. I would've used his statement to me at the police station that there was nothing amiss with Michael, and I would've thrown that up in his face. I would've asked him to point to the police report and to show me where he wrote down that Michael was acting odd and that Michael's car was in the driveway for an hour.

In short, I ordinarily would've made mince-meat out of this guy. He would've completely lost credibility by the time I got through with him.

But in this case...I needed the jury to believe him. He had a good story, one that made Michael look guilty as the day is long. I wanted that story to stay in the jury's mind.

I cleared my throat. "Officer Murphy, have you had experience with men acting like you claim Michael was acting?"

I was carefully laying the groundwork for his testimony to damn Michael even more, all while making it look like I was trying to cross-examine him, and, oops, I didn't get the answer I wanted. Happened all the time.

Be careful, Harper. You don't want this conviction overturned on the grounds of ineffective assistance of counsel. Just do enough, but not too much.

"I have."

"How many times have you encountered men who acted like you say Michael acted at the scene? Non-chalant, uncaring, joking around?"

He shrugged. "A good dozen times, I guess."

"Out of those men that you arrested who acted extremely calmly when you arrested them, how many of those men ended up being convicted for the crime for which they were arrested?"

"100% of the time."

Good, good. "100% of the time? So, you're saying that every time you have arrested somebody who acted extremely calm when there was a dead body in the room, that person was found guilty by a jury of his peers?"

"Yes. That's what I'm saying."

"Nothing further, your honor."

There. That was plausible enough. When Michael filed his ineffective assistance of counsel appeal, I could simply say that I was looking for a different answer there. That I was looking for the officer to say 50% of the time or something like that, and I'd use that answer to springboard to different questions. But he said 100% of the time, so there wasn't anywhere I could go with that, so I decided just to rest.

I sat down and Michael was ready to kill me. I knew this. I could feel his eyes on me, even though I refused to turn my head to look at him. "Why did you do that? Why didn't you question him harder?" Michael's voice was a whisper, but I could feel it. I could feel it in my bones.

I turned to look at him. "Stop questioning me."

I looked up at Judge Graham and saw she was still studying me. She knew that I wasn't on my game. I'd been in front of her enough times that she knew how I usually operated. I was usually aggressive with lying witnesses. I could always break them down.

I closed my eyes and prayed there wouldn't be a mistrial. I needed this conviction. The judge calling a mistrial would be a disaster, because it would delay my plan to try to bring down Gerald. I had decided that bringing down Gerald, and bringing him down quickly, would be the best way to also bring down Judge Perez before the Dowling trial. Assuming I was correct, and Gerald was in on the whole scheme with Judge Perez, I knew he'd sing like Adele about the judge, in order to get a better deal.

I needed that to happen, and I needed that to happen quickly. I wanted everyone who was involved in this sorry affair to burn. Except maybe Kayla. I felt bad for her.

"Call your next witness, Ms. Todd," Judge Graham said.

"The State calls Bradley Cipolla."

Bradley was the guy who would testify about matching up the gun with the bullets. I knew this, because he was on April's witness list and I had also seen his deposition transcript. There wasn't much that I could impeach him with. He was pretty solid.

Brad went to the witness stand and was sworn in.

"Mr. Cipolla, could you please state your name for the record?"

"Bradley J. Cipolla."

"Mr. Cipolla, what is your current title?"

"I'm the lead forensic investigator for the Kansas City police department. I specialize in firearm forensics."

"Firearm forensics. Can you please explain what that means?"

"Basically, I match bullets with guns. That's what I do, in a nutshell."

"Okay. And what kind of training did you complete to become a forensic investigator?"

"I received a Bachelor of Science degree at Colorado State University, with a concentration in criminal forensics. I studied as an apprentice with Officer Dayton Roswell, who was the lead forensic investigator prior to my becoming the lead. Officer Roswell retired last year. My training with him lasted three years, and I learned about bullet striations, gunpowder residue, trajectory and ricochet, pin impressions and bullet tissue damage."

"Tell me about the gun recovered from the landfill. Was it matched up with the bullets found in Judge Sanders?"

"Yes it was."

"And how did you match up that gun with the bullets found in Judge Sanders?"

He cleared his throat. "I matched them by bullet striations."

"Bullet striations. Explain what you mean by that."

"Well, every gun barrel is different. Every gun barrel has a unique pattern of grooves. Because of this, every bullet fired from a certain gun will have that same unique groove pattern. The gun recovered from that landfill was matched to the bullets found in the victim, Robert Sanders, by matching striations."

"And how did you match the striations in this case?"

"I fired another bullet from the recovered gun and matched that bullet up with the bullets found in Robert Sanders. Under a microscope, I can compare the strata on each bullet. Both the bullet fired from the recovered gun and the bullets found in the victim had identical strata."

"The bullets had identical strata? Is it possible for two bullets, fired from two different guns, to have identical strata?"

"No. That is impossible."

"And why is this?"

"Because the strata on a bullet is like a fingerprint. It's unique, because the every gun barrel is 100% unique."

"And what is your professional conclusion?"

"My professional conclusion is that the gun recovered from the landfill was the same gun used to kill the victim, Robert Sanders."

April then went to her table and brought a gun out of a box, after carefully putting on latex gloves. "Is this the gun used to kill Robert Sanders?"

"It is."

"I'd like to enter this gun into evidence as Exhibit A," April said.

"I have no objection," I said.

"It is so entered," Judge Graham said.

"I have nothing further." April sat down.

"Your witness, Ms. Ross," Judge Graham said.

"I have nothing for this witness, your honor."

"Mr. Cipolla, you are excused," Judge Graham said to the officer. "Ms. Todd, please call your next witness."

"The State calls Alan Dennehy," April said, and I sat up in my chair. I rubbed together my hands, knowing this would be the good witness. He was the forensic expert who would testify about the gloves.

After I "accidentally" included my forensic report for the gloves in my document dump to April, she apparently took the ball and ran with it. She formally asked for the gloves, and I gave them to her, without Michael's knowledge. I was really covered there, because April formally asked for them, and I was obligated to give them to her. She then hired her own forensic guy to test the gloves, and I knew the outcome. Alan Dennehy would testify to this.

I looked over at Michael, and saw he had no idea what was coming. He was slouched in his chair, doodling on a piece of paper, looking pissed off. He didn't show any degree of alarm about seeing this guy, though, so I knew that he was about to be blindsided.

Alan came to the stand and raised his right hand.

"Do you promise to tell the truth, the whole truth, and nothing but the truth, so help you God?" the bailiff asked him.

"I do."

April approached. "Please state your name for the record."

"Alan B. Dennehy."

"Mr. Dennehy, what is your profession?"

"I am a forensic investigator."

"Please state your qualifications to be a forensic investigator."

He cleared his throat. "I received a bachelor of science in biology from the University of Massachusetts, Amherst, in 1991. I went on to receive a master's degree in Criminal Justice and Criminology from the University of Missouri-Kansas City, graduating in 1992. In getting both my bachelor's degree and master's degree, I took extensive coursework in DNA analysis and finger and glove print analysis. I became an officer in training on the Kansas City police force in 1993. I was an officer for 10 years, and, in 2003, I underwent an apprenticeship with a senior forensic investigator, Officer Finney, that lasted two years. I graduated from that apprenticeship in 2005, and, since 2005, I have investigated over 3,000 crime scenes using forensic analysis."

Impressive credentials. This guy was unimpeachable. Not that I couldn't make him crack if I was really trying, but I wouldn't try, so I knew the jury would find him extremely persuasive.

That was my hope.

"Okay. Now, Officer Dennehy, did you examine the gun found in the landfill and was matched to the crime scene?"

"I did."

"And did you find fingerprints on this gun?"

"No I did not."

"Did you find glove prints on this gun?"

"Yes, I did."

"How did you recover these glove prints?"

He cleared his throat. "Glove prints are as unique as fingerprints. Each glove has a unique grain, which is found on the surface of each pair of gloves. Most pairs of gloves, over a period of time, pick up dirt and grease, which leaves prints on hard surfaces, such as that of a gun. I dusted the surface of the gun and I retrieved a unique glove print from the weapon."

I turned and looked at Michael and saw he was looking alarmed. He frantically left me a note on the yellow pad of paper. "What the fuck?" was all that note said.

I simply shrugged and turned back to listen to Alan give testimony that would definitively sink my client. Michael would as sunk as the Titanic by the time this guy got through with his testimony.

April started to pace a little bit in front of the witness. Then she went over to her table and put on her latex gloves again, and picked up the pair of leather gloves in a box next to her table.

She approached the witness as Michael wrote another note. "Those are my fucking gloves. How did she get my fucking gloves?"

I shrugged again, and I wrote back. "Maybe one of your enemies sent them to her. I guess you were careless and left them somewhere."

"I'm going to show you a pair of leather gloves," April said to Officer Dennehy. "Can you please identify these gloves for the record?"

"Yes. These are the gloves I used for my forensic analysis of the recovered murder weapon."

"You did the forensic analysis on this pair of gloves?"

"Yes."

"Describe the forensic analysis that you conducted on these gloves."

"I dusted the murder weapon for glove prints and found several. I then received this pair of gloves and I matched the grain on these gloves with the grain I found on the recovered gun. The two prints were identical."

"Was there anything else that led you to find this pair of gloves matched the glove print on the gun?"

"Yes. I found the gloves are frayed and worn on certain areas." Alan took the glove and held it up. "Right here, you can see a wear pattern, a place where the grains of the gloves are not as prominent as other areas of the glove. These wear patterns were identical to the areas of the gun that didn't have prominent glove grain prints. From the grain patterns that I dusted and the wear patterns that I also dusted on the gun, my conclusion is that this pair of gloves were the same gloves that were used to fire the recovered murder weapon."

I had to suppress a smile. This testimony was getting good.

"What the fuck," Michael wrote on a piece of paper. "She obtained those gloves illegally. She had to have. You better call for a mistrial. I won't fry because the prosecutor stole my gloves."

"Relax," I wrote back. "She got these gloves perfectly legally."

I turned back and watched the rest of the testimony unfold.

"And were you able to trace these gloves to anybody in particular?"

"Yes."

"And who did you trace the gloves to?"

"Mr. Michael Reynolds."

I turned around and looked at the jury. They were mesmerized by this testimony, and, when Officer Dennehy stated the gloves belonged to Michael, I saw them look stunned and I heard an audible gasp.

Michael heard it, too. "Do something," he wrote on the pad of paper. "Do something or I will."

I started to panic just a little. What did that mean, "do something or I will?" What did he plan on doing?

April was still questioning Officer Dennehy. "How did you trace these gloves to the defendant, Michael Reynolds?"

"By a DNA sample. When Mr. Reynolds was arrested, he gave a DNA sample. These gloves had leftover DNA inside of them. DNA can be left by sweat, and this was the source of the DNA found inside the gloves."

"I see," April said. "And did you do the DNA analysis?"

"I did."

"And what qualifications do you possess which would enable you to perform a DNA analysis?"

"As I noted before, I received a bachelor of science in Biology and a master's degree in criminal justice, plus I completed a 2-year apprenticeship with Officer Finney. I studied extensively about DNA analysis in obtaining my bachelor's degree, my master's degree and in my apprenticeship. Since I graduated from my apprenticeship in 2005, I've examined over 10,000 individual sources of DNA and have successfully matched 80% of these sources with a suspect."

"And what about the 20% of the DNA sources that you couldn't match?"

"I couldn't match that extra 20% simply because I couldn't obtain the proper suspect's DNA. Those cases have gone cold."

"And what is your expert opinion regarding the gloves that you hold in your hands, and the glove prints found on the gun?"

"My expert opinion is that these gloves," he said, holding up the gloves, "are the same gloves used to fire the murder weapon, and that these gloves belonged to the defendant, Michael Reynolds."

"And did you find any other DNA source on these gloves?"

"No."

"Did you find any other fingerprints or glove prints on the murder weapon, besides these glove prints?"

"No."

"I have nothing further."

"You get out there," Michael whispered. "You get out there and you hammer this guy. Ask him where he got those gloves, because I certainly didn't supply them."

"Ms. Ross," Judge Graham said. "Your witness."

I stood up. "I have no questions for this witness, your honor."

At that, Michael stood up. "This is bullshit! This is bullshit! That prosecutor stole those gloves. She stole them. She can't get away with this!"

While Michael was screaming obscenities and accusations,

Judge Graham was banging her gavel, over and over again. "Mr. Reynolds, I won't tolerate outbursts in my courtroom. If you say one more word, I will have the bailiff remove you and you won't be allowed to participate in this trial anymore. Do you understand me, Mr. Reynolds?"

He sat back down and crossed his arms in front of him. I looked at him, and he was shaking his head, over and over again. "It's over," he wrote down on the sheet of paper. "I'm toast. And so are you. I'll have your Bar license when this is all said and done."

"I'd like to see you try," I whispered.

The rest of the trial was anti-climactic. After the testimony by Officer Dennehy, everything was downhill from there. April called Christina, Ava and Anita to testify. They all testified to the fights they witnessed between Michael and Judge Sanders, and they all testified to the fact that Michael was the only one who had decent access to Judge Sanders' kitchen, because he refilled the pill boxes, so he was the most likely one to have poisoned Judge Sanders. They all testified that Michael had motive to kill Judge Sanders, because Judge Sanders was threatening to tell Christina about his affairs with multiple women, and Christina would have divorced Michael and left him penniless.

I half-heartedly cross-examined each of them, doing the bare minimum - just enough to keep me out of trouble, but not enough to make the witnesses look bad.

For Christina, I stood up and asked one question. "Ms. Sanders, you stated that only Michael had access to the Judge Sanders' kitchen. But you never actually saw him put poison into the orange juice, did you?"

"No."

"I have nothing further."

For Ava, I went a tad further. "Mrs. Sanders, isn't it true that Judge Sanders had a different family?"

"Yes."

"And you wanted to divorce him?"

"Yes," she said with a nod of her head.

"And if you divorced him, you would have to give him half of what you owned?"

"Yes."

"Were you willing to give him half of what you owned?"

She shook her head. "No."

"Nothing further."

As for Anita, I just didn't ask her any cross-examination questions at all.

No matter. After the glove testimony, Michael knew his goose was cooked. He looked defeated, and he no longer cared if I grilled the witnesses or not. He knew, as well as I did, that it was over.

The fat lady was warming up in the jury box.

And I couldn't have been happier.

Finally, after three days of endless testimony, April and I were ready for our closing arguments.

"Ladies and gentlemen of the jury," April began. "A lion of the judiciary was killed on October 19 of last year. He was a respected jurist, a good friend to many, an excellent father and grandfather. He never had an unkind word for anyone. And he was a social justice warrior. He always saw the little guy in his courtroom. He always made sure that the little guy was protected. He was a voice for the powerless. And now his voice is gone. His voice has been cruelly snuffed out in the worst possible way. No longer will the powerless and the meek have a chance to have Judge Robert Sanders as their voice. His voice was silenced on October 19."

She paced back and forth, back and forth, as she continued to address the jury. "You heard evidence in this courtroom that the defendant was eating a bucket of chicken, calmly waiting for the police to arrive, while his father-in-law's body was lying in the kitchen. He didn't care, that was clear - he cracked jokes. He got rid of the gun, but, nevertheless, that gun was recovered. You heard the testimony of witness after witness who stated that the defendant had unique access to the deceased, unique access to the orange juice of Judge Sanders, because he, and he alone, refilled Judge Sanders' pills every week. Nobody else in the house had access to Judge Sanders' kitchen. You heard evidence that Michael Reynolds had motive to kill his father-in-law, because Judge Sanders knew that Mr. Reynolds was having multiple affairs and Judge Sanders was threatening to tell his daughter Christina about these affairs. You heard evidence that Christina Sanders was independently wealthy, but that Michael Reynolds was independently penniless, and that Christina Sanders would have left Mr. Reynolds penniless in the event of a divorce."

April came back over to her table, and then went back to the jury box. She had, in her hand, the pair of gloves. "So Mr. Reynolds had motive, means and opportunity. You heard evidence regarding all three of those elements. But the most important and damning piece of evidence was found in these gloves."

She waved the gloves around, and showed them to each and every juror. "These gloves were worn when the judge was shot in his home. The glove prints left by these gloves were the only glove prints found on the murder weapon."

She stood still in front of the jury, the gloves in her hands. "Let me repeat. There was one set of glove prints found on the murder weapon. One." She held up her index finger for emphasis. "And the glove prints on the murder weapon matched the gloves worn by the Defendant. Michael Reynolds' DNA, and only Michael Reynolds' DNA, was found in these gloves. The inescapable conclusion was that only Michael Reynolds touched the murder weapon."

She shrugged and smiled. "So, since only Michael Reynolds touched the murder weapon, there is only one person who could have killed Judge Sanders. And that's Michael Reynolds. It's really as simple as that. You can't get any closer to a smoking gun, folks."

At that, she sat down.

"Ms. Ross," Judge Graham said to me. "Please present your closing argument."

I stood up, not wanting this charade to go on any longer, but not wanting to be too obvious about my intention. I would have to make a closing argument, but it would short and sweet.

"Ladies and gentlemen of the jury," I said, walking over to the jury box. "I do agree with the prosecutor that a lovely man is dead. I agree that Judge Sanders was a social justice warrior who really cared about the people hurt by large corporations and really did make sure that these people were taken care of. That's indisputable. What is in dispute is whether my client, Michael Reynolds, poisoned Judge Sanders. Nobody ever saw him do this. There were no eyewitnesses. And Mr. Reynolds was far from the only individual who had a motive to kill Judge Sanders. You heard testimony that he started a different family with a different woman, while he was married to Ava Sanders. You heard testimony from Mrs. Sanders that she didn't want to part with half her fortune in the event of a divorce. That gave Mrs. Sanders motive to kill Mr. Sanders, and it also gave Christina Sanders motive to kill Mr. Sanders, as she was interested in protecting her mother."

I nodded and turned to sit down. "Thank you very much, ladies and gentlemen of the jury."

I sat down and the judge banged her gavel. "Okay," she said, "it is time of jury instructions. If you find, beyond a reasonable doubt, that the defendant, Michael Reynolds, is guilty of murder in the first degree, then you must make a finding of guilty. This finding of guilty must be unanimous, in that every single one of you must find the defendant guilty. The prosecutor has the burden of proof, so if you do not find, beyond a reasonable doubt, that the State has met its burden, then you must return a finding of Not Guilty."

Judge Graham continued on. "You must find that the defendant met all the elements for first degree murder under the law. If I may reiterate these elements to you, they are that the defendant knowingly causes the death of another person after deliberation upon the matter. So, you have to find that Mr. Reynolds knew that he was causing the death of Judge Sanders. That's the first element. The second element was that Mr. Reynolds actually did cause the death of Judge Sanders. And the third and final element is that Mr. Reynolds deliberated before killing Judge Sanders. If you find every one of these elements applied in this case, then you must find the defendant guilty of the crime of first degree murder."

"And if you find that Mr. Reynolds knowingly caused the death of Judge Sanders, but that he did not deliberate before causing the death of Judge Sanders, then you shall find the defendant guilty of the lesser offense of second degree murder."

"Thank you for your service, ladies and gentlemen of the jury. You may now begin your process of deliberation."

At that, the jury filed out of the courtroom.

After they left, I got up to stretch my legs. I honestly thought that we would get a verdict sooner, as opposed to later.

I wandered around the halls of the courthouse, and my mind was filled with anxiety. This case was almost over. The smoking gun was the pair of gloves. Surely the jury would do the right thing.

Wouldn't they?

What if they didn't? What if they found Michael not guilty? Or what if they hung? What if I was forced to go through this hell a second time? That would be a horrible scenario. I'd almost want to see him acquitted then have to go through this again.

Almost.

Either scenario would be a nightmare, though. I prayed they didn't hang, and I really prayed they didn't acquit.

I went back into the courtroom where I saw Michael sitting at the table, just staring off into space. He looked defeated.

I didn't go and sit next to him. He still made me want to vomit. Just being near him made my skin crawl.

He turned around when he saw me coming back into the courtroom. "I'll kill you," he said calmly. "You supplied those gloves to the prosecutor. I remember now. I took those gloves off in your office and I never saw them again. I didn't even think about them. I didn't even notice I was missing them. But you must have sent them to the prosecutor. You stole them from me and then used them against me. I'll have your Bar license."

I sat down next to him. "I got a discovery request from the prosecutor, asking me for those gloves. I supplied them pursuant to the discovery request. Nothing more, nothing less. If you try to bring a Bar Complaint against me, it will be your word against mine. I will tell the Bar that I obtained the gloves from you, with your knowledge, pursuant to the discovery request. At any rate, once I got that discovery request, I was obligated to give her what she asked for. Period."

"How come I didn't know about it?"

I shrugged. "I didn't think you needed to know."

He shook his head. "You fucking bitch."

I smiled and walked to the back of the courtroom and sat down. Hopefully, the jury would be in soon. I really wanted to get out of this place and, hopefully, celebrate.

Twenty minutes later, the jury came back in. I took my seat at the table and watched the jury come in, my heart in my throat.

"Ladies and gentlemen of the jury, have you reached a verdict?" Judge Graham asked the foreman, who was standing up.

"We have, your honor."

"On the count of murder in the first degree, do you find the defendant guilty or not guilty?"

"Your honor, we find the defendant guilty."

"Is this the unanimous decision of the jury?"

"It is."

"You are excused," Judge Graham said. "But I would like to thank all of you for your service and sacrifice. The right to be heard in front of a jury of one's peers is one of the most important Constitutional rights that all of us enjoy, and you are integral in ensuring that this right is preserved."

At that, the jury filed out and the bailiff came over to Michael and put the handcuffs on him.

As Michael was led away, he looked back at me. "You're a dead woman," he said, his eyes dead.

"Yes, but I'm free." I nodded my head and tried to suppress a smile. "Unlike you," I said under my breath.

As I gathered my files and put them into my briefcase, I realized something.

I truly was free.

For the first time in 17 years, I was free.

Thirty-Three

Three Weeks Later

"Mom, come and see," Abby said excitedly.

I was finally Abby and Rina's mom. The adoption was formalized the day before, and, over our celebratory dinner at the Red Lobster the night before, I informed them that they were to call me "Mom" from here on out.

The girls were more than excited about this. "Mom, Mom, Mom, Mom," Rina said with a giggle. "I like that sound."

"And so do I, Ladybug. So do I."

That wasn't the only thing that had happened, of course. As soon as Michael was sentenced to life in prison without the possibility of parole, I went to work to make sure that Gerald and Kayla were also on the hook. So, I called the police and gave them an anonymous tip about Gerald and Kayla.

My thought was that Kayla would quickly roll on Gerald, and I was right. I had been following, on the news, the developments of this case, and, sure enough, Kayla was quickly arrested. I knew it was only a matter of time before Gerald was, as well.

"What is it, Buttercup?" I asked Abby when I came into the living room.

"They're talking about that Judge Sanders case," she said. "On the news. Look!"

She pointed at the television screen, where I saw Gerald doing the perp walk out of his office building. The news reporter solemnly informed the television viewing audience that "Gerald Stone was arrested today for his part in the murder of Judge Robert Sanders last October. Michael Reynolds, Judge Sanders son-in-law, has already been tried and convicted for this murder, and Kayla Stone, Gerald Stone's estranged wife, is currently in custody for her role in the judge's murder. Mr. Stone's arraignment for the murder is scheduled for tomorrow. In other developments in this wild murder case, Judge Manuel Perez, who is currently a District Court judge for the Western District of Missouri, also was arrested for his part in the murder of Judge Robert Sanders." The newslady shook her head "These developments certainly are dramatic. Watch this space for additional details on this wild and wooly case. Back to you."

I smiled and called Christina Sanders. "Did you see on TV?" I asked her.

"Oh my God, yes. Yes. Thank God. Thank God. I finally feel safe."

"I'm glad," I said. "Was it Gerald and Judge Perez who were threatening you before?"

"You're damn right it was them," Christina said. "That goddamned judge is as dirty as the day is long. Thank God he's getting his. And so is that damned Gerald Stone. Gerald and Judge Perez tried to force me to take the blame for my own father's murder. They tried, but looks like they're the ones doing the perp walk." She laughed. "They're the ones doing the perp walk, not me."

I had found additional information that linked Judge Perez to Gerald Stone. Anna found payments that Judge Perez was paying to Gerald, hundreds of thousands of dollars. She then hacked into Judge Perez' computer and found thousands of child pornography images, even though the Judge thought that he had deleted them all. We then put two and two together - it seemed that Gerald was blackmailing Judge Perez, because somehow, someway, he found these child porn images as well.

Anna was able to find all sorts of things, deleted or no, so she presented me with this evidence. I suddenly knew why Judge Perez was in on the blackmailing of Judge Sanders. I had no idea why he was arrested for being a part of the Judge Sanders' murder, though. I guessed that Gerald probably gave him up somehow.

"Yep, they're doing the perp walk," I said, as Judge Perez' image flashed across the screen. He was being led out of the federal courthouse in handcuffs. "As they should."

I hung up the phone and Abby came over to me. "Mom," she said. "Can you take me and James to the zoo tomorrow? He wants to go and so do I."

I tousled her hair. "Of course, Buttercup," I said. "I love the zoo, too. Can Axel come along?"

She smiled shyly. "Sure, Mom. I love Axel."

"So do I."

Abby and James had been hanging out together for the past few months, and James had finally asked her to "go steady." I bought Abby a necklace that had two halves, and asked her to give him a half and told her she should take the other half. "That's how we did it when I was in school," I said. "A million years ago."

Abby, for her part, went ahead and gave James half the necklace, and he wore it all the time, she said.

"What about me, Mom," Rina said. "I want to go to the zoo, too."

"We'll all go," I said. "it'll be a lovely spring day. We'll have fun!"

As for Axel and me...we finally were able to make love. Once I buried the past, which I could finally do when I saw Michael get sentenced to life in prison, I finally moved on.

And the love-making was truly glorious.

But not everything was glorious. Things never were for long in the life of a criminal defense attorney.

My mother called the Monday after our family zoo outing. "Harper," she said desperately over the phone. She was sobbing, seemingly out of control. “You have to come over here right away. Right away.”

I rolled my eyes. “Why Mom?” She could be so dramatic sometimes.

“It’s your Uncle Jack,” she said. “Oh, and he was doing so well, too. I just don’t know.”

“What about Uncle Jack?”

“He’s been arrested for murder.”

My heart plunged a million miles. “I’ll be right there.”

The story continues with *Hidden Defendant,* available now!

For information about upcoming titles in the *Harper Ross Legal Thriller* series, sign up for my mailing list! You’ll be the first to know about new releases and you’ll be the first to know about any promotions!!!! http://eepurl.com/hBqhtr

Read on for a sneak peek of *Hidden Defendant.*

Also by Rachel Sinclair

For information about upcoming titles in the *Harper Ross Legal Thriller* series, sign up for my mailing list! You'll be the first to know about new releases and you'll be the first to know about any promotions!!!! http://eepurl.com/hBqhtr

Johnson County Legal Thrillers (Kansas City, Missouri)

Bad Faith

Justice Denied

Hidden Defendant

Injustice for All

LA Defense

The Associate

The Alibi

Reasonable Doubt

The Accused

Secrets and Lies

Until Proven Guilty

Emerson Justice Legal Thrillers (Los Angeles)

Dark Justice

Blind Justice

Southern California Legal Thrillers (San Diego)

Presumption of Guilt

Justice Delayed

By Reason of Insanity

Wrongful Conviction

The Trial

Milton Keynes UK
Ingram Content Group UK Ltd.
UKHW040711201123
432908UK00001B/280